THE GILDED CAGE

LUISA A. JONES

Storm
PUBLISHING

Ebook ISBN: 978-1-80508-095-4
Paperback ISBN: 978-1-80508-096-1

Cover design by: Sarah Whittaker
Cover images by: Alamy, Shutterstock

Published by Storm Publishing.
For further information, visit:
www.stormpublishing.co

ALSO BY LUISA A. JONES

Goes Without Saying
Making the Best of It

This book contains themes which may be upsetting for some readers, including domestic abuse and loss.

"Marriage is like life in this – that it is a field of battle, and not a bed of roses."

ROBERT LOUIS STEVENSON *Virginibus Puerisque, I.i*

To Martin, with grateful thanks for the bed of roses.

PROLOGUE

MAY, 1897

"There's nothing else for it, Ros: you will have to marry. You have none of the usual accomplishments or skills by which you might obtain a respectable paid position, and as much as it galls me to say so, I can't afford to support you. I'm sorry for it, more than you know. I'll keep a house in town, of course, but somewhere smaller – this house will have to be put up for sale. Most of the staff will have to go. Papa's debts... I had no idea the situation was so dire, until today."

Rosamund clenched her fists in her lap but said nothing. The prospect of this dismantling of her entire world was terrifying. Tristram was avoiding her gaze, leaning an elbow against the mantelshelf and drawing great gulps on his cigarette as if his life depended upon it. As she watched him, she saw in the set of his shoulders and the tremor where his fingers held the cigarette how much it hurt him to have to sell their childhood home. She must make allowances: he felt keenly the burden of responsibility which had suddenly been laid upon him along with a barony. Still, for him to speak to her with such brutal candour about the family finances was appalling. She could not have been more offended if he had deliberately and loudly broken wind.

If the loss of their father hadn't been sufficiently agonising, the reality of her situation was becoming ever clearer, like mist on a mirror being wiped away to leave a newly haggard, ugly reflection. Papa had always indulged her, shielding her from the hard facts of life such as financial and household management. He had kept her close, never sending her away to school like Tristram, or even appointing a governess, but teaching her to read and write himself. She had spent almost every waking hour with him. She read to him: never novels, but serious (often tedious) works of historical scholarship. She took dictation as he gathered a lifetime's research into volumes of literary and anthropological musings. She played the piano to him, wheeled him around the garden to admire their magnificent roses, and, on days that were dry but not too warm, took him out on occasional jaunts to the village in the old horse-drawn landaulet.

By the time she turned twenty and still hadn't been presented at Court, Papa had been in such frail health that she couldn't have been prevailed upon to leave him, and he left her in no doubt that he couldn't have borne the separation if she had spent the Season in London and bagged herself an eligible husband. So, in the long hours he spent sleeping, she whiled away her time painting, practising her music, and cutting out pictures and snippets of poems for her collection of scrap books. If she felt sure she could get away for a couple of hours at a stretch, she would ride her horse across the lush fields of the Dales. It hadn't been an exciting life, but she had been content to know she was loved, and that her presence was fundamentally necessary to the happiness of another soul. Without him, she was alone. It had come as a shock to realise that there was no one she could turn to now.

Papa was gone and, it seemed, she was not merely unnecessary, but surplus to requirements: a financial burden on her brother, even with her modest lifestyle. As Tristram was seven years her senior, and spent much of her childhood away at school, then in the army, they hadn't grown up to be close. Papa hadn't actively discouraged her from having friends of her own age, but they had spent so much time together, and socialised so little, that she had never really had the opportunity to nurture friendships.

For almost the first time in her life, she would have to contemplate venturing into society beyond the local parish. Their childhood home would be forever lost to the Pelhams, with its exquisite gardens, rambling corridors and dusty old books that had formed the backdrop to her entire existence. The thought of it made her want to curl up and hide away, or, better still, metamorphose into a tree like the nymph Daphne, and stay in her beloved garden untouched by any man for ever.

But Tristram hadn't finished. He had tossed his cigarette butt into the fire and was now pacing the room in obvious agitation. She cringed as he started talking about money again. Papa had never discussed such things with her. Once again, the pang of loss clawed at her.

"Finding a husband won't be easy. You have little to recommend you. Your skill at languages is five hundred years out of date; your paintings are banal; I've never known you to finish a piece of needlework. You can barely even dance. You're too pretty to be a governess: even if you had the necessary skills, no wife with any sense would have you in the house. You've never even learned how to manage a household or perform as a hostess, as Papa would not spare you—"

"At least Papa didn't think me as utterly useless as you evidently do." This was too much. There might be an element of truth in his words, but surely Papa wouldn't be the only man who could appreciate the brain behind her face? If it was true that marriage was her only option, there must be a bachelor or widower somewhere who might enjoy playing chess and conversing about literature and legends, instead of expecting her to while away her hours in meaningless dancing and petit point? She wasn't entirely lacking in accomplishment: she could ride competently; she could sing and play piano quite well. Her paintings were only dull to Tris because he had no interest in flora and fauna. No doubt if she were to paint a battle scene, he'd find it captivating.

Nevertheless, she'd be a fool not to acknowledge the potential difficulties in finding such a suitor. Shyness rendered her tongue-tied in wider society, except with people she knew well, and a lack of female influence and company meant she knew next to nothing about the mysteries of fashion and flirtation. When she looked back now, her girlhood seemed like an idyllic golden age, one from which she had been abruptly ejected only a week ago. The doors of that time were now shut and bolted so firmly against her, it might as well have been someone else's life.

Now, she was in mourning, and would be for the next year. Even if she wished to transform herself into a social butterfly, it would be impossible during that period. At least that was some consolation – her brother would have to support her for the next twelve months. After that, she might feel ready to turn her thoughts to matrimony. But even then, she couldn't imagine hurrying to snare a husband. If she was to be a man's lifelong companion, it would be foolhardy in the extreme to rush into such a decision. Better to take her time and choose carefully...

Tristram delved in his pocket for his cigarette case and lit up yet again, a sure sign that his nerves were on edge. He had been tense and downcast ever since Papa died. Yet he would feel better once he was back with his regiment; she, on the other hand, faced uncertainty. If he would just slow down, give things time, Rosamund was sure everything would fall into place. He'd find some money from somewhere, and she would look after things at home for him while he was away, helping him to make savings by learning how to manage a household in a thrifty and responsible way. Perhaps one day she would meet the right man, someone gentle and kind like Papa; but it wouldn't trouble her if she ended her days as a spinster, so long as she could stay here at Ambleworth Hall with her memories and so much ancient beauty around her.

"We can't rush these things, Tris," she said, moderating her tone to placate him. "Given time, perhaps, a suitable match will be found—"

"If you wanted to have a choice in such matters, you should have urged Papa to allow Aunt Agatha to present you at Court. If you'd had a season at seventeen or eighteen, like any normal girl, you might have caught yourself a fine young husband – but, as it is, beggars can't be choosers."

It was hopeless to argue. Feeling more alone than ever, she bade him a cool good night and left him to his smoking and musing, determined not to allow herself to be infected by his anxieties. There was enough pain in sorting through Papa's personal effects and writings, without troubling herself over a future she couldn't begin to envisage.

The matter was so far from her mind that when, one afternoon several weeks later, Tristram led an unfamiliar gentleman out of the house and along the terrace to greet her, she found nothing significant in it.

Sir Lucien Fitznorton had been a friend of Papa's, Tristram said, and certainly the middle-aged gentleman he introduced seemed appropriately mournful as he lifted his hat and bowed over her hand. Greying and generously bewhiskered, Sir Lucien's claret-coloured nose and florid cheeks, together with a portly figure inadequately disguised by his expensively cut coat, were suggestive of an indulgent lifestyle which couldn't have been more different from Papa's almost Spartan abstemiousness.

"Miss Pelham, you are everything your father described to me, and more besides. I only wish we could have met in happier circumstances. The loss of your dear papa must be very painful to you," he boomed, making her wish she could shrink back into the shadows.

"Thank you, Sir Lucien. Yes, it is painful indeed."

"Your brother has suggested you might show me around your gardens? I'm considering improvements to Plas Norton, my country estate in Wales, and am sorely in need of inspiration."

Meekly, she set down her basket and pruning scissors and allowed him to accompany her along the gravel path, but not without first casting a mutinous glance back at her brother. He had for some reason dropped several paces behind and gestured at her in what was presumably intended to be an encouraging manner.

"It is some time since I last saw your father, my dear, but he spoke of you so often I almost feel I know you. You were quite the treasure to him."

"You are very kind, Sir Lucien."

"I have a daughter myself, and if she grows up to show even half the filial devotion you showed to my dear friend, then I shall be a happy man."

Rosamund smiled politely. "I'm sure she will return your love in good measure," she murmured.

"Hmm. It is a matter of great sadness to me that my little Charlotte has no mother to guide her since my wife passed away. I am often in town, and so she frequently lacks any parental influence at all."

Rosamund nodded. Having lost her own mother at a young age, she could easily imagine a young girl growing up lonely on a country estate with her only parent frequently away. "Is your daughter – Charlotte, you said? – is she very young?" she asked.

"She is. Very young, and very precious to me. I had hoped that one day I might have a son. But..."

He paused, leaving her to finish the sentence in her mind. *But for that he would need a wife living.* Her breathing quickened. Was that what Tristram hoped for? That she would marry this fat, florid old man thirty years her senior to bear him children?

She started paying more attention. His manners were perfectly correct, but there was something intense, almost predatory, in his lingering gaze, giving her the impression he was comparing what was before him against what he had been led to expect. She led him around the rockery and the water garden, pointing out the most exotic and interesting specimen plants and the conditions in which they thrived most happily; but for all his talk of needing inspiration for his own garden, he showed little more than a perfunctory interest. Instead, he maintained a lengthy, one-sided discourse about his factories, his mining, his recent investment to expand his exports, and his house and estate. Why he would imagine she might find any of this interesting was beyond her – unless, of course, he was trying to lure her towards marriage by creating an impression of wealth and standing.

He paused next to a particularly beautiful shrub, which he ignored as if it were perfectly invisible, and addressed her with an alarming directness.

"Miss Pelham, it was your father's dearest wish, as expressed to me himself the last time I saw him... and it is most certainly also mine, that you might do me the honour—" Here he broke off, although she couldn't tell whether his sudden attempt at discretion was because he guessed he had startled her, or for dramatic effect.

Realising her mouth had fallen open in an O of horror, she collected herself, closed it again, and merely stared at her hand, which he had seized in his own.

"Sir Lucien, I assure you I have entertained no thoughts of marriage—" she began, but then noticed Tristram's fierce, desperate expression behind them. He had engineered this moment, she realised. The two of them must have discussed it together and decided to broach it like this. All that talk of his motherless little girl and his wealth had indeed been to establish his eligibility and attract her interest.

"I realise this will be somewhat unexpected," Sir Lucien was saying. He licked his lips, and the sight of his shiny wet tongue sliding out amongst his whiskers made her shudder inwardly. "Let me assure you I have already ascertained from your brother that my suit will not be unwelcome."

She felt hot and cold. It was a deal, then, already negotiated and shaken upon. Tristram had given her warning, she supposed, when he told her some weeks ago that she must marry. But for him to imagine she would be content with this – it was a betrayal of their sibling bond.

"It is. I hadn't anticipated..."

She was thankful for their gloves. Her hand lay captive in his, and he turned it over and stroked the palm as if trying to comfort her. Every instinct urged her to pull it away and hide it behind her back like a child. Sir Lucien's voice had receded a long way off, drowned out by a ringing in her ears as the sunshine grew brighter, white dotted by a million black pin pricks and stars.

As her vision cleared, she became aware of Tristram gripping her elbow. He gave her a fierce little shake.

"Am I to congratulate you, Rosamund?" he asked, with such desperation in his expression and his hand on her arm that she lost all hope.

She nodded, helpless in the face of his determination, and lowered her gaze to blank out the triumph in their faces.

ONE

ROSAMUND

FEBRUARY 1914

Rosamund knew the blow was coming, yet when it landed it still came as a shock. The force of it sent her crashing against the unyielding polished walnut of the headboard. Metal in her mouth: she'd bitten her tongue again. Not badly this time.

She knew what would follow, too, and regrouped by drawing into herself. Focus on the strange ringing noise from her eardrum, still whining from the blow. Don't think about the remorseless jab-jab-jab into tender flesh, or the scraping nails, or the suffocating weight, pushing her into the mattress as if she mattered no more than the bed itself. Her muscles cramped, rebelling against her mind as it reasoned with them to go limp and stop resisting. She couldn't help the tension that sent her into a spasm, even though it would only make things worse.

She crawled into the depths of her own mind to shove this nightmare into the box she kept there, the box containing all the other terrors, and willed herself to breathe. Swallow the nausea; she'd let that out later, but not now, not with her face squashed into the mattress. *Breathe in. Out. Be small. Be quiet; insignificant.* Be so inconsequential that he would forget there was pleasure to be found in her flesh.

Sometimes, if she counted in her head, or visualised a piece of sheet music and how her fingers might translate it to the piano keyboard, she could gain a few precious moments of dissociation. But not tonight.

She let the pinpricks of light in her eyeballs and the ringing sound engulf her, until at last the pain couldn't be blocked and a cry escaped her throat.

He had made her howl like an animal, and she despised herself for it as much as she detested him. This was what he did: he made her something less than human. A creature, devoid of pride or self-respect. Without dignity. A piece of meat. Made sordid, contaminated by the filth that spewed from his mouth and his Thing, like a beast itself in the way it rose up and sought her out as prey.

Her cry had excited him further. She ground her teeth, hating herself for her inability to deny him that pleasure, and told herself at least it would end sooner now. The only power she had over him was her endurance. Broken she might be, but he would not destroy her. Not while there was breath in her body.

She was alone in this. There was no knight on a noble steed coming to slay the dragon and carry her to safety. Her only weapons were fortitude and the small acts of defiance that kept her from sliding into an abyss of despair. Sixteen years of this marriage had taught her that it was pointless to try to fight him with physical strength: he was nearly three times heavier than she, and brutal when he wanted to crush her.

When he was finally finished, he rolled aside and slumped against the pillows while his breath slowed. She lay still, her naked skin exposed and sticky, counting a hundred places that hurt to varying degrees; then twisted carefully onto her back. The dull ache of bruises; the sharper sting where her tender, dry flesh had torn. The throb of her lip – she had bitten down on it to keep herself quiet. Her thighs were raw and scratched from the raking of his fingernails.

At least now he was done, and would need to rest before launching his next assault. It was exhausting, never quite knowing what he would do next; always wondering what he would demand of her and living on a knife-edge of fear. And then, when he attacked, like a coiled snake striking... Why did she still feel shocked every time? How could she still feel such incredulity that a human being could take delight in injuring and debasing another creature, when years of experience had taught her over and over that he could?

"A gentleman would treat his wife like a lady, not like a whore," she said now, the bitterness of her tone unmistakable despite the soft quietness of her voice.

Sated, he seemed amused rather than angry. His face loomed over hers, breath reeking of his customary cigars and late-night brandy, and she forced herself to look into his eyes, ignoring the skittering of her heartbeat.

The fine linen of her nightgown was bunched around her stomach; she moved a hand to push it down, but he caught her wrist in his great paw and wrenched her arms up, above her head, in a grip that would leave a fresh set of bruises.

"Do you imagine yourself to be better than a whore, my dear? I see very little difference... saving that, unlike you, whores generally have womanly grace and charm, and are prepared to work hard for their bed and board. And you are amply rewarded for your services. I would remind you that it is only your submission that earns the clothes on your back and puts food in your mouth. What use are you to me apart from this? If I didn't gain at least this small pleasure from keeping you, I wouldn't have hesitated to have you put away years ago."

His contemptuous sneer widened as his eyes traced over her nakedness like a burn, making her shrink further against the mattress. "You are a failure in every respect. You have failed to provide me with a son; you are useless as a companion or as a hostess; you are a hopeless chatelaine; you can't even manage to look like a woman." He prodded her hip with a hard finger, his eyes cold with distaste. "Look at you, scrawny as a boy. I had arses plumper and riper than yours at school. Eat more, or I'll make you sorry."

She didn't doubt that he meant it, but held onto the kernel of satisfaction it gave her. The only aspects of her body and her life that he couldn't control were her stomach and her mind. Her refusal to eat more was a small act of rebellion against his demands, the pride afforded by such resistance overcoming the gnawing pain in her stomach. Sometimes he would send the footman out on some pretext, and stand over her to force her to eat more, cuffing her on the side of the head where the bruise wouldn't show, or pinching the tender skin under her arm if she refused. In recent years she had learned to eat just enough to deflect his attention, then retreat to her bathroom and push her fingers down her throat to purge herself. She couldn't prevent him from invading her body, but she would do everything in her power to make that body repulsive to him. At least that way she could deny him some measure of his perverse enjoyment.

Abruptly he released her wrists and she rubbed them to ease the throbbing left behind. The mattress dipped towards him as he heaved himself up to sit on the edge of the bed, reaching for his robe. She tensed, the tiny hairs on her back rising in revulsion at the prospect of rolling towards him. She never touched him voluntarily.

He was going. Gingerly she drew her nightgown down and dragged the bedclothes over herself. She lay curled into a ball, shutting down her mind. His words were only words, and the bruises and grazes were only pain. The click of the door told her lungs they could fill themselves with air again, and her limbs that they could let go of some of their rigidity. He had at last left her alone.

Sometimes she felt it would have been better if he had killed her years ago. He had come close once, when her head hit the grate as he knocked her down. He must have been alarmed when she still hadn't woken by the time he finished using her, as he had called for Nellie, her maid, to wave smelling salts under her nose. She cried when she woke, that time, and didn't contradict him when he railed against her stupid clumsiness and told Nellie that she had tripped and knocked herself out.

She rarely cried any more, even when he flung his cruel words or used her like his personal toy. She was just a doll to him, to be played with or tossed into a dusty corner on a whim. Not the sort of soft, pretty doll that demands to be picked up and held, but an ugly porcelain one with a cold, prim mouth and dead eyes, blank-faced even when she was screaming inside. One day, she was sure, he would forget himself and smash her to pieces in a fit of pique, consigning her to history. There was a part of her that wished it would happen soon, but somehow the instinct to survive had always managed to overrule her desire to die. He hadn't made it happen tonight. Was she glad, or disappointed?

For now, it was enough to have made it through another of his visits to her room. He would sleep in his room at the other end of the corridor, and she would be safe until morning. So she gathered up the pains, along with her feelings, and locked them up deep inside. They were too dangerous to be released. Where might they go if she set them free, and what further damage might they cause? The boxing of them hadn't come naturally: for the first year of her marriage she had waited and prayed for her brother to realise what was happening to her and come to her rescue. But Tristram was at first away with the army, and then was killed in the war against the Boers. She'd had to accept that this was her fate.

In some ways her life resembled a fairy tale: one in which an enchantress had cast a dreadful curse on her that robbed her

of her mother and father, and then condemned her to marry a
wicked ogre. The curse had transformed her, laying a filthy
disguise over her former self. There could be no fairy tale
ending for her – of that she was sure. No passing prince or
chivalrous knight would come riding to release her with a kiss of
true love, even if he could look past the pollution staining her
soul. No, the only way this curse could be undone was by death:
either his or hers. To Rosamund, trapped in this prison of a
marriage, it mattered little which.

TWO
NELLIE

Nellie Dawson entered Lady Rosamund Fitznorton's room at half-past eight precisely, as she always did. Through the gloom, she noted with some irritation that the bed was a mess, with the sheets and blankets all askew, some of them dragging onto the floor. She set down the tray with her ladyship's cup of tea – black, and piping hot, just the way she liked it – and then moved to the window to draw open the curtains.

Milky morning light poured into the room, illuminating the heavy mahogany tallboy and armoire, the sinuous grey-green print of twisted briars on the walls, and the thick, dark carpet that must be a horror for the housemaids to keep clear of dust specks and ash from the fireplace and Sir Lucien's cigars.

Her ladyship lay curled in a foetal position in the centre of the large four-poster bed, the rumpled opulence of its plum-coloured silks and pristine white linens at odds with her waiflike appearance. She was as thin as one of the orphans in the local workhouse, her hair escaping its night plait in unruly tendrils and her skinny arms marked with fresh bruises. It was always like this when Sir Lucien was home. Nellie was no fool: she could see better than anyone that the master of the house was a brute. It was a common enough situation within marriage, as far as she could tell, whether they were gentry or ordinary folks; and one of the reasons she had never been seriously tempted to attach herself to a man.

Briskly, Nellie marched to the adjoining bathroom and set the taps running in the deep bath, adding a dash of lavender salts. As much as it wasn't nice to think of Sir Lucien mistreating his wife, in reality her ladyship suffered no more than many of the foundrymen or miners' wives in the village did, and with a whole lot of creature comforts to make up for a bit of roughing up now and then. Look at the depth of this bath – and as much hot water as she could ever wish for. No tin tub in front of the kitchen fire or lugging cans of water up and down stairs for Lady Fitznorton. Nellie swished the water with her hand, enjoying the scent: a soak in this fragrant heat would soon soothe any number of bruises, she was sure. Lady Fitz always said lavender reminded her of her childhood.

It was hard to feel too much sympathy for someone who got to wrap herself in towels as thick and soft as goose down, then dress in a fresh set of fine linen undergarments every morning. Lady Fitznorton wore clothes of a quality that Nellie could only dream of. She slept by herself in a soft, warm bed that could fit an entire family. She ate and drank all kinds of fancy delicacies from goodness knows where – when she could be bothered to. It was criminal, the way the rich wasted food. While Sir Lucien scoffed down enough in one meal to feed a working-class household for days, her ladyship left most of hers untouched, congealing on her plate. Perhaps she'd eat more if she had the trouble of cooking for herself, but she had never had to prepare her own meals, beyond occasionally browning toast on the fire if the mood took her. Those lily-white hands with their manicured nails had never tackled anything more strenuous than picking up a cup and saucer.

Maybe if they'd had to grow up in a family of seven hungry

children, never having an item of clothing or a pair of boots that hadn't first been worn out by an older cousin or sibling, they'd be a bit more grateful for what they had and waste less. And maybe Sir Lucien would treat his wife more gently if she wasn't so cold, so constantly sullen and silent. She was like a wraith, bringing an air of gloom around the house. If Lady Fitz had any sense she'd simper and please him, show a bit more gratitude for her many advantages, and make things easier for herself. It would cheer things up for everyone if she had a bit more life in her.

While Lady Fitznorton slipped falteringly from the bed and sank into the depths of her bathtub, Nellie busied herself laying out her clothes for the morning. Her ladyship would be travelling into Pontybrenin with her husband and stepdaughter after breakfast, to see them off on the train to London, so needed an ensemble suitable for either motoring or for the carriage. Given Sir Lucien's enthusiasm for his new motor car, Nellie guessed he would take that. She selected a tailored jacket in French navy blue with a matching skirt and a wide-brimmed hat with an ample veil to protect her ladyship's complexion from engine smuts.

Such impractical clothes, they were. How could anyone do anything useful in a skirt so fashionably narrow at the ankle? It was a wonder Lady Fitz could even climb the stairs. Her employer's silk stockings and exquisitely cut clothes with their softly draping fabrics and intricate lace trimmings were elegant, but they couldn't create a convincing illusion of womanliness. Her ladyship's bust needed artful padding and pushing from her steel-boned corset to create an illusion of womanly curves. Admittedly it was fashionable to be slender now, so her tiny waist was to be envied; but that was all Nellie approved of in her ladyship's looks.

Lady Fitz's extravagant wardrobe set her as high above her servants as did her pale skin, even if its alabaster-smooth surface was marred with a few scrapes and bruises. Her garments were fastened with so many hooks and buttons, she would have to be a contortionist to dress or undress herself. Only someone with a lady's maid to fasten them and laundry maids to spend hours over the cleaning, pressing and goffering of them could wear clothes like those. Only someone who didn't have to be up at five to rake coals or sweep floors could take so much time over dressing.

Lady Fitz emerged from the bathroom in her chemise and drawers and submitted to the lacing and hooking up of her corset before stepping into the centre of the petticoat Nellie had laid out on the floor. She was moving carefully, and looked tired and wan, despite the hot bath which should have brought some colour to her cheeks. She'd taken a pasting last night, then. Nellie took extra care when dressing her, seeing the marks on her arms and the way she winced on being touched. While she folded up the nightgown and towel from the chair in the bath-room, she noted in the corner of her eye the way her employer set her jaw before easing herself slowly onto her seat at the dressing table. Nellie pursed her lips. However frosty and dismal her manner, no woman deserved that kind of handling. It wasn't right.

Nellie had no great liking or respect for Sir Lucien, or for any man who used a woman with so little care, come to that. He was clever, rarely leaving marks where they might show, but it was obvious from the way his wife moved some mornings that he left her sore. Thankfully, he usually left the maids alone. There had been one, a housemaid, who'd had to leave in disgrace, and blamed him for her condition, saying she'd tried to refuse him. Mind, Nellie had seen her sly smiles and the way she'd batted her eyelashes at the footman. Brazen, she was. Giving men coy looks like that, it was like waving a tray of sweets around under the nose of a little boy and then grumbling when he pinched one. Girls like her had no business complaining when men took advantage.

She brushed out her mistress's long, dull brown hair with vigorous strokes, adding a few drops of sweet almond oil. She enjoyed the rhythm of it, and seeing the way she could add a little gloss. Even though it lacked much in the way of natural curl, and often seemed as lacklustre as the head it grew from, with her brushing and crimping irons Nellie had the knack of making it look its best, and there was always satisfaction to be found in doing a job well.

Sometimes, while brushing, or while mending her ladyship's clothes, she allowed her mind to wander and consider looking for a position elsewhere. It would be nice to work for someone who appreciated the fine things that surrounded her. Someone who took an interest in what she wore, who might even perhaps take Nellie along to the fashion shows in Paris, or out to parties where she could exchange tips and tricks with other ladies' maids. It would add some interest to the job to work for someone who wanted the latest hairstyles instead of putting up the same plain cottage loaf or chignon day after day. Lady Fitz tolerated Nellie's daily backcombing, her padding with hairpieces, the pinning and the curling with a disappointing lack of enthusiasm. The only things she seemed to have any enthusiasm for were playing the piano or going for solitary walks in the gardens.

Still, it was better than being Miss Charlotte Fitznorton's maid. That girl was a spoiled little minx. Not even nineteen yet, and her petulant ways had already driven two maids to leave. Whatever the disadvantages of working for Lady Fitz, at least she didn't have to deal with temper tantrums.

This morning, her mistress was particularly quiet. The face reflected in the mirror was pinched; her mouth had a downturn that made her look sour.

At last, Nellie grew bored with the silence. "Will you be

travelling in the new motor car this morning, m'lady?" Although it wasn't strictly correct for a lady's maid to speak unless first addressed by her employer, she had been Lady Fitz's maid for near enough ten years now, and knew this slight informality would be tolerated.

Her ladyship seemed to find it a great effort to speak. "I expect we shall, Nellie," she said at last.

"I thought so. Sir Lucien seems very pleased with it."

Lady Fitz didn't respond, but fiddled with her cuffs, presumably to ensure the lace covered the marks on her wrists in their entirety. She had rearranged her expression and gazed impassively into the mirror while Nellie deftly manoeuvred the final few pins to secure her hair in place.

"I saw the driver polishing it this morning," Nellie went on. "He seems very competent. I heard one of the lads asking him about how the engine works, and he knew all the answers. It sounded very complicated – quite beyond my understanding, I must say."

Her efforts at conversation were rewarded with a fleeting moment of eye contact in the mirror and a slight nod. Conversations with her employer were always somewhat one-sided, but Nellie was not deterred.

"His wife is sister to Wilson's wife, I hear. You know Wilson – the groom? I expect that's how he heard about the position. And I hear his son has been engaged alongside him as an apprentice mechanic. I expect it will be useful for him to have help with maintaining the motor car."

Her ladyship looked away towards the window. Nellie abandoned the topic of the new driver, unsure if Lady Fitz had even been listening.

"Will Sir Lucien and Miss Charlotte be in London for long?" she asked now, offering up a choice of earrings. Lady Fitz gave them only a cursory glance; Nellie awaited her instructions.

"The pearls will do. I expect they will be away for two or three weeks."

So this was to be an extended visit to Sir Lucien's fearsome sister, with her ladyship left at home in the country where she almost always stayed. There, her silent reserve couldn't be the cause of social embarrassment. She spoke so little in company, she was widely understood to be aloof, or, worse, socially inept. It was no wonder, really, that Sir Lucien got impatient with her. A man in his position needed a wife who could fulfil her role and help him, one who could run a sparkling country house party or garden party, or even just a simple dinner party, and dazzle with brilliant wit and use subtle wiles to find out from the other wives what their husbands were up to.

Lady Fitznorton never sparkled. She was as dull and wooden as this dressing table – heavens, even her hair had more life in it than her face. As far as Nellie had ever seen, she was quite incapable of being charming, assured or amusing. There was rarely any expression of emotion, whether a smile or a snarl, on those carefully composed features.

It wasn't that Lady Fitz was ugly. She might even be called handsome if she ate enough to put a bit of flesh on her cheeks and wore a bit of rouge and a smile, Nellie supposed. It wasn't natural for a woman to be so buttoned up inside herself. It wasn't normal.

She stepped back now, her work done for the time being, and Lady Fitznorton rose stiffly to her feet. Watching, Nellie was unsure whether the hesitancy of the other woman's steps towards the door was due to physical pain or her customary lack of enthusiasm for breakfast. Their eyes met briefly.

"What did you say the new driver's name is, Nellie? I must try to remember it later," Lady Fitz asked in her soft, low voice. She had been listening, then.

Nellie wasn't surprised she'd want to address him by name when she met him. To give her credit, Lady Fitz was always polite to her staff. She wasn't one of those spiteful mistresses who would smack careless fingers with the back of a hairbrush or jab a maid with a hat pin if displeased.

Nellie beamed, always glad to be a source of information. "It's Cadwalader, m'lady. Joseph Cadwalader."

That caught her ladyship's attention: she looked up at Nellie with what could almost pass for a smile. "Like the last king of Britain, who was ordered by an angel to give up his throne and become a pilgrim."

"I wouldn't know anything about that, m'lady. I never heard of any King Cadwalader. Just the chauffeur." Really, it was odd the things Lady Fitz talked about sometimes. Too much reading in her youth, and not about anything that was actually useful in real life.

"Geoffrey of Monmouth, Nellie. My father taught me... oh, never mind. It took me back for a moment, that's all."

The spark of interest had passed. Nellie had no idea who Lady Fitz was talking about, but she knew nothing good would come of the melancholy expression that had once again settled on her features from all this talk of kings and her father.

"I'm not familiar with your Geoffrey chap, but I do think Cadwalader is a fine-looking fellow in his uniform," Nellie said with an arch look. "Heads will turn when you drive through Pontybrenin, m'lady, and not just because of the car."

There was no response. Squashing a sigh, she opened the door and stepped aside to allow her employer to pass.

"Never mind, m'lady. I won't keep you any longer from your breakfast."

THREE
ROSAMUND

Rosamund stared at the mound of steaming kedgeree on her plate, her stomach churning at the prospect of such strong flavours in so large a quantity. She had already eaten most of a dish of porridge with cream, served by the footman on her husband's orders.

She risked a peep along the table towards Sir Lucien. He was watching her, eyes as cold as those in his ancestors' portraits on the walls, as if daring her to refuse to eat. She picked up her knife and fork and raised a dainty mouthful to her lips. If she chewed slowly and sipped at her glass of water between mouthfuls, she could avoid having to clear her plate before it was time to depart for the station.

Seated below a painting of a hind being torn apart by hounds, her stepdaughter was tackling a plate of bacon, kidneys and scrambled eggs with enthusiasm, chattering to her father about their plans for their visit to the capital. She didn't bother addressing Rosamund, having never made a secret of her irritation at her stepmother's distant and quiet demeanour. Sir Lucien wouldn't challenge Charlotte's rudeness, perhaps because he found his wife equally enervating. He was always amused by his daughter's vivacity, and she used his affection to persuade him to indulgence. He must surely know he was being played, but never seemed to mind.

Rosamund watched him smile and pat her hand, his adoration of his daughter plain to see. The pangs of envy she had felt when Charlotte was little and she had hoped to be a mother to her had long passed. There was no room in Charlotte's heart for Rosamund, who couldn't find her petulance amusing. Charlotte had had little interest in her stepmother's retellings of ancient legends or sitting down quietly together to draw and paint. She preferred her governess and her father, who indulged her whims and allowed her to while away her hours in idleness.

Over the years, Rosamund had schooled herself to detach her emotions and expect nothing, for by expecting nothing she could never be disappointed by Charlotte's rejection. Besides, Charlotte was welcome to her father's attentions: Rosamund had no desire to attract his notice. Now, while he was distracted in conversation, she motioned to the footman to take away her plate. There wasn't time for her husband to insist she ate more before the moment for their departure arrived.

Sir Lucien and Charlotte's luggage had already been despatched to the station along with his valet and her maid before the family prepared to leave in the new motor car. It had been brought around to the front of the house where it now stood, engine idling, its navy-blue paintwork gleaming in the weak winter sunshine. This was Rosamund's first opportunity to see it, and certainly from her position under the tall gothic arches of the porch it appeared considerably larger and more comfortable than their previous motor. The rear compartment resembled a traditional carriage, its navy panels picked out with a thin coach line of red. It had a canvas roof at the back with a hinge like the hood of a giant perambulator. It would be pleasant to drive along with it lowered in the summer.

"Ah! There she is – my beauty," Sir Lucien rumbled,

patting the vehicle's long blue nose with evident satisfaction before climbing into the front seat where he obviously intended to sit beside the driver. "Look sharp, Cadwalader. We don't have all day."

The driver, smart and broad-shouldered in his tailored navy-blue coat with its matching cap, looked every bit as fine as Nellie's description. He hesitated, strangely awkward, with a flush rising to his clean-shaven cheeks.

Clearing his throat, he answered in a deep and melodious voice: "Of course, sir. If I can just see the ladies in…?"

Rosamund was not surprised by her husband's obvious irritation. He was not accustomed to being kept waiting, but as this vehicle had no separate door for the driver, he would have to exercise some unaccustomed patience until she and Charlotte were seated in the back, then wait for the chauffeur to slide across the front seat before him.

Cadwalader opened the rear door, stepping aside politely, and Charlotte pushed in front, prattling excitedly about their journey and ignoring him as he handed her in to the enclosed compartment. Rosamund was relieved when he closed the door on her and her shrill girlish voice was muffled for a moment.

"Lady Fitznorton."

She had been gazing across the lawns to blank out her irritation at her stepdaughter's insistence upon being first into the car. Now she turned her attention back to the motor. The driver was waiting, holding the door on the other side and offering a hand to help her climb in. She placed her gloved hand in his and glanced up at his face before putting her foot on the step.

"Thank you, Cadwalader," she said, and was struck by the warmth that came into his eyes. They were an unusual colour, somewhere between green and hazel; in that brief exchange, she hadn't time to decide which, but the image lingered. He acknowledged her courtesy with the slightest of smiles and a nod, then saw her settled before closing the door and walking around to slide across the front bench into the driving seat.

Charlotte leaned across Rosamund to open the little flap in the glass panel between the ladies' compartment and the front seat. "Oh, Papa, if it rains you'll get wet sitting there at the front," she said.

It was certainly true that there was little to protect those at the front from the elements. A cool blast of spring air whistled through the flap and Rosamund dragged a travelling rug across her lap.

Charlotte tapped imperiously on the glass and Cadwalader turned.

"Open this, would you?" she demanded. "I want to be able to talk to Papa."

Cadwalader unlatched the glass panel and slid it out of the way.

Rosamund leaned back and pulled her travelling rug more tightly around her knees as they set off. The car was comfortable and elegant, its grey cord interior well-padded. There were brocade-trimmed straps to hold onto when rounding corners, and a less luxurious folding seat for a maid's use. Tasselled blinds could be pulled down for additional warmth and privacy, but Charlotte was having none of that, determined to have her father's attention.

It gave Rosamund some satisfaction to observe that Sir Lucien was equally determined to ignore his daughter's chatter. He was fully engaged in establishing Cadwalader's opinion of the Wolseley engine. Finding herself snubbed for once, Charlotte soon lapsed into a sulk, staring out of the window.

"So, Cadwalader – you're a local man, I gather?" Sir Lucien was clearly inclined to be jovial this morning. He liked to believe he had the common touch, asking his staff inquisitive questions that he imagined made them like him, although Rosamund suspected that his tendency to forget their answers and ask the same questions the next time he saw them probably undermined any respect he might have won.

"Yes, sir," came the driver's reply. "We lived away for a while, in England – that's when I got my training on motors at the Wolseley factory in Adderley Park – but when we heard about this opportunity, we moved back to be nearer to my wife's family."

"It was a bit of luck that you did. We had the devil of a job finding someone competent to maintain a motor of this calibre in such a backwater. I was contemplating sending one of the engineers from the works off to train, but your application saved me the trouble."

Cadwalader gave a polite nod of acknowledgement and Sir Lucien pressed on.

"How is your lad getting along? Making himself useful, I trust, as your apprentice?"

"Yes, sir. He's a fast learner. Thank you for taking him on – we're grateful for the opportunity."

"And do you have any other boys?"

Rosamund had only been half-listening, but there was a moment of silence in which Cadwalader paused, which struck her as odd.

"Yes, sir. We have four boys now, and three girls..." He fell silent, negotiating the junction of the rutted road out of the Fitznorton estate and onto the public highway.

Now? Rosamund wondered.

Cadwalader's voice deepened, turning gravelly. "We had another son, but scarlet fever took him; and we lost our youngest daughter last year."

That explained his hesitancy. Rosamund gazed into her lap, all too easily able to understand the pain of such a loss.

Sir Lucien had no such sensitivity. "Five boys! Well, you're a lucky man. I'd have done better to marry your wife, not mine.

I'm afraid if mine was a brood mare instead of a woman I'd have sent her to the slaughterhouse long ago."

Charlotte snorted in amusement, her boredom momentarily relieved by her stepmother's embarrassment.

Rosamund felt a hot blush rise to her cheeks, exacerbated by the startled glance she saw Cadwalader throw at Sir Lucien before he fixed his attention firmly back on the road. Quite apart from her husband's vulgar remark about her, how could any man of sense describe a father who had suffered such grief as *lucky*? Grinding her teeth, she was relieved to glimpse the railway station ahead. The time for their departure was not far off now, and the constant throbbing tension in her temples would gradually ease without Charlotte's insolence and Sir Lucien's cruelty plaguing her days.

Charlotte pushed herself forward the moment the door was opened, obliging Cadwalader to hand her down first; she ignored him, hastening to take her father's arm as they made for the platform to await the train.

"I'm very sorry for your loss, Cadwalader," Rosamund said quietly. "I hope you will be kind enough to overlook any insensitivity on Sir Lucien's part. I'm sure he meant no offence."

His expression barely changed. But there was something in his eyes that hadn't been there before: an understanding, as if they had exchanged a sudden insight into the misery in each other's souls. His was the face of a man who had known sorrow and joy: both were etched there in the lines fanning out from his intelligent hazel eyes and the deep grooves on his forehead. For a moment, his gaze held her as warmly as an embrace. When he held out his hand she took it reflexively, realising her own was trembling.

"Would you mind waiting here with the car?" she asked, momentarily bereft without the support of his hand. She was so unused to kindness, especially from a man, and yet she was quite sure it was what she had read in his features.

"Of course, m'lady."

Reluctantly, resisting the desire to look back at him, she moved away into the railway station and once again assumed her habitual emotionless mask. It wouldn't do to reveal any weakness to Charlotte, who was more than capable of exploiting it through spite, or to Sir Lucien, who would take pleasure in planning ever more inventive ways to amplify her pain.

Standing back, she huddled under her fur collar and watched the loading of the travelling trunks, the efficiency of the staff making her presence entirely redundant. If not for her husband's insistence that she should make this public display of family unity, she would have remained at Plas Norton and exploited the dry weather to wander the gardens. She was well schooled to patience, though, and to a pretence of contentment, and somehow she summoned a sort of gracious half-smile when Sir Lucien bent to drop a kiss onto her cheek and bade her farewell. She even managed to maintain the appearance of calm as the train puffed and heaved its way out of the station, carrying her tormentors away for at least two weeks.

Two weeks. Fourteen whole days in which she would at last be able to breathe.

FOUR

JOSEPH

Joe snapped his book shut with a guilty start as a shadow fell across his lap. Lady Fitznorton was waiting beside the car, looking faintly surprised to see him reading. How typical of the gentry – she probably assumed her servants were barely literate. What else was he expected to do while he waited? As he climbed out hastily to assist her, his stomach growled a reminder that it was a few hours since he had eaten. He hoped she hadn't heard.

"M'lady," he said, the greeting covering a multitude of situations: an apology, in this case, for keeping her waiting by failing to notice that she had returned, and an invitation to step into the back seat. He put his hand on the door handle to open it, but she surprised him by walking around the car and standing next to the front door.

"I'd like to ride in the front on the way back?" she asked, making it sound like a question instead of a statement. As if he had any say in where she sat.

"As you wish, m'lady. But you might find it cold. There are no windows at the sides..."

"That's quite alright. I can use one of the travelling rugs."

He primed the engine and cranked the starting handle with a sharp, practised jerk of his arm. It started immediately with a roar and he climbed back into the front, sliding out of her way into position behind the steering wheel and offering a hand for her to climb in. He'd noticed that her movements were considered and perhaps a little stiff, much like the way she spoke. The other staff described her as cold, a Snow Queen with a face as frozen as her heart. It was true that he hadn't yet seen her smile, but he'd been aware of her blush earlier when her ass of a husband had insulted her. And he'd noticed her trembling when she'd offered her condolences outside the station, which she hadn't needed to do. So common sense told him she couldn't be as unfeeling as the others had suggested. Perhaps she just didn't have all that much to smile about.

He leaned over to tuck a woollen travelling rug around her lap. There wasn't much to her, he realised as he draped the rug over her legs. For a woman who could afford to dine on caviar and champagne every day if she chose, she was a thin little thing, her thick travelling coat concealing how delicate she was. And she smelled wonderful, like flowers. Nothing like his Mary, whose soft, warm torso generally smelled of sweat, cooking and, until last year, milk and baby sick. Not that she would be smelling of babies anymore. Not since Annie's death had left them both broken.

Cross with himself, he pushed away the memories that had a habit of drifting into his mind like a persistent ache. They set off in silence, Lady Fitznorton staring straight ahead, her face expressionless. He wondered why she had been so keen to sit at the front when it meant she would be buffeted by the cold. Glancing at her surreptitiously, he saw her shiver as icy air blew in through the vehicle's open sides.

"Are you alright, m'lady? It's quite chilly up front. Would you like me to stop and help you into the back?"

She shook her head at once.

"No, no – I enjoy the fresh air. And this car is much more practical than the old one, now that we have a canopy and the windscreen. We shall have no further need for goggles."

Her mouth softened slightly in what he interpreted as a faint hint of a smile. It was a shame she was so serious. A smile would take years off her. Behind that veil she had full lips that looked made for smiling. Or kissing. He swiftly crushed that thought and stared straight ahead. It wouldn't do to allow his imagination to stray in that direction.

Curious eyes followed the car, which must surely be the newest and fastest in the area, given Sir Lucien's standing as the biggest landowner and industrialist between here and Merthyr Tydfil. The policeman at the main crossroads in the centre of Pontybrenin saluted and held up the other traffic for them, including a smart couple in a single-cylinder car who watched them with obvious envy. Children in ragged clothes ran alongside with grinning faces and he waved back, waiting until he was well clear before speeding up lest he cast up a cloud of dust or startle the horses pulling carts. As they passed the forbidding walls of the town's workhouse, Joe looked away with a shudder, thankful to have the skills and aptitude to enable him to earn a decent living. God forbid any of his family should ever end up in there.

Pontybrenin wasn't a large town, at least not compared with his recent years in the bustling, smog-covered urban sprawl of Birmingham, so before long they were on the outskirts, passing narrow slate-roofed terraced cottages and small workshops. Now he was able to open the engine up and feel the thrill of controlling a large machine at speed.

"It must be quite exhilarating, being able to drive," Lady Fitznorton said suddenly, putting a hand on the door to steady herself as he rounded a bend. "Travelling so fast, one could be miles away in quite a short time."

He hoped he had managed to conceal his surprise that she

had made an effort to start up a conversation. "It's marvellous, m'lady. I'll never go back to working as a coachman again, not now I've trained on motor cars. And this model is a beauty. She'll do as much as forty-five miles per hour, on a fairly straight and flat road. A Silver Ghost could do more than that, of course, but then it has more brake horsepower..."

He broke off, realising she'd probably not intended for him to start wittering on about specifications. She'd only been making a polite observation, and he'd gone and made himself look like an idiot by responding as if they were having a proper chat. Worse, he might have made her think he was criticising Sir Lucien for not owning a Rolls-Royce. He should keep his mouth shut, lest he should blot his copybook with his employer's wife when he'd only just started in the job.

They had reached the edge of the Fitznorton estate, but were still a couple of miles from the big house. Joe eased his pressure on the accelerator pedal, careful on the rougher road for fear of dislodging stones that might damage the car's paint-work or windows. The deer park spread out to their right, silvered in places with the remnants of the night's frost, and dotted with occasional trees, each with their own little protective fence. Mountains brooded behind it, rough-hewn and dark today, although he knew they would be transformed by summer sunshine. To their left was a dense area of woodland that Joe would bet had more than its fair share of pheasants and rabbits. A poacher's paradise – although doubtless Sir Lucien had a vigilant gamekeeper to keep them at bay, and to stop them fishing in the lake.

The trees were mostly bare of leaves at this time of year, but it didn't take much of a leap of imagination to picture them a few months from now, a palette of greens, or in autumn when they would be bound to look glorious. Not for the first time, he was glad he'd taken up the opportunity to bring his family here: even allowing for the factory and mine on the other side of town, this was a healthier place for the children to grow up than the dirty city they'd lived in before.

"You seemed quite absorbed in your book," Lady Fitznorton said after another minute or so. "Is it good?"

Again he glanced at her, surprised that she was interested in his opinion. It didn't seem to fit with the stony, silent figure he had been led to expect. Yet she seemed genuinely curious, and as he couldn't think of any reason not to, he drew out the slim volume from where he had tucked it between his hip and the arm rest, and passed it to her.

"H.G. Wells. *The Time Machine*. I haven't read this one." She turned the book over and opened it to flick through the pages. "I believe Mr Wells is quite the outspoken socialist..."

He was suddenly wary. Perhaps this conversation was intended to trap him into admitting socialist leanings? "I wouldn't know anything about that, m'lady," he said, rather than give his thoughts away.

"I read *The War of the Worlds*, but I found it rather frightening. What's your opinion of this one?"

This felt like safer ground. "Well, m'lady... I like the idea of a machine that can travel through time. If I could build a machine like that, I'd go into the future, perhaps fifty or even a hundred years into the future. I'd love to see the motor cars and aeroplanes then. Mary – my wife, that is – Mary says motor cars will go out of fashion. 'Joe,' she says to me, 'don't you lose your knack with horses because one day those filthy dirty engines might fall out of favour.' My Mary's right about a lot of things, but I can't see that happening, myself. Progress never goes *backwards*, does it?"

She remained silent, her face as elegant and immovable as carved marble. Emboldened, he asked her, even though it wasn't his place to do so: "What would you do, then, m'lady, if you could travel through time?"

Her chestnut-brown eyes widened and she snapped the book closed, laying it down on the seat between them.

"I believe I'd prefer to travel backwards in time. If I could go back, there are things I could do differently."

There was a finality in her tone; she remained tight-lipped and silent for the rest of the journey, and Joe didn't dare interrupt her thoughts. Perhaps he had overstepped the mark. And yet, he had a feeling her silence wasn't because she was annoyed at him. It must be something else. He brooded on her words.

With a life as charmed as hers it was hard to imagine her having things she wished she could change. Her husband was a peculiar one, though, with that horrible joke he'd made about her being no good as a brood mare. And now he came to think about it, the daughter hadn't shown her much respect, either, pushing in front all the time and sulking out of the window. If she'd been one of his kids, she'd get a clip across the ear for that sort of behaviour.

It was odd: Lady Fitznorton had the air of a woman carrying her own private grief. Joe was sure he hadn't just imagined an emptiness in her, a need for human warmth. In spite of what the other servants had said, she hadn't seemed at all aloof. On the contrary, she'd been courteous and seemed genuinely interested in his opinions. He certainly hadn't expected that. Or to feel that, if she wasn't who she was, he could almost have liked her.

FIVE

NELLIE

Nellie always looked forward to her pudding. Not because she was greedy, although she did have a weakness for sweet things, but because once the main course was finished, she could leave the other staff in the servants' hall and retire with the more senior servants to the housekeeper's comfortable sitting room, where they could relax and talk in private. Today they had bread and butter pudding, Nellie's favourite, drenched in custard.

"I haven't stopped today," she grumbled. "Himself must have given Lady Fitz a pasting last night. Her arms were black and blue when I took her tea up, and the bed all askew. She was moving like an old woman, stiff as a board, so Lord only knows what other bruises she had where I couldn't see 'em. And as for her nightdress, when I checked it..." She paused for dramatic effect and shook her head, a gesture mirrored by Mrs Longford, who put down her spoon and clucked her tongue. "Torn to shreds, it was. I did my best with it, but I had to replace half of the lace, it was fit for nothing."

The butler's attention was caught at that. His spoon paused halfway to his mouth, and his sharp, unblinking gaze made

Nellie wish she hadn't mentioned the torn nightgown. "Perhaps she likes a bit of rough handling? Some women do, I'm told."

"Rubbish!" the housekeeper exclaimed. "I don't know who's told you that, Mr Phelps, but they were obviously having you on. It isn't right for him to treat her like that. Baronet or no, he's no different from some brawling thug in the pub in town."

Mr Phelps was having none of it. "It is not for us to judge our betters, Mrs Longford," he declared in the lofty tone he liked to use. It never failed to rile Nellie, and this time it seemed Mrs Longford was just as annoyed by it.

"Betters, you say? Betters my foot. Think of the size of her, compared with him, and the way he treats her. He's no better than an ape, and she's like a delicate little butterfly in his paw. Yes, Mr Phelps, there's no need to look at me like that. He's like an animal, treating her like that."

Mr Phelps arched his brow at Nellie. "You see where your gossip leads us, Miss Dawson? Dangerous talk, that's where."

Nellie ignored Mr Phelps's huff of annoyance. He pretended to disapprove, but she knew he enjoyed discussing the salacious details of their employers' lives as much as she did. And besides, they were safe enough to share in here, now that the hall boy had gone back to the servants' hall to finish his meal.

"You'd think he'd be too old for all that, by now, but he seems to be getting worse, if anything," she said.

Mrs Longford shook her head. "He was always like it. You weren't here when the first Lady Fitz was alive, but I remember she used to scream the place down sometimes. Not often, mind you, because it was a whole lot livelier here then: they used to be forever hosting parties, or going off to town or to other people's parties instead. Her maid, Miss Everett, was hardly ever here, they used to gad about so much. But I suppose it must have made him a bit more careful, because he couldn't very well go knocking her about with half the nobility to hear her calling him all the names under the sun, could he?"

Nellie licked the last of the custard off her spoon and laid it back in her bowl. The first Lady Fitz's maid must have had a very different life from her own. She must have forever been packing and unpacking, and travelling about the country with trunks. The chance to see a bit of the world and to mingle with other ladies' maids would be nice, but she probably wouldn't like all that endless to-ing and fro-ing. She liked to sleep in a familiar bed of a night, and there was comfort in the constant routines here. Working for this Lady Fitznorton might be dull and predictable, but that also made her everyday tasks relatively easy.

"What was she like, his first wife? Was she like this one?"

Mr Phelps chuckled into his napkin at that. "Not in the slightest."

Helpfully, Mrs Longford supplied more details. "Had a terrible temper, she did. Of course, she was French, like Sir Lucien's mother. A hot-tempered, impetuous people, the French. I expect that's where Miss Charlotte gets her petulant ways from. I remember the late Lady Fitz used to slap Miss Everett if she didn't like the way she'd done her hair, and throw things across the room in a temper. Expensive things, mind. I soon stopped putting the really nice vases in her room, I can tell you. She had a nasty tongue on her, too: I saw poor Miss Everett in tears no end of times."

"I couldn't imagine the current Lady Fitz behaving like that."

"Glaciers don't move fast enough to throw things," Mr Phelps said drily, helping himself to another bowlful of pudding. He hovered his spoon over the bowl, his brows drawn together in a frown. "She's like winter drizzle, this one. Cold, miserable, and dampens everyone's spirits. When you think about it, it's not normal, is it, for a woman in her position to be such a recluse? I mean... she isn't quite all there, I don't think? There are times, now and then, when I think about looking elsewhere, for a more sociable place: a family that holds a few parties, with opportunities to meet people with a bit of life about them."

Mrs Longford hid a mischievous grin behind her cup. "That's understandable, Mr Phelps. But then you remember that her quiet life in the country with no guests to serve saves you no end of work. And that all those lively people attending parties would have no interest whatsoever in you. To them, a butler, or a housekeeper for that matter, might as well be a chair in the hall: useful to make their lives more comfortable, but not something to excite their curiosity."

Nellie sat back in her chair. Her instincts told her Mr Phelps was wrong about their mistress. "I probably know her better than anyone on the staff, and I'd say it isn't that she's stupid. It's as if she's lost. And maybe, I wonder, even a bit shy? She doesn't know what to say to all those fancy people, so she says nothing at all, and they can't bear it because they're so used to being fawned over. That's what *I* think isn't normal. All that money, all that deference, and people like us to spend our lives at their beck and call, but when all's said and done, none of them are really *happy*. No more than the rest of us."

"Hmph. You haven't been here long enough to remember what happened the last time they held a party. Anyway, I'm not interested in whether they're happy or not," said Mr Phelps, polishing off the last of his pudding and setting his spoon down. "Just as long as they're satisfied with the running of this house. The rest... Well, the rest is none of my business." On that pronouncement, he folded his napkin, tugged his waistcoat down over his portly stomach, and the meal was over.

The two women made to follow him from the room, but Mrs Longford laid a hand on Nellie's arm. "Don't go losing any sleep over her ladyship, now. I know it can't be pleasant, dealing with all that, but there's nothing you can do to change it. She made her bed when she married him, and she'll just have to lie in it. All the sympathy in the world won't help her."

"I never said I sympathised," Nellie said. But as she went up to her room in the attics to tackle some more mending before Lady Fitz might summon her again, she wasn't sure if this was entirely true.

SIX
MARY

Mary was bone-weary, although it wasn't yet mid-afternoon. Up at six, fingers blue with cold, she had cleaned out and lit the range and filled the boiler with water to get it hot enough for washing and brewing a pot of tea. Her eldest daughter Maggie had made a start on cooking porridge and fried eggs for breakfast, while twelve-year-old Dolly emptied the chamber pots into the toilet at the end of the yard. The little ones had been fractious that morning, especially Miriam, the youngest, who had wanted to stay in the warmth of her bed when Dolly got out.

She didn't feel settled in this house yet. The paint was cracking off the floorcloths in the downstairs rooms, and the walls were painted in an ugly, drab colour that did nothing to lift her spirits. Patches of black mould in the corners kept coming back however much she scrubbed. There was no linoleum upstairs, just bare boards that let in draughts around her feet when she got up. She'd need to make some peg rugs to give them something warmer to stand on while they dressed. In the kitchen, the range seemed to have a mind of its own, and she hadn't yet got the knack of it. Worse, there was no tap, so all their water had to be brought in from the pump in the yard, and the dirty water collected in a pail to be taken back out again.

While Joe might feel he'd gone up in the world because this house was bigger than their last – and she'd have to agree with him that the air was most likely healthier here on the edge of the Fitznorton estate than it had been in Birmingham, where black smuts were forever landing on her laundry – she missed her indoor plumbing and being on a street with neighbours to talk to while she scrubbed the front step. She held her tongue, though, knowing she'd better not complain too much when it was she who had urged him to take the job with the Fitznortons after her sister Peggy wrote to them about it.

Poor Peggy was struggling, with her newest baby only a few weeks old, two other children to care for, and her own health none too strong. It was no wonder she'd wanted her elder sister close by, and Mary was glad of the chance to offer some help. As soon as her own younger children had run off back to the village school after their dinner hour, she packed a freshly baked loaf of bread into a basket, wrapped a warm shawl around her shoulders, and walked the short distance to Peggy's cottage.

Like their own tied cottage, it was on the fringes of the Fitznorton estate, on the side nearest the village, which was an easy walk away. With its baker, grocer and butcher, the village was a convenient source for most of the items Mary needed on a day-to-day basis. For a wider choice of shops, like the ironmonger, chemist and fishmonger, she had to walk four miles in the opposite direction, following the path of the river to the drab, smoke-choked town of Pontybrenin, noisy and dominated by the chimneys of the factory and foundry. Ugly though they were, Mary was grateful for the opportunities the local industries afforded her eldest son Leonard, who had found employment almost as soon as they moved. In the next valley, beyond the town, was a colliery, one of many that plundered the Welsh soil for its mineral riches for the benefit of men like Sir Lucien, whose own house was well upstream and away from the smoke that hung over his enterprises like a widow's veil.

Peggy and Wilf's cottage was smaller than her own, a reflection of Joe's relatively high status among the staff. Mary felt a puff of pride as she let herself in, remembering how Joe had worked his way up since his days of managing the horses. She called up the stairs to let Peggy know she had arrived, then set to work in the scullery, washing up the breakfast dishes the children had left behind. A shame Wilf hadn't done it, knowing his wife was still in a weakened state after a difficult birth, but there it was. He was up and out to work early, and couldn't afford to be late with a growing family to provide for.

"I'm glad to see you," Peggy said from her bed as Mary brought her a cup of weak, sweet tea with some bread and jam. "Look at this little one. There's not an ounce of fat on him. I try to feed him, but no sooner than he starts suckling, he falls asleep. Do you think he's getting enough milk?"

"Have you tried waking him to feed more often?"

"Over and over."

He did seem a fragile little mite. The golden tint to his face, almost like a deep suntan even though he had never yet been outdoors, made Mary suspect jaundice. But there was no sense in voicing her thoughts and adding to Peggy's worries.

"All mothers find things to fret about. Before you know it, he'll have left school and he'll be telling you he wants a job in a factory." She attempted a smile, but the previous evening's argument with eighteen-year-old Maggie still rankled.

"Are you alright? You look a bit down in the mouth again."

"Just a difference of opinion with our Maggie. Joe and I have tried to convince her to go back into service, if she can get a position with the Fitznortons; but she says she's had enough of skivvying. Thinks she's too good for scrubbing floors and cleaning out fireplaces these days. She's made up her mind to ask for work at the factory. Says the money's better and she'll enjoy it more. As if enjoyment has anything to do with work."

Peggy raised an eyebrow. "Probably best not to mention that to the pastor. He doesn't hold with girls working unless they're in a job that gets them ready to run a home and be a good wife... Kids, eh? Like you said, there's always something to worry about."

She gazed down again at the baby lying fast asleep and milk-drunk in her arms. Her lip trembled and Mary patted her hand.

"No sense in distressing yourself," she said briskly, to stop Peggy dwelling on her fears. "He's in the Lord's hands. You'll be having him christened soon, won't you?"

To Mary's relief, Peggy nodded. It would be as well to have the Lord's blessing on the little lad, as he had a look of one who might not be destined to remain long in this world. She reached down and stroked her forefinger against the baby's clenched fist. Instinctively, he grasped it. She smiled, though her heart contracted with remembrance of her own lost infants and the knowledge that she would never again experience the pull of a baby's rosebud mouth at her breast. Just for a moment, her arms longed to cradle the weight of her own baby again.

Her eyes pricked, and she tore herself away, busying about the house with duster, mop and scrubbing brush until she had regained control of herself. Activity: that was what she needed. If she kept busy until she was too tired to think, she could numb the yet-raw grief that dogged her. Being busy was how she got through each day.

When she had worked her feelings off and felt able to converse without any dangerous currents of emotion catching her off guard, she climbed the stairs again to sit beside Peggy on the bed. The painted iron bedstead creaked and dipped under her weight.

"How are you feeling?" she asked, casting a critical eye

about the room. Peggy's dark hair hung lank about her shoulders and her nightgown looked as if it needed laundering. Mary felt sure something wasn't right with her sister, but guessed it was probably the usual tiredness any mother felt, tending a small baby and keeping a household going without any domestic help.

Peggy dragged a hand over her face. "I'm worn out, Mary. I did get up earlier, honest, to do the breakfast, but then this one was rooting and crying again so I thought I might as well bring him back to bed while his sisters are at school. I'll get up to do tea before Wilf comes home. I'm just so tired – I don't remember feeling like this for so long after the others. And Wilf doesn't understand. He thinks I need to tidy myself up a bit, get on with things."

"Get on with things? Surely he can manage until the babe is a bit stronger? I can send my Dolly over to help a bit with the house, if you want."

"I don't just mean that. Other things. You know. Between man and wife." She lowered her eyes, her face crimson.

Mary sucked in her cheeks. "Oh. It's only been a couple of weeks."

"*Four* weeks."

"Then he'll have to take no for an answer."

"It isn't that simple, though. I mean, I wouldn't mind it myself, but..."

"It was that simple with my Joe. After Annie, I said no more. He blustered and sulked about it in the beginning. He's even tried it on now and then. But he knows I mean it, and he's left me alone. He hasn't touched me in twelve months or more. So you tell your Wilf it's too soon. You've not even been churched yet: he should be ashamed of himself. What is he, an animal?"

"Mary!"

The baby's hands flew up, fingers outstretched like the

points of stars, and Peggy shushed him, eyes alight with laughter at her sister's outrage.

"Of course Wilf isn't an animal. I'm not against it. It would be nice – just not yet, not when I'm looking like this, all sweaty and leaking milk down me, and with this little one in bed with us. But do you really mean it? You and Joe don't—?"

Mary shook her head, feeling awkward now after seeing the inquisitive gleam in Peggy's eyes. She had revealed too much and made herself the butt of a joke, it seemed. It wasn't fair for all that hurt, and all that strife between husband and wife, to be seen as ridiculous by someone younger and more fortunate, who could have no idea what it was like to have her heart plunged into an abyss of grief.

She smoothed her skirt and donned her shawl, glancing at the clock on the mantelpiece for form's sake, as if she was only getting up because it was time to go and not because she couldn't bring herself to stay any longer. It wasn't Peggy's fault that she couldn't understand. She was young yet, and still filled with optimism that all her babes would thrive. Mary leaned down to press a farewell kiss on her forehead, cupped the little lad's soft head in her hand, and sent up a silent prayer that it would indeed prove to be so.

SEVEN
ROSAMUND

Rosamund had woken early. Only the faintest glimmer of light shone around the edges of the velvet curtains. She stretched out her toes, allowing herself to luxuriate in the warmth of the bed. Its four posts reached up to heavy, shot-silk drapes in deep crimson and green, pleated and joined in a central boss. They made her feel closed in, those drapes. She kept her eyes closed and focused on the softness of the sheet and the weight of the blankets and coverlet.

The only times she felt safe were when her husband was not at home. At other times this bed, this room that wasn't truly hers as long as he could invade it, always held the possibility of danger. But now, with him away, the oppressive cloud that hung about her when he was here had begun to lift, allowing her spirits some rest, if not peace. For the time being, at least, she was free to eat her breakfast on a tray in her room. He would never allow it when he was home, as he used breakfast as an opportunity to control her activities, making her eat under his watchful eye.

She thought back to her youth, when her bedroom at Ambleworth Hall had been her private sanctuary. She had loved to retreat there with a book, to sit in the window seat or clamber back into bed to read under the eiderdown on cold days while Papa took his afternoon nap. But those were different times. A time when she was loved and indulged, as her mother had been.

There was no one to love her now. And it was hardly surprising: she had done such disgusting things at her husband's bidding, submitted to depraved and unnatural acts to satisfy his will. Such a filthy creature as she didn't deserve kindness or gentleness. She could only be thankful that her father would never know the depths to which she had sunk.

Her neck muscles were tense, even now. Her shoulders were always taut. Perhaps she would ask Nellie to knead them later. She flexed her fingers – it had been a couple of days since she last played the piano. It would do her good to play again this morning. Rain was lashing against the window, so it wasn't a day for a walk.

When she thought about it, there was so little to do. She closed her eyes, ashamed of herself. A woman in her position should be involved in local affairs, a patroness of charities such as those for miners' widows and children. There was certainly a need for it, after the mine disaster last year that had rivalled the one at Senghenydd for its death toll. She should be organising events, engaging in social visits, being appointed to committees, and telling people what to do. But whenever she tried to imagine pushing herself forward, issuing invitations, or being charming in company, she froze. What could she possibly offer, contemptible, damaged plaything that she was?

She knew she wasn't normal. She'd tried, when she was first married, to play the hostess. But she'd felt so broken then, not yet numbed to the nightly assaults that crushed her spirit. Their first dinner party had been a disaster: she'd descended the wide, carved oak stairs wincing at every step, feeling as if she was plunging underwater. The voices of the gathered local gentry seemed to roar in her ears, sucking the breath from her, and when she arrived in the hall and saw dozens of heads swivel towards her, hungry in their eagerness to appraise the young bride, her lungs and limbs had simultaneously failed her. The massed faces swam before her eyes like a mob sent to attack her, and as her evident distress changed their expressions to either alarm or contempt she sank onto her knees, gasping for air and clinging to the barley twist newel post as if it was the mast of a ship sinking beneath stormy waves.

She recalled her husband's sister, Blanche, taking charge, ushering their guests away into the dining room, leaving her alone with Sir Lucien. As the doors closed against the throng his thick, pitiless fingers unclenched and seized her by the hair to drag her back upstairs to her room. She had trained herself not to think about what followed. The way her bladder let go, the crowning humiliation as he tore at her clothes and flung her against the bedpost; the blow that sent her to the floor, and then the kick that left her winded. He hadn't time to punish her further then; she knew that would come later, when the guests had gone. For the time being, he had left her lying in her torn, urine-soaked gown, locked in, completely alone.

Over the years, her bedroom had become both her prison and her refuge. A place to nurse her bruises. A torture chamber he visited whenever he chose. He had no more regard for her protests than for her closed door. She and her room were his property, for him to enter and desecrate at will. She had no freedom to choose what happened in this room, any more than she had a choice over the furnishings. The house remained as his mother and his first wife had left it. She would knock the whole place down, if she could.

It was small comfort that she was never again expected to participate in any of his parties. The village fête still took place in the grounds each year, but Plas Norton's chatelaine was not required to open it. Other ladies in the district had their charitable works and committees, which Rosamund was not expected to support. No doubt, after witnessing her collapse, they saw her as too weak and unstable. And they were right, really: she was a failure. She was not up to the role for which her station in life should have prepared her. When she read in the newspapers or magazines about women campaigning for suffrage or raising money for good causes, she could no more visualise herself doing the same than she could imagine herself flying an aeroplane or mounting an Antarctic expedition.

In some ways, her enforced reclusiveness suited her, shielding her as it did from the possibility of others seeing any hint of her degradation. Charlotte had had to learn from her aunt Blanche how to behave in company. There were even peaceful times, when her husband visited his friends or spent time at his London house. And Rosamund had learned how to shield herself from the curiosity of her servants by constructing a shell of icy propriety. Even in front of Nellie Dawson, she rarely displayed any emotion. It was better that way; better for the staff to see her as a social misfit than as the filthy, debased creature she knew she really was.

If only she could be different. Braver. More confident; at ease in her own skin and in her station. Then, she might have a chance of shaming her husband into leaving her alone. She could be living an entirely different existence, one filled with satisfying good works and interest; an exciting, even a useful life. But it seemed an impossible dream, a vision of a different person entirely. Seated at her dressing table each morning and evening, while Nellie brushed and fussed with her hair, she would cast her gaze down at the silver brushes, the hair pins and hat pins, the sundry bottles and pots. She'd look anywhere but into her own eyes, unable to face the darkness she would encounter in their depths. How could a woman who struggled even to look at her own reflection in the mirror ever become that person?

Nellie's familiar knock at the door came at half-past eight, as it always did, and Rosamund sat up while the maid plumped up her pillows and arranged her breakfast things on the lap tray before opening the curtains.

A magazine lay on the tray and Rosamund leafed through it idly while nibbling the first slice of toast. An article caught her eye, timely given the direction of her thoughts earlier. After describing the outrageous acts of a Canadian suffragette who had taken a meat cleaver to a painting of Venus in the National Gallery, the writer went on to denounce all the militant actions of the "unwomanly" suffragettes.

Rosamund frowned. It was hard to disagree with the journalist, considering the malicious criminal damage and disorderly conduct espoused by Mrs Pankhurst and her ilk. But there was a part of her that admired the women's passion and determination, even though she found many of their actions reprehensible. How unfeminine they were, the article claimed, with their violent actions and immoral rejections of the traditional domestic role. Why, their leader Mrs Pankhurst even employed a woman as her chauffeur, making use of her motor car to spirit her away from events, thereby preventing her rightful capture by the police.

Rosamund read those few sentences again. A female chauffeur, aiding and abetting a criminal! It should be shocking, yet it sounded thrilling. This wasn't the first time Rosamund had read about female motorists, of course. She had been aware that they existed, and that some respectable ladies even competed in races. But this was the first time she had ever read about a woman using her driving skills to escape.

She thought back to her first journey with Cadwalader, when she had been so struck by his easy competence at the wheel and the swift pace of the new motor car. Could she, perhaps, learn to drive it herself? Sir Lucien's first motor had been slow, loud and dirty, and she hadn't been enamoured of it, preferring to travel in the horse-drawn landau or even by pony and trap. But travelling in the new Wolseley limousine-landaulette was a very different experience. It was a big machine, though, and she had no idea how complicated it might be to operate, or how far she might be able to travel in it. But if she could find a way to learn, so many possibilities could open up before her. She remembered her journey to and from the station: every junction they passed had seemed to represent other roads, paths leading away from this gilded cage she lived in and towards freedom. In a car and on her own, without any servants to tell where she went, she might have a chance of getting away.

She folded the magazine and laid it down, feeling suddenly energised. The scent of her bath salts drifted from the adjoining bathroom, beckoning her to get up.

"Nellie, I'd like you to go into town today for me. I'd like you to go to the library, and also pay a visit to the bookshop and stationer. See if they have any books or magazines about motoring for ladies."

Nellie paused in her task of laying out clothes on the back of a chair. "Yes, m'lady... if you're sure?"

Ignoring Nellie's doubtful frown, Rosamund drank the last mouthful of tea and pushed the tray to one side before heading to the bathroom. She wanted to bathe, not engage in conversation about her half-formed plan.

She didn't know yet whether learning to drive was a realistic objective, but it had to be worth trying to find out if there could be a way. She needed a project, and what better than one with the potential to change her life completely?

EIGHT
JOSEPH

Joe lay underneath the car, trying vainly to ignore the ache in his back. The cold floor of the motor stable was about as comfortable as a mortuary slab. Beside him, his sixteen-year-old son Stanley peered intently up at the damaged part he had just pointed out.

"How do you think we should go about fixing it, then?" he asked the boy, keen to make him consider how best to solve the problem, instead of giving him the answer too easily.

"We could send to Wolseley for a new part?" Stanley said, his voice hesitant. Uncertain, he looked at his father for reassurance; Joe kept his face carefully expressionless. "On the other hand," the boy added, "that might take a while. So we could – maybe – take it off and make another one ourselves?"

"Are you asking me or telling me?"

"Er... Telling you?"

"Well done. That's exactly what I would do for a simple job like that." He laughed at his son's obvious pleasure in getting the answer right. "Now, you get on your bicycle and ask at the hardware shop in town for a five-inch flat file. And while you're there, you might as well ask for some emery powder too. Tell them to put it on the Fitznorton account."

Stanley nodded and scrambled out from underneath the car, moving as nimbly as only a young and wiry lad could. Joe reached again for his spanner, but a sharp kick on his ankle from the boy's steel-capped boot made him yelp.

"What was that for?" he growled, mystified when the boy coughed loudly and kicked him again, a gentler nudge this time. He looked around for the source of the problem, and was immediately arrested by the sight of a pair of feet in black leather shoes polished so smartly the light fairly bounced off them. Above them, oyster-coloured stockings clung to slim ankles. Ye gods, those stockings were a thing to behold: they had the smooth sheen of silk, as far removed from Mary's wrinkly black woollens as a diamond was from coal.

"La— Lady Fitznorton's here," Stanley stammered, his voice half strangled with nerves.

Of course she was. Who else around here would have stockings like those? With a grunt, Joe slid out along the floor and rose to his feet, dusting himself down. He picked up a rag and began wiping his hands, stepping around the motor car to see Lady Fitznorton waiting patiently, gloved hands demurely clasped.

"Off you go, then, Stanley," Joe said, and the boy needed no encouragement to seize his bicycle and wheel it outside, relieved to avoid the need to exchange polite greetings with his employer's wife.

Lady Fitznorton had her back to the open door, and her hat down low, making it hard to see her face in the shadow. Joe moved towards her, wiping the oil off his hands, so as to have a clearer view of her expression. It was as carefully blank and guarded as it had been the first time he met her.

"What can I do for you, m'lady?" he asked.

"I'm in need of your assistance, Cadwalader."

"I'll help you in any way I can, m'lady." He hoped his answer was suitably helpful, but non-committal. It wouldn't do to promise anything until he knew what he was letting himself in for.

"I want you to teach me to drive."

He hadn't seen that one coming. Realising his mouth had dropped open, he snapped it shut again. Her gaze was earnest and steady, making it impossible to take her request as a joke. Lovely eyes, she had: soft, unblinking and a rich shade of brown. They made him feel like an animal caught in a snare.

"I said, I want you to teach me to drive," she said again, sounding less sure of herself.

"That's what I thought you said. I'm just – well, a bit surprised, if I'm honest."

"Many distinguished ladies drive, you know," she began, her chin tilted upwards as if she had rehearsed this argument in her mind. "I've been reading about it. You'll have heard of the racing drivers Miss Levitt and Miss Thompson, I'm sure; and there's the Duchess of Sutherland, the Countess of Kinnoull, Lady Wimborne... I believe the Ladies' Automobile Club has hundreds of members nowadays. Thousands, probably."

"I know all that. This is a big car, though, and a complex machine. The best cars for ladies are small and light, with only a single cylinder. This has four."

She wasn't discouraged. "Once I've mastered the skill of driving, I'm sure my husband will buy me a smaller car of my own. But he won't be willing to purchase another motor car unless I prove to him that I can drive competently. Cadwalader, I've given this matter a great deal of thought. I'll listen to all of your instructions and heed your advice. I won't do anything foolish, I assure you."

He scratched his head and turned to put the rag down on the workbench. "It's none of my business, of course – but where would you want to go driving off to?" he asked, curious to know why she was so keen to learn.

"Oh... Not far."

"Well, if you want to go much beyond walking distance without anyone to help you, you'd need to learn some vehicle maintenance. It's dirty, and often heavy work. You'd have to know how to replace a sparking plug, for instance. And if you get a puncture... You'd struggle to change one of these wheels."

"I see." Her face fell, but soon regained its determined set. "In that case, I'll stay on the roads within the estate when I'm alone, and if I go further afield I'll take you or your boy with me."

It was hardly his place to refuse a request from his employer's wife, however foolish or strange it might seem to him, but this seemed like a particularly daft idea. For the sake of form he'd have to at least appear to go along with it, initially at least... Luckily, he had in mind an easy way to get out of it without having to go against her wishes.

"I'll teach you if you meet certain conditions," he said.

"Anything you ask."

He raised an eyebrow at her eagerness. *So much for the Ice Queen.* It seemed there was fire aplenty when she wanted something.

"Driving a motor car like this requires a certain amount of physical strength."

"I'm stronger than I might appear."

"Perhaps. If – and I mean *if* – you can manage to use the starting handle, and provided Sir Lucien permits it, then I'll help you. But if you don't have the aptitude for driving, I'll tell you – and then you have to promise to give up the idea."

"Agreed."

"If you prang Sir Lucien's pride and joy, I won't take the blame," he warned her.

"Of course you shan't. I take full responsibility."

"Hmmm." He rubbed his top lip thoughtfully. "Let's try you with the starting handle then, shall we? You look as if you've no more strength than a lamb, but if you're sure you want to give it a go...?"

He wasn't seriously worried, knowing that once she'd tried it she was sure to give up this silliness. He adjusted the controls inside the car to prime the engine and make sure all was safe, then ducked back out again, pointed to the crank handle at the front of the car, and took hold of it to demonstrate how it was done.

"You need to make sure you have your thumb on the same side of the handle as your fingers – like this. Cup the handle, don't grasp it. If you don't, and the engine backfires, you could break your arm."

Her eyes widened at that, but she nodded eagerly.

"Before you even touch the handle, you need to make sure that the engine isn't in gear and the handbrake is on – otherwise the car could run you over."

She nodded again.

"It's important," he said, to ensure she took his advice on board. This was already feeling like a mistake.

"I understand."

"Now – never press down on the handle. Push it inwards until you feel it slip into a notch, then pull it. When you feel it resist, let go. Can you remember all that?"

She raised a delicate eyebrow, then repeated his instructions back to him perfectly.

"Right. Well, then. If you still want to – off you go."

Excitement radiated from her as she stepped to take his place.

"Ready?"

She nodded, then positioned her hand carefully, checking with a glance back at him that she had done so correctly. At his nod, she pushed the handle inwards, then yanked it up. Just as he'd expected, the engine remained silent.

"There's a knack to it," he said. With luck, she'd fall at this first hurdle and that would be the last he'd hear about this foolish plan.

Frowning, she bent again to seize the handle.

"Mind your thumb!" he exclaimed, grabbing at her arm before she could injure herself. Her cuff pulled upwards as he caught it, revealing a set of what looked like black, oily finger marks on her wrist. He went cold, shocked by what he had seen as much as his own boldness in touching her. There was only one thing that could have caused those marks. He wasn't stupid – any mechanic knew what finger marks looked like. But those were bruises, not oil. And it wasn't hard to imagine how she got them.

"Has your husband agreed to this idea of yours?" he asked.

"I haven't mentioned it yet." She averted her gaze, adjusting her sleeve.

His eyebrows flew up in alarm.

"I want it to be a surprise," she said, airily, still without meeting his gaze. "It would be such fun to take him out for a drive. If you teach me in secret, one day I can surprise him. He's sure to find it frightfully amusing."

Joe knew a lie when he heard it. He thought it highly unlikely that his employer would be pleased to learn that his wife had been keeping secrets from him.

"Let me try again," she said, turning back to the starting handle and positioning her hand carefully this time. She put more vigour into it, and the engine almost caught.

He was on the point of telling her to abandon the idea when she put all her strength into the handle and almost toppled over in surprise when the engine spluttered into life.

"I did it!" she exclaimed.

"So you did."

His stomach plummeted in the face of her determination; but then he looked up and saw that her face had lit up with a triumphant grin that threatened to split it from ear to ear, transforming her in an instant. He basked in the radiance of her unexpectedly lovely smile, warmed by it like the glow of an oven door opening on a cold morning. Against all common sense he grinned back, shaking his head with a wry awareness that there was no going back on his word. What had he got himself into?

"You'd better get yourself a motoring coat," he said.

NINE

NELLIE

Nellie wasn't sure what surprised her most: her ladyship's notion of learning to drive, or the enthusiasm with which she looked forward to it. There was a brightness about her, utterly unlike her customary disinterest, as she riffled through magazines and catalogues to order a fashionable new motoring wardrobe. For once, she was consulting Nellie about her sartorial choices with genuine interest in Nellie's opinions, instead of paying merely desultory notice and agreeing to whatever Nellie suggested. And whenever Nellie went about her daily tasks, laying out Lady Fitz's clothes or styling her hair, she would read out sections from a book she had purchased, as if it were her new gospel.

"Miss Levitt says I shall need a butcher-blue or brown linen overall with long sleeves, Nellie. And we must purchase some Antioyl soap. Listen to this: 'If it has been necessary to use bare hands for a repair you will nearly always find some grease on your hands, and this it is impossible to remove with ordinary soap.'"

"M'lady, you're surely not intending to work on the motor yourself?"

"According to Miss Levitt I shall have to learn to carry out some of the running repairs myself, if I'm ever to drive alone."

Nellie had a feeling she'd soon be sick of hearing the words "Miss Levitt says". Who was this Dorothy Levitt, anyway? Some jumped-up young miss turning sensible ladies' heads with her silly book inciting them to go off driving on their own, racing and hill climbing and suchlike. It sounded like a reckless, hare-brained scheme that could do her ladyship's reputation no good. As if she wasn't already seen as odd enough.

Still, this new interest had its benefits. It was as if her ladyship had had a sudden awakening. There was a whole new vivacity about her. Nellie guessed that this was partly down to his lordship being away, as she was always less withdrawn when he was in town, but this time was different. This time, she was taking an interest in life. She was enjoying herself. From time to time she would catch Nellie's eye in the mirror and, instead of lowering her lids like shutters, she would relax her face in the faintest smile. Naturally, Nellie reported the change to the other senior servants. It seemed Mrs Longford had noticed a hint of animation about her, too.

Dour and cynical as always, Mr Phelps was quick to dismiss it as a phase. "It won't last. She'll realise cars are dirty and heavy and complicated, and look for something more ladylike to do."

"Well, I for one am glad to see her looking a bit brighter," said Mrs Longford, and Nellie couldn't help but concur.

"I'm surprised at Cadwalader, going along with it. Barmy, that's what it is. The very idea of it is ridiculous."

"You know as well as we do, Mr Phelps, that those who pay our wages can ask us to do whatever they want. It isn't for Mr Cadwalader to refuse her ladyship's request."

"She isn't the one who pays him, though. Sir Lucien does, and I'm not sure what he'd think of Cadwalader's working hours being frittered away on pandering to her ladyship's whims."

"What he doesn't know can't hurt, can it?"

But Phelps said nothing, and Nellie felt a sense of foreboding. Whenever Sir Lucien telephoned the house, it was the butler who answered. Had he said something? She wouldn't put it past him to stir up trouble for Lady Fitznorton, disliking her as he did for her frigid demeanour.

Anger flared in Nellie, making her forget her own reservations about her ladyship's new hobby. Who was Phelps to deny a bored and lonely woman some pleasure? Phelps's world was a narrow one, with limited horizons and Sir Lucien at its axis. He didn't have the capacity to understand anyone who aspired to something more. To a man like him, a woman like Lady Fitz learning to drive was a sign of her overreaching the natural confines of her world, like the story Nellie had heard at school about a boy flying too close to the sun on artificial wings. For her to crash and burn would seem to him nothing more than divine justice.

Nellie despised small-minded men – they struck her as dangerous. She'd have to be careful what she said about her ladyship's driving lessons in future, and hope that they didn't lead to disaster.

At the time arranged for her ladyship's first lesson, Nellie followed her to the motor stable and hovered in the background until at last Mr Cadwalader noticed her and opened the rear door for her to climb into the back seat. It was comfortable, not unlike a carriage, with its plush cord upholstery and silk brocade trimmings. With the glass closed between the passenger compartment and the driver, she couldn't hear much of what was said, but she was able to watch and thus preserve her ladyship's reputation. No one could say there was anything improper about Lady Fitznorton sitting next to the chauffeur and taking instruction when her maid was sitting right behind them.

It seemed to take an age before her ladyship was even permitted to sit in the driver's seat. At first, Cadwalader took them out around the estate, keeping up a constant commentary that Nellie was sure would bore her almost to sleep, although from what she could see through the glass panel her ladyship seemed fascinated. After a while they returned to the yard and he continued the instruction.

It must all be very complicated, Nellie supposed, suppressing a yawn as she watched him lecturing Lady Fitz and poking and prodding about the car. He lifted the cover from the engine and folded it over onto itself, pointing out a multitude of features while her ladyship nodded eagerly, her face fierce with concentration. Why she was so keen to attempt something so inordinately complicated, Nellie had no idea. The horn was tried, its sudden parp-parp making Nellie jump, along with the horses in the stables further along the yard, no doubt. And then, after much fiddling about with switches, and a trip around the front of the car and another lecture, her ladyship bent to the handle.

Within moments, the engine started up its clattering rhythm and Lady Fitz looked up, a great, beaming grin on her face such as Nellie had never seen on her before. Agog, Nellie watched her exchanging smiles with Cadwalader, nodding obediently as he hurried to point out more of the controls, and looking like the cat that got the cream as she slipped into the driving seat. Nellie couldn't have been more surprised if her employer had turned cartwheels in the stable yard.

Lifting the brass-edged flap in the glass between the rear compartment and the driver's seat, she called through. "All's going well then, m'lady?"

"Oh yes, Nellie. Everything is going swimmingly." Her ladyship flashed a glance back at her with eyes that fairly sparkled with excitement, her cheeks dimpling like a young girl's. Nellie dropped the flap and sat back, stunned into silence. This was a turn-up. She could hardly wait to tell Mrs Longford about it, smothering an inner grin as she imagined her surprise. Could she even find the words to make the housekeeper believe such an unlikely report of her mistress's sudden attack of gaiety?

Just as suddenly, even as she was thinking of words like *glee* and *vivacious*, something went wrong. Cadwalader's face was a picture of confusion and concern, and he was bundling out of the car as Lady Fitz fled towards the house like a hind with a pack of hounds after her.

"What's happened?" Nellie asked through the communication flap, stunned by the sudden about-turn.

"I don't know," Cadwalader said. He killed the engine and opened the door to the rear compartment. Frowning, he recounted what had transpired. "I'd explained everything she needed to know to get the engine started. She cranked the handle just as I told her, got it going and – well, you saw for yourself. She was pleased as punch. I talked her through the controls and we were just about ready to go when she gave me the most dreadful look and told me to let her out." He took off his cap and scratched his head, clearly at a loss to explain the sudden change in their employer's demeanour.

"What did you say? You must have said something that she took amiss."

"Well... I started talking about the steering. I explained that it's heavy. And I made a sort of joke. I said, 'once you're moving it's like a horse: just point its nose in the direction you want to go.' And I asked if she'd ever ridden a horse, although I imagine she has, a woman of her position. She looked at me – such a look, as if I'd stabbed her through the heart – and then she practically shoved me out so she could make a dash for it."

Nellie covered her face with her hands and groaned.

"What? What is it?" He reached out and seized her arm.

She pulled it back at once, loath to permit that sort of familiarity.

"She had a horse... it was before I started here. Mrs Longford told me about it once, and I've never forgotten the story."

"What happened?" It was obvious that he was mortified and confounded in equal measure.

Nellie saw no alternative but to tell him what she had heard. She lowered her voice.

"It was long before I came here, so I can only go by what I was told. Apparently, she had a horse when she was a girl, and it was brought here when she was first married. She used to ride it most days. But one day, something went wrong. There was an accident, the horse reared up or something, and she fell. It turned out she was expecting, without realising it, and..." Nellie hesitated, uncomfortable with the idea of discussing such matters with a man. But one look at his face showed he knew what she meant. He was a married man, of course, and had a family of his own. She should have remembered.

"She lost her baby because of the horse?"

Nellie nodded. "Because of the fall."

"So that's why she got so upset when I asked if she rode. She was thinking about the baby she lost." He cursed under his breath and turned away, as if he imagined he understood. But he didn't. He hadn't understood it at all.

"No. I don't think that was it. Or at least, it wasn't only that. You see, he shot it, Mr Cadwalader. She loved that horse, and when Sir Lucien found out about the baby, that her horse had cost him his heir... he went out to the stables and shot it through the head."

Cadwalader's face drained of colour. There was a pause in which his thoughts showed in his face – the kind of thoughts it was safest not to share if he valued his job. Nellie recalled hearing that he'd worked with horses before he trained to work on engines. He plumped down onto the sill, dragging his fingers through thick brown silver-streaked hair that was surprisingly unruly when not contained by his chauffeur's cap.

"That's it, then. She isn't likely to forgive me for bringing those memories back. What a prize idiot I am," he murmured.

Nellie felt a pang of sympathy. "You weren't to know." She reached out to pat his shoulder, but gathered herself in time and folded her hands neatly in her lap. She couldn't go around touching the male servants, even when she felt sorry for them. Even when they were kind-hearted and had a face that was open and amiable.

"Ah well. There's one good thing about it. She'll give up on the idea of driving now. I don't suppose he'd have wanted her to do it, so at least she'll be spared any further grief from that quarter." He sighed and got up, holding out a hand to help Nellie down from the car.

She guessed he was probably right. Lady Fitz would more than likely be too upset, and then, when today's events had had time to sink in, too embarrassed, to ever attempt driving again. But as Nellie walked back to the house, uncertain of the state she would find her ladyship in, she couldn't help feeling sorry that the new hobby that had infused so much freshness and zest into both of their lives would now be over.

TEN

ROSAMUND

Rosamund stood at the window in the library, the warmth of the afternoon sunshine seeping into her soul. The last few cream and claret goblets of the magnolia trees across the lawn danced in the breeze to tempt her outdoors, and she headed impulsively upstairs to her room to summon Nellie. She would change her clothes and go out, take a walk to the orchard, and enjoy the springtime blossom before heading past the lake and up to the summerhouse, if she had the energy to climb the hill. Nellie helped her into a sensible tweed skirt and sturdy outdoor shoes, then selected a suitable coat, hat and gloves.

She swept back downstairs and out of the front door, nodding at Phelps on her way out. His beady gaze followed her, but she paid him no attention. Later it might rain again, but for now she had time to dream and to make the most of the fresh air as she strode across the gravel towards the gardens. Still, the back of her neck prickled. Even outside in the grounds, she couldn't entirely shake Plas Norton's oppressive atmosphere. The windows of the house were like eyes, their gothic arches brows. Cold and blank and hard, she felt them staring until she reached the orchard, where she was hidden by the trees on her way to the lake beyond. Here, her shoulders dropped and she lifted her face towards the sky, taking in the scent of blossom mixed with the damp smell of the Welsh earth that cloyed on the soles of her sturdy shoes. She breathed it in, then gave a startled exclamation as a flock of rooks broke cover and burst upwards through the branches.

Her thoughts turned, as had become their new habit, to her driving lessons with Joseph Cadwalader. He had been instructing her for several weeks now: three sessions per week at her insistence, although he had initially expressed the view that one or two should be sufficient. She had argued that she needed to make rapid progress if she was to impress Sir Lucien on his return, and he could hardly refuse to do as she asked.

Although her first lesson had been something of a disaster, thanks to Cadwalader catching her off guard with a joke that had brought back memories of the most distressing kind, they had gone more smoothly since. He had attempted to apologise at the beginning of her second lesson, which she quickly dismissed with a peremptory gesture. The last thing she wanted was for either of them to dwell on distractions. She wanted to learn, and as quickly as she could; for that, she would need to keep her wits about her. There was so much to co-ordinate when driving, even more so than when playing the piano, with the fingering and pedals to master; but she found she relished the challenge.

Once again, during that second lesson, he began the lesson by driving around the estate, explaining the controls and how to manoeuvre the car. Then, to her surprise, they stopped at a lane on the edge of the woods.

"Your turn now," he said with a look that was half-mischievous, half-nervous.

She was stunned into immobility, gaping at him from the passenger seat, all at once terrified of the idea of trying to control this enormous beast of a machine. As he indicated for her to swap seats, her mind swam with images of dreadful accidents and the consequences if her husband took against the idea of her using his motor car. But once she had slipped down from the car, he stood patiently holding the door for her, with an air of expectation; and with Nellie's curious face watching from behind, she could hardly back out. She had embarked upon this, and must face the next step of the journey.

"Come on. You said yourself, hundreds of women can do this." Cadwalader grinned and gestured for her to get back in ahead of him. It was impertinent of him, and they both knew it, but it gave her the push she needed. Within moments she had replaced him in the driving seat, and when she drove at a snail's pace into the yard and drew to a stop in front of the motor stable she felt she could burst with pride.

Before learning to drive, she had found it necessary to live in a way that many might find quiet, perhaps even dull, in order to maintain a level of equilibrium. Living with Sir Lucien was like living on the slopes of a volcano: she never knew when the rumbling undercurrents might erupt into a storm of violence. She tiptoed through her days with him, dreading the nights when he might choose to visit her room. Stillness and tranquillity had been her refuge, the medicine she took as an antidote to her husband's casual cruelties.

Sometimes she tried to imagine Cadwalader's life, and the liveliness of a cottage filled with children. Her own home was almost silent: no laughter or shouts of childish excitement brightened the rooms. Before driving, she could easily have gone for weeks without laughing once, or hearing a laugh that was genuinely joyful. With Sir Lucien and Charlotte away, there was no murmur of conversation from the drawing room. If she happened to pass a housemaid on the stairs, the other woman would turn and face the wall. No pleasantries would be exchanged except with the senior servants, and those conversations generally had a practical purpose. The only time she ever had anything approaching a meaningful conversation was when she discussed the car with Cadwalader, or suitable clothing for motoring with Nellie.

Nellie, of course, was something of a handicap during Rosamund's lessons. For the sake of form she always sat in the back of the car, even though being subjected to an audience while trying to learn such a difficult new skill made Rosamund uncomfortable. She feared her maid was secretly laughing at her, and that she might gleefully report her frequent mistakes to the other servants. Strangely, she never had that sense with Cadwalader. He was a good teacher: patient but firm, and clear in his instructions and explanations. When he laughed at her, he did so without malice.

She couldn't recall a time since her marriage when she had been more at ease. With her husband and Charlotte seemingly content to remain in London for several more weeks, the fear she had been accustomed to living with like an unwelcome ghost had receded. Her times with Cadwalader were the highlight of her week. For the first time in years she had something to look forward to, and the melancholy that had blighted her existence for almost her whole adult life showed signs of lifting. She had even begun to allow herself to eat more, without feeling the old desperate need to slink into her bathroom and purge herself. She could almost convince herself now, inhaling the lush, ripe air of the morning, with nature bursting with colour all about her, that she might, perhaps, be – she hardly dared use the word – *happy*.

The hill where the summerhouse stood was not steep, so she was soon at the top. She tugged open the door, finding it sticky and swollen from the spring rains and disuse. It smelled musty inside, and the windowpanes were festooned with cobwebs that made her shudder. She would have to ask the head gardener to send someone up to clean and air it.

She liked being up here, alone and away from the confines

of the house. In the distance it sat squat and grey, as if it had been dropped there to crouch in the parkland, strangely out of place and unlike the vernacular Welsh cottages and longhouses. The towers at its corners gave it some pretensions, but it was neither ancient nor grand enough to inspire awe or admiration. Built by Sir Lucien's grandfather when the family's booming industrial wealth improved their standing and enabled them to purchase the land, its mock-gothic style was already old-fashioned. She had no fondness for Plas Norton, having never felt she belonged there, but she could appreciate the grounds, where she had spent many hours walking.

The lake looked small and black from here, and the rhododendrons standing between it and the hill impenetrably dense. They would come into their scarlet blooms soon, she supposed. The year was moving on, another year stuck here in this empty life spent either dreading her husband's return or enduring the torment of life in the shadow of his presence. But it never helped to dwell upon him.

She gave herself a mental shake as she rose and dusted herself off, her need for refreshment giving her the impetus to head back to the house. Things were starting to change this year, she reminded herself, and once she could drive competently without supervision who knew what she might be able to do? Descending carefully in her sturdy shoes, holding her skirt up and stepping around the sheep droppings that dotted the hill, her thoughts focused on possibilities, and on the person who could help her make those things happen: Cadwalader.

She felt safe with him – well, perhaps not safe exactly. There was a frisson that sometimes put her on edge and made her tongue-tied around him. She was very aware of his masculinity: his broad shoulders and strong arms, his long legs in his leather boots when he sat beside her on the front seat of the motor car. His eyes sometimes caught her attention so strongly that she quite forgot to listen to what he was saying; he would frown slightly, the groove in the centre of his forehead deepening, and repeat himself with exaggerated patience.

When she had performed well in a lesson and he nodded and smiled, she wanted to dance with the delight of knowing she had pleased someone. His praise was a drug she found she craved. She hadn't experienced anyone's approval since her wedding, when Tristram had clapped her shoulder and praised her good sense. *Well done, Rosa,* he'd said. *You'll be well taken care of now.* How wrong he had been. But Cadwalader did take care of her, by understanding her need to build her confidence gradually. He showed it in small ways that she felt went beyond the deference of a servant to a lady, like noticing when she was tiring or being quiet when she wasn't inclined to converse. Although, those times were less frequent with him than with anyone else. She enjoyed their interactions and found him surprisingly interesting.

His voice was low and pleasant, with a lilting Welsh accent that set him obviously apart from her own class. He was not well educated – how could he be? But it was apparent in his conversation that he had intelligence as well as practical skill. He was considerate, but never obsequious, and though he was paid to attend to her, he seemed genuinely to care about her needs and wishes. He couldn't be more different from her husband. In other circumstances, if their lives were different, she felt she could think of him as a friend.

Drifting along her usual walk through the grounds, pausing to appreciate the emerging lilac blossom, she sighed at the impossibility of ever calling such a person "friend". They inhabited different worlds. Mutual liking and respect – and she was sure she hadn't imagined his liking her, too – could never be enough to create such a relationship between them. They could never be on first name terms, could never sit across the table from one another at dinner. She could never invite him to tea or call upon his wife, as one might expect to do with a friend of one's own class. Their lives were separate, and must remain so. She knew it, and wanted to kick out at a world that prevented her from acknowledging her deepening affection for the only human being in the world who didn't seem to despise her.

She had a powerful sense that other people disliked her, a chill that made her feel constantly uncomfortable. Even at home, the servants showed her deference because they must; yet she was under no illusions. Phelps's cold gaze made her uneasy. Mrs Longford, the housekeeper, and Mrs McKie their Scottish cook, were polite, but she knew they must disapprove of her for always deferring to their decisions about the house and menus. Even Nellie, who had been her personal maid for a decade, had sometimes betrayed her true thoughts with a dismissive sniff on days when Rosamund was unable to summon the will to rise from her bed. She never felt that cold-ness from Cadwalader. In fact, she thought now as she skirt-ed the corner of the house, he was quite the kindest, best and most wonderful person she knew. A greater gentleman, in his own way, than the so-called gentlemen of her acquaintance.

The sound of shouting roused her from her reverie. It came from the courtyard, harsh yelling closely followed by thuds, muffled cries and a shriek of alarm. Rosamund's heart pounded with a fear that had become instinctive after years of subjection to casual violence. What should she do? Her feet itched to turn and run the other way, but a sense of duty made her take a deep breath and head towards the noise.

"Get him off me!" came a half-strangled cry. A hubbub of voices rose in argument and rebuke.

Rosamund arrived on the scene as Phelps, red-faced with indignation, stepped between two men who had been grappling in the yard, their booted feet kicking out and fists flying. One of them, the taller man, she recognised by his shock of red hair as one of the stable hands. His hands clutched at his face while Phelps held him at arm's length. Blood dripped between the man's fingers, turning his shirt-front scarlet. His nose must be broken, Rosamund thought, and moved past Phelps to see who could have done it.

Joseph Cadwalader stood apart, cradling bruised and bleeding knuckles and shaking with fury. His eyes met hers briefly with a flicker of what she hoped was shame, then he looked away towards his son Stanley, whose face was contorted with distress. Biting his lower lip, the boy stared back pleadingly at his father. Was it fear of his father that made him look so anxious? Had young Stanley seen Cadwalader turn to violence before? She blinked, unable to reconcile what she was seeing with her earlier thoughts.

Cadwalader was beginning to calm down, it seemed; his nostrils were no longer flared, and his stance had straightened from the tense edginess of the fighter. Phelps was remonstrating with the other man, whose muffled protestations were less panicked now. Rosamund looked at the blood in distaste, resisting the sudden lightness in her head and the nauseous churning of her stomach.

Phelps's florid countenance had turned an unusually virulent shade of puce, no doubt induced by fury at his staff being caught in such blatant misconduct by the mistress of the house. She would let him deal with the stable hand, as was appropriate to his position in charge of the other male servants. A chauffeur, though, was not technically subject to the butler's jurisdiction.

"Phelps, I trust you can deal with this man. Cadwalader, in the absence of Sir Lucien, you must explain yourself to me. Such behaviour is intolerable." Her voice was icy, like the splinters in her heart that had appeared at the sight of his bloodied knuckles. It seemed all men were untamed, vicious beasts at heart. She'd been a fool to believe her chauffeur was in any way a gentle man. He had betrayed his true nature: violent, as other men were violent. She must recognise it, and steel herself to deal with him, however scary the thought. Turning on her heel, she marched into the house.

She didn't need to check that he had followed; she was aware of his presence behind her as surely as if he had been attached to her on a leash. She went into the library and stood before the window, looking out, not wanting him to see how his potential for violence frightened her.

"Close the door," she said, cursing herself for the way her voice trembled.

The latch clicked. For the first time since their first journey home from the station, they were alone together. Should she be afraid, now that she had seen this darker side of his character? She sensed him waiting, could almost hear his mind whirring as he wondered what she would do. She was asking herself that very question. What action should she take against him? What would her husband say if she sent him packing? What would he say if she didn't? Anger rose in her chest: how dare he put her in this position?

Swallowing the anger, she faced him. He looked her in the eye, his mouth twisted; he appeared calm but not, it seemed, contrite. He flexed his fingers gingerly, covering the bloody knuckles with a handkerchief.

"I can't begin to express my disappointment..." she began, then broke off to look towards the door. Someone would almost certainly be behind it, listening. He followed her gaze and she saw understanding dawn in his eyes.

She must speak cautiously. She couldn't treat him with any sign of particular favour for the sake of the help he had given her before this. Doubtless the servants already gossiped about the amount of time she had spent out driving with him. If not for Nellie's constant presence she dared not imagine the level of speculation.

"Would you care to explain to me why you assaulted one of my husband's employees?"

"M'lady. I apologise for any distress I have caused you, and for any trouble I have caused to Mr Phelps. I assure you..." He seemed to be searching for words. "I am not in the habit of *assaulting* people."

"Then why did you do it?"

"He deserved it."

The arrogant simplicity of his reply made her catch her breath. "*No one* deserves to be beaten," she hissed, moving behind a chair and gripping its back. She thought of the times Sir Lucien had claimed she deserved her treatment at his hands because of her stupidity, her weakness, her failings.

"Begging your pardon, m'lady, but some men do. He..." Cadwalader sighed and shook his head slightly as if he couldn't hope to make her understand. "He was acting the fighting cock with my Stanley. Hopefully I've taught him to argue with men, not boys half his size." A muscle twitched in his cheek.

"Is that all? Is there nothing else you wish to add in your defence?"

With her eyes she pleaded with him to give her more, a better reason than that; to show that he wasn't a brute after all, and that she could still trust him.

"No, m'lady. That's what happened. And I hope he's learned his lesson and that will be an end to it."

In the silence between them, the ticking of the clock seemed magnified, reminding her that a decision would have to be made soon. She should probably send him away, tell him his services were no longer required and that he and his family would have to leave their cottage by the end of the week. But she couldn't bring herself to say the words. As always, she hid her feelings as best she could behind a frigid mask. She couldn't bear to look at him any longer, knowing the man she had respected had sunk so low.

"My husband will decide what is to be done. I must warn

you that he may not be inclined towards leniency. For now, you had better resume your duties."

She had no intention of involving Sir Lucien if she could avoid it, but hopefully invoking his name would give Cadwalader pause for thought, and she could put off making a decision about his fate until she had had time to think.

He closed the door softly on his way out. As she allowed herself to sink into the chair, she heard him speak curtly to someone in the hall, before his footsteps receded. Someone had been out there, then. The footman lurking as Phelps's eyes and ears while he dealt with the other fellow, no doubt.

She took in a deep breath, inhaling the scent of old books and tobacco which always transported her back to her youth. This was her favourite room in the house, the only one in which she came close to feeling at home. In the library she could tuck herself away with a book in a winged chair and make herself almost invisible, while retreating in her mind to other worlds, other lives in which adventures and excitement were to be had, and dangers were almost always overcome.

How different from her own, cursed life. When she looked up into the mirror above the fireplace, she hardly recognised the thin, pinched creature staring back at her. A creature beneath contempt who had done unspeakable things in secret. Just looking at her own face made revulsion flood her mouth like bile. She looked away, scanned the books on the shelves, the view from the window, anything to shut out the sight of the darkness in her own eyes.

She had been a fool to believe Cadwalader was different. He was as beastly as any other man who used violence to impose his will on another. He didn't even seem to feel any regret for his actions, only for the inconvenience he had caused by getting caught. He had even tried to justify himself.

Yet... when she thought back over it now, she believed he told the truth when he said he was defending his son. His gaze had been sincere as he explained himself, and his gestures frank. He hadn't tried to embellish the tale as a liar might do, to present himself in a better light, but had put his case simply. She remembered the expression on young Stanley's face: perhaps his fear hadn't been of his father, but *for* him, and the danger he might face in coming to the boy's rescue.

As much as she hated the idea of letting such a horrible incident pass, it didn't seem fair for it to cost both Stanley and Joseph Cadwalader their jobs, especially if they had been acting in self-defence. The whole family lived in a tied cottage; if Cadwalader was sacked, they would all be made homeless, even the youngest children. She couldn't bring herself to inflict such hardship on them.

Moreover, in spite of her disappointment and disgust over today's incident, she had her own selfish reasons for keeping him on. If he went away, she could no longer continue learning to drive, and the only golden hours in her life would be gone. She was struck by how much she would miss him. His smile, the reassuring way he explained everything she needed, and the way his eyes lit up every time she mastered something or showed an improvement in her level of skill. The man he had been, until today.

She was left alone to brood on this for no more than five minutes before Phelps announced his entrance with his customary discreet knock. His highly polished shoes made no sound on the thickly carpeted floor as he glided over to the centre of the room.

"Yes, Phelps?" She moved behind the desk, its solidity like a shield before her, and sat down to await his report. There was something about the man that made her shudder. Perhaps it was her suspicion that his obsequious manners were a mask designed to hide his dislike. Or perhaps it was memories of the spark of eagerness in his eyes each Christmas when she was obliged by tradition to open the dancing with him at the servants' Twelfth Night ball. His fingers spread across her back with such obvious relish, it made her want to shove him off and run. But, as always, she was trapped – forced by convention to comply.

"It seems, my lady, that Wilson's nose is not broken, despite appearances earlier. He has asked me to relay to you his sincere apologies for his appalling behaviour, and his assurance—"

She couldn't bear to listen to any more excuses.

"Very well, Phelps. Cadwalader said much the same. I am satisfied that no such incident is likely to reoccur, and in the light of their apologies, it seems unnecessary to take any further action. We both know the difficulties involved in finding another driver suitably qualified and experienced. And, as we can't show favour to one over the other, when there are no witnesses as to how it started, and we can't know for certain which of them is more to blame, they both must stay."

"My lady, you are right of course, that we can't be sure which of them is more to blame. We also can't be sure how Sir Lucien might wish us to proceed. Therefore, might I be so bold as to suggest that this matter should be discussed with him before any decision is taken?"

She paused. The last thing she wanted was to consult her husband, for fear he might return home or send Cadwalader away. "It seems a trivial matter with which to burden him when he is so caught up with business in London—"

"Nevertheless, as it concerns the moral character of his employees, I am sure he would wish to be kept informed."

He had her. If she refused to discuss this with her husband, it would look as if she was hiding things from him. Tongues would wag, and Phelps would probably be the first to suggest that she had her own reasons for protecting the chauffeur. He wouldn't be wrong. As much as she hated what he had done today, the idea of never seeing him again was painful to contemplate. He had changed her life by giving her a reason to look forward to her days as well as the possibility of a means to escape. If Cadwalader left, what would she do?

She looked Phelps up and down, taking in the portly figure and florid beaky nose that suggested he availed himself rather more frequently than he should of the contents of her husband's wine cellar. The almost feminine softness of his bearing and the oily, slippery way he spoke couldn't be more different from Cadwalader's straightforward, honest masculinity.

It took a huge effort to keep contempt from chilling her voice even more than her usual cool tones. "In that case, Phelps, if you feel this is too much for you to deal with, by all means refer the matter to Sir Lucien when next he calls."

"Very good, my lady."

The prospect of speaking to Sir Lucien filled her with dread. Even the sound of his voice through the telephone earpiece had the power to make her knees turn to liquid. And yet somehow, without giving her feelings away, she would have to find a way to convince him to keep Cadwalader on.

ELEVEN

JOSEPH

Joe and Stanley walked home in silence that evening. Joe wasn't proud of what he'd done, but was unshaken in his conviction that he'd been right to do it. He brooded over what had happened, his face grim as he faced the strong possibility of dismissal from his job and the ruination of Stanley's training. Stan wouldn't be able to carry on working at Plas Norton with Joe gone.

With no savings to speak of, he would have to find another position quickly, but that would be more complicated now: being sent away from here in disgrace would mean he'd have no character reference. He'd start looking at the situations vacant tomorrow, and write to some servants' registries in the hope of finding work based on his experience and previous character. He'd only worked here for a matter of weeks: perhaps he could lie and say he was without work for that time. By moving away, he'd have a chance of finding an employer who didn't know Sir Lucien Fitznorton, and nobody would ever need to find out what had transpired here. His skills would be in demand, of that there was no doubt. The real shame would be losing the accommodation and having to move his whole family on, when his eldest two, Len and Maggie, had found work in a local factory. And he'd be sorry to never see Lady Fitznorton again. He had enjoyed teaching her to drive and had come to admire her determination and quiet good humour even more than her physical charms. Her obvious disappointment in him today had stung.

His footsteps slowed as they neared their cottage and he paused on the bridge, watching the stream rushing below.

"You go on in," he told Stan gruffly. "I want to stay out here for a bit."

The boy nodded and went to the door. Joe saw him look back, silhouetted in the light from the house before stepping indoors and removing his cap. Joe stayed outside for perhaps ten minutes, until the chill of the evening began to seep into his bones and the familiar ache in his lower back made him seek the physical comfort of his own hearth.

The smell of coal fire and mutton stew greeted him, and he shut the door on the chilly night air, grateful for the cosiness of home but unsure what he would say to Mary.

She was in the kitchen with a face like a wet Monday morning. Seeing him come in, she moved to the coal-fired range to ladle a portion of stew and some boiled potatoes onto a plate.

"You were a long time outside." The note of accusation made her voice sharp. "The little ones are in bed. It was getting too late for them to wait up for you any longer."

She sawed a slice of bread off the loaf and buttered it, then cut it in two and plopped the pieces onto the edge of his plate. They lay there, their edges absorbing gravy while Joe took off his cap, coat and boots. He went to the sink, rolled up his sleeves and washed his hands using the ewer of water, all the while saying nothing. He'd been hoping to persuade Sir Lucien to get a tap installed, to make Mary's life easier – but there wasn't much likelihood of that now. Indoor plumbing would be the least of their worries soon.

Stanley wiped the last smears of gravy off his own plate with a crust and got up.

"That was good, Mam – just what I needed after a long day."

Mary remained expressionless, watching Joe with her arms folded across her breast. Stan looked warily at his parents, sighed quietly and left the room, closing the door behind him.

The atmosphere was sour and cold, in spite of the warmth from the range. Wishing Stan had stayed, Joe sat down at the scrubbed pine table. He picked up his fork, eyeing the plate of steaming stew, and poked at a lump of mutton. It was hard to muster up any enthusiasm under Mary's reproachful gaze.

"At least the children have an appetite for my cooking," she remarked.

Joe set his fork down. Where had she gone, the lovely girl he had been in such haste to marry? He remembered the soft voice and the sweet smile that had made him so eager to make her his for ever. Her face was hard now, her mouth bitter and thin. She wore her hair scraped back uncompromisingly and dressed in nothing lighter than sepulchral dark grey. He understood why, and sympathised; but it was like living with a spectre, not a woman.

"I heard about what you did, Mary."

Her eyes met his, defiant and wary. "Shouldn't it be me saying that? You're the one who's been fighting, risking your job. How will we eat if Sir Lucien throws you out? Where will we live? I don't suppose you thought of that, did you?"

"So you do know what happened today. Did Stan tell you?" She nodded.

"Did he tell you why?"

Her lips pursed, sour as a crab apple.

Joe pushed his plate away. "We're the talk of the village, thanks to you. Why did you have to go clecking to Peggy about us? Didn't it occur to you that she'd tell her idiot husband, knowing that he works with me? How do you think Stanley felt when he overheard Wilf telling the whole stable yard that Lady Fitznorton has nothing to fear from driving instruction with me because I'm not man enough to interfere with her virtue? What was it like for Stan, do you think, to hear his father being laughed at? And how do you imagine it was for me, knowing that thanks to you they see me as less than a man? They think I'm a fool because you told Peggy nothing happens in our marital bed."

He paused, his agony plain to see if she cared to look him in the eye. But she only looked at her hands, red-raw and dry from housework.

"You're a stupid, selfish, thoughtless woman, Mary Cadwalader." He couldn't keep the pain or his bitter rage from his voice, but regretted his words the moment they had escaped his lips. He buried his face in his hands. It wasn't in his nature to hurt anyone, yet here he was insulting his own wife, the mother of his children. It might be how he felt, but the words should have been left unsaid.

"How dare you?" she spat back at him, angry as a hissing cat. "I did nothing wrong. Peggy was upset. She told me he wanted to force himself on her, even though she hadn't been churched yet after the baby. So I explained that things are different with us—"

"Yes, and she drew her own conclusions. And then she shared her thoughts with Wilson, and he's told every man I work with. I couldn't let him get away with saying those things. Even if I'd been cowardly enough to let it pass, our Stanley would have punched him – and Stan would have come off worse. At least I had a chance of beating him in a fair fight."

"You shouldn't have hit him. You should have turned the other cheek—"

"And have them all think they're right? That I'm not a man, that I'm weak, not even the head of my own house? If I still have a job at the end of this, I need to be able to hold my head up among them. You might not understand, it might not be a woman's way, or the Christian way, but that's how it is. It's the way that working men respect."

She shook her head, and he realised it was hopeless to explain.

"If you lose your job over this, and especially if our Stanley loses his, I'll never forgive you," she said.

He looked down at his knuckles, swollen and grazed. They were sore, but not nearly as much as his pride.

"So be it. You can add it to the list of all the other things you'll never do, and all your other reasons to hate me."

TWELVE
NELLIE

Mr Phelps's sly sideways glance at the hall boy and his air of smug self-satisfaction were enough to tell Nellie that he had something to say.

"Careful, boy!" he boomed at the poor lad, whose hand trembled even more, further endangering the portion of steaming hot rice pudding on its way to his bowl. The boy wavered, then finally dropped it in safely and stood back, nodding gratefully when the butler dismissed him.

"Useless boy. He'll never make a footman," Mr Phelps grumbled, scooping up an ample spoonful of pudding.

Mrs Longford raised an eyebrow. "No wonder, the way you keep berating him. I could practically hear his knees knocking from this side of the table. You mustn't be so harsh with the poor little mite."

"Poor little mite? He's lucky to be employed in this household. He's fed, isn't he, and housed, and getting a training that will set him up for life. One day he'll thank me for setting an example. No point in letting them grow up soft."

"He'll need to grow another six inches or more to make a footman," Nellie remarked. Luckily, the lad was young enough to have a few more years of growth in him yet, but she couldn't imagine his scrawny little limbs ever reaching the dizzy heights of six feet, which would greatly improve both his chances of employment as a footman and his future wages.

"Enough about the boy. I'll soon have him licked into shape. Tell me, how is her ladyship this evening? Has she recovered from the events of this afternoon?"

So this was why he had been looking pleased with himself. Mr Phelps was an inveterate gossip, despite his occasional protestations that their employers' affairs were none of his business. He loved nothing more than to speculate or pass on titbits of news.

"She has been resting all afternoon. I took tea up to her at five, but she said she had a headache. That's all I know," Nellie said. There was nothing unusual about her mistress taking to her bed, but clearly on this occasion Mr Phelps knew something she didn't.

"There was a scuffle among the outdoor staff, I understand?" Mrs Longford asked, prim-mouthed as if there were sour lemons in her bowl instead of rice pudding.

This was news to Nellie, who had been mending for much of the afternoon, enjoying the peace and quiet of her room and the rhythm and precision of her meticulous hand-stitching.

"A disgraceful business. They behaved like ruffians, and I have told Sir Lucien so. I'm not surprised her ladyship took to her bed. She'll be fretting at the prospect of her fancy man getting his marching orders."

"*Fancy man?*" Nellie's cheeks flamed.

"Cadwalader. He was the one throwing punches – all in defence of his manly prowess. She took him off into the library afterwards, tried to make light of it to me in the hope that I'd keep it quiet, but I made it very clear that Sir Lucien must be told. A duty which I have performed this evening."

"You made it clear that there's never been any kind of

impropriety, I hope? You do realise I am always with her when they go out driving? They couldn't do anything – anything remotely indecorous – without my knowledge."

Mr Phelps's eyes gleamed. He said nothing, but shrugged as if unconvinced.

"Tell him, Mrs Longford. Lady Fitznorton is never alone with Mr Cadwalader. I've sat through every tedious and occasionally terrifying minute of her lessons and never once has anything untoward occurred. And I resent the implication that I might suffer such a thing to go on in my presence. Or, for that matter, that her ladyship might encourage or desire such a thing. I know you don't like her much, Mr Phelps, but to imply to Sir Lucien that she's immoral... You do realise what the consequences might be?" She realised she was gripping her spoon so hard her hand was hurting, and dropped it on the tablecloth. She'd lost her appetite now, anyway.

Mrs Longford, calm as ever, did her best to smooth things over; but Nellie's head was spinning with the thought of what might happen if Mr Phelps succeeded in convincing their employer that his wife had taken a lover.

It wouldn't surprise Nellie if Sir Lucien killed Lady Fitz if he believed she had made a cuckold of him. And if he didn't kill her, his revenge would still be savage and wickedly cruel – of that she was sure given the way he treated her even when he had little to complain about. Lady Fitznorton didn't deserve that.

And what would be the consequences for Nellie herself? If Sir Lucien believed she had aided her mistress by turning a blind eye to adultery, she would lose her job. She would be cast off without a reference, forever disgraced. Her reputation would be besmirched by association with Lady Fitznorton, and she'd never get so good a position again. She'd end her days as some downtrodden maid of all work, sleeping in a damp basement with raw hands and joints that wouldn't give her a moment's peace. And all because Mr Phelps wanted to curry favour with his master at her ladyship's expense.

No doubt he was jealous of Cadwalader for his – what did he call it? – *manly prowess.* Joe Cadwalader was a fine-looking man, tall and broad-shouldered with a ready smile and a pleasant disposition. It wasn't only the glamour of the chauffeur's uniform that made him stand out like a peacock among sparrows. There had been a moment when, looking at him, Nellie could have been tempted herself, but he was already married, and even if he hadn't been, Nellie had no wish to exchange her current role for that of wife to a working man. It was doubtful that any woman had ever longed to caress Phelps's thinning thatch of hair. Next to Joe Cadwalader, he looked like a sullen little pig. And now he was behaving like one, too.

Nellie pushed back her chair and stood up, holding her head high and dusting down her skirts. She couldn't stand to share a table with Mr Phelps for another moment.

"Mr Phelps, you should be very careful what you say. Slander is a serious offence, and I will not hesitate to defend her ladyship's reputation and, by association, my own. I am horrified and, frankly, disgusted that you would suggest I would permit any liberties to be taken in my presence. Think very carefully; very carefully indeed. If you're going to make any kind of suggestions to Sir Lucien, you need to be absolutely sure of your ground. Because when he realises you're wrong, it won't be Mr Cadwalader getting the push. It'll be you."

Phelps glared back at her, gimlet-hard. "It is you who should be careful, Miss Dawson."

Sweat prickled down Nellie's back as his words sank in. He was loathsome, but it would be a fatal mistake to make an enemy of him. The sensible thing to do would be to back down, but her outraged principles choked the words of apology in her throat. Mute, she opened and closed her fists, wishing Mrs

Longford would step in. In the event, she was saved by the hall boy, whose timorous tap at the door interrupted them.

"Lady Fitznorton is ringing for you, Miss Dawson," he said, his eyes widening as he took in Phelps's choleric face and Nellie's defiant posture.

"I'll speak to you later, Miss Dawson," Mrs Longford said, her face long and pale as Nellie took her chance to slip out of the room.

THIRTEEN
LUCIEN

"Ah, there you are my dear. I understand you have had an eventful day."

Lucien smiled into the telephone mouthpiece, picturing his wife's reaction to his call. It gave him great satisfaction to hear the slight tremble in her voice as she replied. No doubt her knees had turned to jelly as soon as Phelps called her to the telephone. He kept his tone pleasant, but inside he was simmering at the idea that she might have made decisions about the tenure of his staff without consulting him.

"There was a minor incident, but it has been smoothed over."

"Has it, indeed? Why don't you tell me about it?" His tone was silky, couched as a suggestion, merely an expression of interest; but he knew she would hear it as it truly was. An order.

She cleared her throat nervously before replying. "One of the grooms was hurt. He was fighting with your driver. As I expect you have heard."

He took a deep puff on his cigar. Of course, she would know that Phelps had already reported the details of the incident. It was daring of her to imply that he needed no more information from her, though. He should widen the jaws of his trap. If she had indeed acted on her own initiative, she would have to face the consequences.

"I understand you decided to keep both men on?"

"I made no such decision. I asked Phelps to deal with the groom while I dealt with the driver. He—"

"And how *exactly* did you deal with him?"

"Naturally, I told him that you would be notified of the incident, and that you would decide what's to be done."

He could picture her so easily, chin raised in one of her fearful attempts at defiance, her swan-white neck taut and her generous mouth thin with tension. How he loved to frighten her. Those limpid, long-lashed eyes would dart about, looking for a means of escape or searching for dangers in the shadows. He closed his eyes, imagining her breast rapidly rising and falling as her breathing quickened, even as her limbs froze on the spot. He could almost smell the sharp, familiar tang of sweat breaking out under her arms. It made him miss their games. He had been in London too long.

"I understand you have grown somewhat attached to Cadwalader since I came to London."

"Attached? No, not at all. He has... He has merely been useful. I have developed an interest... an interest in your new motor car. He is maintaining it in an excellent condition, ready for your... your return."

She faltered, as if she could hardly bring herself to speak of his homecoming, and he kept her waiting while he pondered his next move. More than anything, he wished he could catch the next train back. He'd come unannounced, take her by surprise. He'd crush her. He'd watch pain and panic drown her as he broke her to his will. But it was out of the question for the moment.

"Tell me, my dear: what do you think I should do about Wilson and Cadwalader?"

"It isn't my place to tell you what to do."

Very true, but he wasn't going to let her get away with that. It was obvious from Phelps's reports that she was spending too much time with the driver, and therefore it stood to reason that she would want him to be kept on. Reason enough to let the man go. Despite the difficulties of finding another chauffeur, there couldn't be any possibility of Rosamund believing she could have her own way in his house. He pushed her again, relishing the prospect of her squirming in his trap. He'd get her to admit to wanting Cadwalader to stay, and then punish her by getting rid of the man.

"No, it isn't your place, but nevertheless I am interested to hear your views."

"Well, then. If you insist upon knowing my opinion: I think they should both go."

He was thrown by her unexpected response. "You want me to sack them? Both of them?"

"You know how I abhor violence. The idea of any of the staff – *your* staff – behaving so dreadfully, is quite deplorable. Sending them away would set a clear example to others and send a message that fighting will not be tolerated."

It came to him that her condemnation of the men for fighting was an attempt to censure him for his own moments of violence. He smiled to himself, amused at the idea that she might believe she could use this as an opportunity to not only criticise but also inconvenience him. Did she really imagine he cared about her opinion, except that it gave him a way to spite her?

"Do you know how much trouble I had finding a suitable driver?"

"I understand, but even so... You asked my preference."

He sniffed, took another puff of his cigar, and declared his verdict.

"It's fortunate for you, then, that you left the decision to me. According to Phelps, the men quarrelled over some domestic foolishness. Their wives are sisters. It's all blown over by now, and nothing more to be said about it. I can't afford to lose skilled men because of an inconsequential squabble. Think of the difficulties it would cause on Friday when I return home, with no driver to fetch me from the station."

"Friday?" Her sharp intake of breath was like nourishment to him.

"I've been away from you for too long. But I haven't yet determined the arrangements, my dear. I'll get the butler here to tell Phelps when I have."

He hung up, savouring her discomposure. She'd be fretting about his imminent return for the rest of the week, no doubt. He'd keep her dangling until Friday morning, wondering whether he'd be back in her bed that night. During his physical absence, it comforted him to know that she would have not a moment's peace. Such sweet revenge for the way she drove him to distraction with her coldness and her failure to appreciate everything he could have offered her if she had only been different.

He stubbed out his cigar and then stumped up the wide stairway towards his room, gripping the elegant, polished banister to haul his heavy body up the long flight. It was time to dress for dinner, and his punctilious sister Blanche would not forgive tardiness. Nor would she understand if she knew how often his thoughts turned to his wife, whom she had never liked. He imagined Rosamund now, trembling at the prospect of his homecoming. Even at this distance, he could so easily make her feel the strength of his power over her. He'd make her feel the full force of it when they were alone.

He would never forget his first night with Rosamund. She had been young, softly dimpled and shielded from men, and he had known from the moment he first saw her in the garden at Ambleworth Hall that he had to have her. She was everything her father had described and more: bright and pure, as sharp and clean to his jaded palate as a sorbet after a rich meal. Aptly named, too, with that rosebud mouth and the fresh bloom of youth on her cheeks.

His first wife, Charlotte's mother, had been a wealthy widow, quick-tempered and sure of herself and what she wanted from marriage. He had found her difficult to manage. Rosamund, he hoped, would be easier to tame. He had also thought that her ancient family connections might benefit him, bringing him closer to the possibility of a peerage and a seat in the House of Lords. Most of all, this time around he sought purity: an innocent girl untouched by any other man, like a holy spring he could plunge himself into for cleansing. A well-bred virgin he could mould to his ideal, one who would be in awe of him and whose sole desire and purpose would be to please him.

All through their wedding day, the deliciousness of antici-pation and the strain of maintaining his control every time he thought of her yielding white flesh brought him to a snarling peak of tumescence by the time they were finally alone. She went to bed that night knowing nothing, expecting nothing more from him than fatherly kindness. She had never even been kissed. He had naturally expected her to find the physical aspects of marriage surprising, and had anticipated that she might show some maidenly reluctance at first. But he had had confidence that this would soon be overcome by gratitude. After all, he was her saviour, rescuing her from grief, from insecurity and the possible financial ruin of her family after her father's mismanagement of their estates. She would respect him, adore him even. Her brother's desperation to rid himself of the financial burden of her support had played into his hands. Tristram may not have wanted her, but Lucien did. He wanted her, body and soul. She could be everything his first wife hadn't been. She possessed not only beauty and good breeding, but was still suffiently young and inexperienced to be shaped into his perfect consort.

What he hadn't expected was open revulsion. She didn't even try to spare his feelings by hiding her disgust as he drew back the bedclothes and perched on the mattress beside her. She recoiled from his touch, shoved his hand away and exclaimed when he reached over to kiss her, protesting against his physical proximity with those lovely brown eyes wide with horror. In that moment she crushed his pride, and he had resolved that she would never do so again. He had given her a chance to please him, and she had thrown it back in his face. If she couldn't love him, then he could at least make her fear him.

In its way, his anger at her aroused him as much as her innocence. He read the dawning fear in her eyes as he crushed her mouth with his own and tasted the metal and salt of blood on his tongue, sweeter than any other triumph he had known. Sex was strength. Sex was power. Every bruise he left on her body gave him pleasure, such as a boy might gain from leaving the first footprints in virgin snow. When he felt her blood hot and sticky against his thigh, her terrified whimpers soft against his ear, it was as great a thrill as if he had struck oil.

Even now, after all these years, every time he thrust his hardness into her, it was as great a conquest as an explorer planting the flag into new territory. He had never lost that sense of puissance, of greatness, every time he took her against her will. Lucien knew what the Roman poet had meant when he wrote that he both hated and loved; he knew the excruciating pain of it, and the relief to be gained from vengeful cruelty.

He had no intention of going home on Friday. There was still too much to be done in London. But when he did go back, he'd slake this thirst for her flesh that still, at times, threatened to overwhelm him. He'd make her wish she had never interfered in the running of his house. He'd find out if there was any truth to Phelps's insinuations about her interest in his driver. And if there was, then by God he'd make her sorry for it.

FOURTEEN
NELLIE

Nellie picked up the tray with its plate of toast still untouched, and set it down on the chest of drawers near the bedroom door. She hated seeing good food go to waste – a result of her upbringing, when food had been scarce and precious.

"You didn't eat your toast, m'lady." The neglected supper meant her ladyship hadn't eaten since breakfast: a bad sign, in Nellie's experience. She cast a critical gaze over Lady Fitznorton's drawn features, pale and pained against the pillowcase.

"I wasn't hungry, Nellie. One of my headaches... I'd like to undress for bed now."

Nellie nodded and shook out a nightgown, then attacked the seemingly endless column of tiny pearl buttons on the back of Lady Fitznorton's blouse, helping her to shrug it off and slide out of her skirt and petticoat before she slipped like a wraith into the bathroom. At least this would mean an early night for Nellie, who had a dull headache herself after her altercation with Mr Phelps. Of course, she wouldn't be able to take to her bed and give in to it, the way a lady could. If called upon, she'd still have to get up and do her mistress's bidding.

Folding the bedclothes down and smoothing the counterpane, Nellie swallowed her resentment and gave herself a mental shake. It wasn't Lady Fitz's fault that she'd had her run-in with Mr Phelps. Well, it was in a way, but only indirectly. Even if she'd never had her hare-brained idea of learning to drive, Sir Lucien and his butler would no doubt have found fault with her for something else.

With her slender shoulders covered again by her night-gown and wrapper, Lady Fitznorton waited in her seat at the dressing table, her gaze cast down at her lap. Not for the first time, Nellie noticed that her ladyship seemed to avoid looking at her own reflection. She frowned, tugging the pins from the neat chignon and dropping them into the crystal dish on the dressing table. The lighter mood of recent weeks seemed to have dissipated, leaving them back where they had been before: Nellie working in silence while her employer brooded, looking as if she would slump into a heap if not for her life-time's habit of straight-backed deportment preventing such a lapse.

Catching up the heavy hank of brown hair in her left hand, Nellie began brushing it with long, rhythmic strokes that made it fall in a shining curtain down her ladyship's narrow back. The movement soothed her as much as the sensation of the silky hair crackling under the ministration of the brush.

"Are you happy, Nellie?"

Startled by the sudden question, Nellie lost her rhythm, but swiftly caught herself and realised Lady Fitznorton's dark eyes were watching her, intense and unblinking, in the mirror.

"Beg your pardon, m'lady?"

"Are you happy? With your life, I mean. With your work."

At a loss as to how to answer, Nellie stared at her as if she had grown another head or started doing circus tricks, and after a pause Lady Fitznorton looked away. She snatched up one of the hair pins and fidgeted with it, twirling it in her fingers.

"I'm sorry, Nellie. It was a foolish question. If you were

*un*happy, I'd be the last person in whom you'd feel able to confide."

Nellie set down the hairbrush and deftly sectioned Lady Fitznorton's hair ready for its night plait. Something must have brought this on. Nellie could only assume that her employer's odd mood must be linked to the incident earlier, or the subsequent telephone call from Sir Lucien.

"I'm not unhappy, m'lady. I hope my demeanour hasn't suggested that I am?"

"No, no; perhaps my imagination ran away with me." Then, as Nellie reached past her for a ribbon to secure the long plait: "Your happiness does matter to me, you know. I'd hate to think... That is, what I am trying to say, is that I'm very grateful to you for your loyal service, and for your discretion. I hope you know how much you are valued."

Nellie's cheeks grew warm. She wasn't ordinarily given to sentiment, or to giving much thought to her employer's feelings, but in spite of herself she found she was touched by this sudden expression of appreciation. It wasn't usual for a member of the gentry to speak so; as a general rule they rarely expressed thanks for any service performed. If they did, Nellie supposed they would be saying thank you a thousand times a day.

"It's very kind of you to say that, m'lady, and I'm glad to know that you're satisfied with my work."

"It's true. I'd be lost without you, Nellie."

Lady Fitznorton caught hold of Nellie's hand and squeezed it, her eyes brimming with tears. Awkwardly, Nellie patted her hand, groping for the right thing to say.

"Are you alright, m'lady? Has something brought this on?"

"No, no. Forgive me, I'm just... just tired." She sucked in a gulp of air and blinked away the tears, nodding as if to reassure herself as much as her maid.

"A night's sleep will do you the power of good. Let's get you into bed now, and with a bit of rest hopefully your headache will have gone by morning."

Nellie guided her by the elbow to the bed as if she was a nursemaid with a child, saw her settled and pulled the coverlet over her. She seemed to shrink against the pillows, tiny in the great, heavily draped bed as if it was trying to swallow her up.

"It will all seem better tomorrow," Nellie added. But the frightened, forlorn look on Lady Fitznorton's face as she put out the light and left her alone in the room had her wondering.

FIFTEEN
MARY

It was the first service of this Sunday, and usually Mary's favourite time of the week. It was not, admittedly, the way it had been when she was younger. Back then, she used to feel a glow enveloping her in Chapel, her spirit kindling during an impassioned prayer or a rousing hymn. Worship made her feel lighter, bubbling up like a cake rising in the warmth of a gentle oven. After the deaths of her two children, it had changed: now, Chapel was less stirring and more healing, like a mother's embrace.

Slipping into an empty pew near the back, Mary was painfully aware of the gossip that had sprung from her ill-advised conversation with Peggy. How many of these folk knew her most intimate secrets? Holding her head high, she nodded to her neighbours but avoided meeting their curious eyes, keeping her attention on her children and giving Stanley a sharp nudge to remind him to remove his cap. The children hated Sundays, having to wear their best clothes and not being allowed out to play. They trooped in behind her, unmoved by the plain wooden cross above the pulpit and the rows of solemn faces peering down from the balcony. Ten years after the Welsh Revival, congregations had dwindled a little, but Mary still felt a little pop of anticipation every time she entered a chapel. Perhaps today would be the day when the Spirit would touch her and heal the chasm that had opened in her heart when Annie followed Alfie to the grave that they had left behind in Birmingham.

"Good morning, Mrs Cadwalader," said the robust woman in the pew in front. Her rheumy eyes scanned the children, fidgeting in their starched Sunday clothes. "I see Mr Cadwalader isn't with you again. Such a shame you couldn't persuade him to come. I suppose he's out and about, driving Lady Fitznorton around? You'd think the gentry would allow him time for worship on the Lord's Day."

She shook her head, disapproving, and Mary's cheeks reddened. She knew how bad it looked, and her heart sank at the idea that people had taken note of it, but Joe hadn't set foot inside a place of worship since Annie's funeral. She was frightened that he might lose his salvation if he turned his back on the Lord, but she found it so difficult to talk to him about spiritual matters these days. To talk to him about anything. All she could do was pray that he would eventually feel the need for fellowship and decide for himself to return.

The low babble of chatter abruptly stopped, rousing Mary from her thoughts. The pastor was scaling the steps into the pulpit, hauling himself up as if his knees troubled him, pausing at the top, his fierce glare sweeping the silent congregation. His bushy white eyebrows drew together in a frown.

"Let us pray," he boomed, in a voice that matched his commanding presence. All heads bowed in one fluid movement. Mary sent a sideways glance along the pew and prodded her eldest daughter Maggie to take the hymn book off Teddy and Jack, who were playing a silent game of tug-of-war with it.

"Heavenly Father, we come before you as filthy rags, unfit to approach the Throne of Heaven..."

Satisfied that the children were still at last, Mary squeezed her eyes shut and listened to the pastor. As always, he was afire with righteousness, railing in his rich, melodious voice against the sins of his flock. And his prayer listed so many sinners: atheists; Catholics; Jews; fornicators; drunkards; adulterers; liars; idolaters; gamblers and cheats all came in for his condemnation. All, he declared, were seething with evil. Every week he reminded his gathered congregation that the way to heaven was narrow, and the way to hell wide, and all were doomed to fall short of the glory of God unless they were washed in the cleansing blood of the Lamb.

It was a relief when his prayer finally ended and the first hymn began, signalling the time for the younger children to troop out to the Sunday School room for their lessons. Twelve-year-old Dolly had been pleased last week at being asked to help out with the younger children, and Mary was equally gratified, taking this as a sign that they had been accepted by the community and were no longer seen as newcomers.

The hymn ended and Mary sank back down, her hips aching against the hard, narrow pew. This week, the pastor's sermon was on the subject of the godly family. As he berated the women of his flock for their vanity and frippery, she gave a complacent nod, knowing this was one sin from which she was safe. But when he castigated them for failing to submit to their husbands as to the Lord, the way Sarah submitted to Abraham, her knuckles whitened on the well-worn cover of her Bible. It was as if the pastor had looked into her mind and seen that she was not a good wife to Joe, with this reminder that it was wrong to refuse her husband what he wanted. Or – the mortifying thought struck her all at once – had Peggy's gossiping reached even his ears?

Her heart warred with her desire to please God and her

husband. Unquestionably she was dishonouring both. To add to her distress, intense heat began radiating from her chest and up her neck into her face. Perspiration prickled on her top lip and her forehead. *Not this, not now.* She fumbled for her handkerchief, knowing her face had turned scarlet, the embarrassment making her discomfort even worse. Even as she dried her face, her armpits felt moist, and she prayed that her dark grey cotton blouse wouldn't betray her with damp patches. She hated it when this rush of heat overcame her, as it often had in recent months; it was bad enough when it happened in the privacy of her home, where she could at least splash cool water on her face and wrists, and fan herself. But here, in front of everyone, and with the preacher's eyes watching her as if he could see into the depths of her soul, he would know from her crimson countenance that his sermon had hit home.

With her stomach in knots, she hardly dared look up again, but forced herself to for fear of making her shame even more obvious. To make things worse, when she did, she noticed more than a few glances in her direction from women who quickly turned away when they caught her eye. Peggy was sitting a few rows in front with a friend who nudged her and sneaked a glance back, covering her mouth with her hand but not before Mary had glimpsed her grinning. Peggy, at least, had the grace to lower her eyes to avoid Mary's hurt expression.

She stared down at the limp handkerchief in her lap, thinking about the way things were with Joe. She'd always known it was pointless to be angry with God for taking their children back to His bosom where they'd be happier and safer than they would ever be in this world. Joe's rage made no more sense to her than cursing the sun on a hot day, or the rain when the streets filled with puddles. It was the way of things to bloom and then to die.

Mary could forgive God, trusting in His mercy in a way her husband never could. It was Joe she couldn't forgive – for his

failure to act, for his bitterness, and his cloying need for her
body. Now, facing the sidelong stares of the gossips, that tide of
anger roiled in her again, spoiling her peace and making her
worship a pointless act: if she couldn't forgive Joe, she could
expect no forgiveness from God. Her very soul was in peril. If
nothing else, she knew she should count herself fortunate that
her husband had never forced himself upon her or punished her
for her disobedience, as many a man would consider it his right
to do. Still, she couldn't imagine how she could ever back down
from the stance she had taken. Too many hurtful things had
been said on both sides.

Soon enough it was Maggie's turn to squirm as the pastor
turned his attention to children who disobeyed their parents,
and in particular young girls who thought themselves too good
for jobs that prepared them for marriage and motherhood, who
should take decent work like domestic service instead of leaving
their natural environment to work in filthy factories where they
would be lured into sinful ways and corrupt, blasphemous talk.
At the edge of her vision Mary noted the defiant way Maggie's
chin lifted, and resolved to speak to her later. It was all very well
for her eldest daughter to refuse to go skivvying like her mother
had done, and for her to claim, truthfully, that the wages were
better in the factory, but it didn't do to draw attention to herself
by glaring back at the preacher so brazenly.

Unusually, Mary left the chapel feeling more troubled than
when she entered. Even the hymns had failed to bring her
either joy or comfort as they customarily did. She kept her head
down, herding the children out and avoiding eye contact with
anyone. They had nearly escaped through the gate when
Peggy's hand tugged at her elbow.

"Mary, don't rush off. Is everything alright?" Peggy's smile
was artificially bright. Her baby was bundled tightly in a shawl
and she joggled him in her arms. He still looked a scrawny little

mite. A baby's cheeks should be plump and rosy. It made Mary's mouth go dry just to look at him.

Her anger dropped away, leaving her weary.

"Yes," she said. "There's nothing to worry about, Peggy. Everything is absolutely fine."

SIXTEEN

ROSAMUND

As the days passed, Rosamund's tension grew. Friday loomed on the horizon like a monster lurking in the shadows, bringing the prospect of her husband's return from London. However much Nellie cajoled her to eat, she could manage only a few mouthfuls of dry toast before her throat seemed to close over and her stomach rebelled. Her head felt as if a metal band had been screwed tight around it, and she developed pains in all her joints that no amount of bathing in scented water could assuage. By Friday morning she wanted nothing more than to hide in her bed and fall asleep for a hundred years, until the danger had passed.

"Perhaps a walk would lift your spirits, m'lady?"

The light bursting into the room as Nellie threw back the curtains hit Rosamund's eyes like a blow from a fist.

"I couldn't, Nellie. Please, close the curtains again and let me rest." It took all her energy to form the words, her mouth like parchment.

"Tea, then. At least take a few sips."

Nellie was waiting expectantly with the tray. It seemed there would be no peace unless Rosamund made some effort to comply; she forced herself to a sitting position and allowed her maid to fuss about plumping up the pillows before sagging back into their softness. Taking a sip of the strong, black tea, she couldn't help but grimace.

"Did you add sugar to my tea?"

"No, m'lady. Mrs McKie did. She's quite put out that every meal she's sent you this week has been sent back practically untouched. I wouldn't be surprised if your next offering from the kitchen will be bone marrow broth to build you up, if you don't start perking up soon."

Rosamund sighed and drained the last few sips, earning a satisfied nod from her maid before being permitted to sink down and draw the covers back up over her shoulders. She couldn't expect anyone else to understand the way she felt after her husband's telephone call. It had taken all her strength of will to outwit him, and all the while she'd been convinced he would see through her ruse and that Cadwalader and his whole family would be out on the streets.

Sickened though she had been to see the driver fighting, she couldn't bear the thought of him suffering, or even worse the prospect of never seeing him again. Through the long hours she had spent in her room since the incident, he had filled her thoughts: his patience when he explained the workings of the motor to her; the humour and kindness in his eyes, and the way their colour seemed to change – sometimes hazel, sometimes green, depending on his mood or perhaps the colour of the sky that day. She pictured his smile, so natural and unguarded when he was pleased with her, and how it warmed her because it showed she had done well. Sometimes she imagined how his hair would feel under her fingers: would the salt and pepper curls be as soft and springy as they had looked when she'd seen him without his chauffeur's cap? Would his rough, deft work-ing-man's hands be gentle if he touched her cheek, the way she sometimes dared to imagine he might want to? But such thoughts were pointless. With her spirits as heavy as her limbs, she allowed herself to drift back into sleep, the pillows and coverlet the nearest thing to a warm embrace that she was ever likely to experience.

When Nellie next appeared, she held out a salver with a letter on it.

"This has come for you, m'lady. Can I fetch anything else? Another cup of tea? Are you ready for your bath?"

"No, thank you Nellie." Rosamund's heart plunged at the sight of the familiar handwriting on the envelope. The letter was from Sir Lucien. Before Nellie could leave, she called her back. "Would you read it for me, and tell me what it says? My head is still too painful..."

Looking faintly embarrassed to be reading her mistress's private correspondence, Nellie took the letter over to the window and slit the envelope open to scan its contents in the chink of light beside the curtains. Rosamund curled onto her side and waited, hugging her stomach as it churned.

"It's from Sir Lucien. He says he won't be able to return today after all, and he hopes you won't be too disappointed." Nellie's voice faltered at that, and she pressed her lips together before sliding the letter back into its envelope. She must know, of course, at least something of what he was like. How unlikely it was that Rosamund would be disappointed by his decision to remain in London.

"Are you sure?" Rosamund put a hand to her forehead and sat up. "He says he *isn't* coming?"

"He has business to attend to, he says, but it shouldn't delay him for long. He will let you know when he intends to return. Actually, m'lady, now that you're awake, I have something to ask you... I've had a letter myself today. It's from my mother. She isn't at all well, and she's asked if I could go home to look after her. Not for long, just for a few days. Would that be alright, m'lady?"

Rosamund was barely listening, overwhelmed by her sense of relief. She felt dizzy with it, as if she was drunk. Her reprieve, however temporary, made everything seem better.

"Of course you must go, Nellie, if she needs you. But not today. If you will wait until tomorrow, I'll even drive you to the station myself. I'm sure I'll feel much better by then, and Cadwalader will be able to carry your bags. I couldn't spare you today, but by tomorrow... I'll be back on my feet, and you will have had time to instruct one of the housemaids as to my needs."

She dropped her gaze to avoid seeing the way Nellie's face fell.

"Could you ask Mrs McKie to send up a boiled egg? My appetite seems to have improved this morning. After that, perhaps I'll be able to get up."

"Very good, m'lady. And then, when you're ready, I'll show Sarah how you like your hair done. She's a good girl, is Sarah: I'm sure she'll serve you well while I'm away."

SEVENTEEN
JOSEPH

After his fight with Wilson, nearly a week passed before Joe saw Lady Fitznorton again. She didn't come for her driving lesson at the usual time, and sent no message to indicate whether she wished to continue with the instruction. When a letter from Sir Lucien was rumoured to have arrived on Friday morning, he assumed the worst and expected Phelps's heavy tread in the gravel outside the motor stable at any time, come to pass on the news that he had been dismissed. But Phelps didn't come. He and Stanley continued working as usual, with uncertainty hanging over them like a condemned man's dread of sentencing after a trial. He felt as badly for Stanley as for himself: it wasn't the boy's fault this apprentice-ship would end prematurely, and it might not be easy to find another.

He was polishing the car and brooding over his likely fate on Saturday morning when a movement in the corner of his eye made him look up. His heart leapt with a combination of fear and pleasure before sinking again. He straightened and smiled at the unexpected sight of Nellie Dawson wearing a powder-blue coat and hat he had once seen Lady Fitznorton wearing.

She was carrying a battered valise and a smaller bag, and he moved to take them from her.

"Miss Dawson. I didn't recognise you in that get-up. I thought you were Herself for a minute there."

To his amusement, colour rose to Nellie's cheeks as she handed over her bags and fluttered her hands over the surface of her coat.

"Oh, this. Yes, she gave it to me as she'd tired of it and there's a mark on the sleeve that I couldn't get out. It's a bit of a squeeze to get into it, mind, even though it was loose on her."

"You look very fine. Are you going somewhere special?"

Although she flushed again at his compliment, Nellie's face was solemn. "My mother is ill so I'm going to nurse her for a couple of days. Unfortunately her ladyship can't spare me for longer, but she did very kindly suggest that she could run me to the station in the motor car."

"Did she, now?" The sun behind Nellie made Joe squint, and he lifted a hand to shade his eyes just as the lady in question emerged from the house wearing a loose navy-blue coat and a hat he hadn't seen before.

"Is this a convenient time to resume my lessons, Cadwalader?" she asked, coolly polite as if she had never caught him fighting and looked at him as if he'd broken her heart. "As Nellie is unfortunately having to leave us for a few days, I thought it an ideal opportunity to attempt the drive into town. If that's alright with you, of course?" She phrased it as a question, but he could hardly demur.

He stowed Nellie's valise in the luggage rack on the roof and opened the doors for each of them to seat themselves in the car before donning his cap and jacket and bending to the starting handle. He wasn't annoyed at the sudden interruption to his work: Stanley had plenty to do, and at least the trip into Pontybrenin would give the engine a good run.

Sadly, it soon became apparent that lessons would no longer

be as they had been before. There was no conversation and Lady Fitznorton seemed tense. She was an apt pupil and had made excellent progress, handling the car competently on the long road through the estate even after a week without any practice. While it was obvious that she was more nervous when driving in the town, her eyes darting to check for pedestrians, edging along slowly to avoid startling any horses, she managed to reach the station without incident. Then, with Nellie safely despatched to her train, it was just the two of them in the car.

She navigated back through Pontybrenin towards the Fitznorton estate without difficulty, and as she turned in past the lodge at the main gates Joe could remain silent no longer.

"Well done, m'lady. You drove perfectly today."

She didn't return his smile – not even a flicker. In fact, he could almost believe she was deliberately avoiding any eye contact with him at all. His face fell, disappointment dousing all the pleasure and pride he had felt at her achievement. Up to now he had believed she valued him as a teacher and appreciated his instruction. He might even have imagined, before, that she enjoyed his company. But today she seemed stiff and uncomfortable.

Worryingly, he found that when he moved his hand quickly she flinched, making him think back to the day he had grabbed her arm and seen bruises on her wrist. Perhaps those weren't the only bruises her husband had inflicted over the years. After witnessing his scrap with Wilson perhaps she thought him capable of the same brutishness towards a woman. The idea that she might now see him as a threat made his heart sink.

It was a beautifully sunny day, with the countryside at its most lush and green after recent rain. With her handling the car so well on the road through the Fitznorton estate he should have been able to sit back and enjoy the view if he hadn't been so concerned by her silence.

"I think it's obvious that you don't need my help any longer, m'lady," he said. "You'd manage perfectly well without me if you went driving on your own."

To his surprise, instead of looking pleased she stared at him in obvious dismay. They had been rattling along downhill, the noise of the engine rising as it gained momentum, but now she brought the car to an abrupt halt as soon as they came to a wider part of the track, braking so suddenly that the wheels locked and he had to put out a hand to steady himself.

"What's the matter...?" he began, taken aback by the abrupt change in her behaviour.

"Let me out, please."

Obediently he opened the door and slipped out of the car to allow her to pass, then gazed at her from across the hood. "M'lady—"

"Please – don't say any more." She gestured vaguely towards the woodland further along the track and said, in a voice that sounded brittle, as if she might snap at any moment: "There may be bluebells in the woods just along there... I have a mind to take a walk."

He stared after her slight figure as she set off, the dark blue coat flapping in the breeze. Despite stumbling once or twice, she hurried towards the trees so quickly that he could almost have believed she feared pursuit.

Joe slumped back in the passenger seat and brooded. This wasn't the first time he had said something that caused her to take to her heels. Was there anything in what he'd just said to cause offence? He went back over the past few minutes in his mind, but no reason presented itself. On the contrary: he had praised her driving. He'd told her she had achieved her objective of being able to drive by herself. What could she possibly have found so upsetting about that?

He wasn't a man who liked to sit around idly. At first, he stayed in the car, restless and fidgety, wishing he had a book to pass the time. Accustomed as he was to hard work, he hated inactivity. After a while he climbed out of the car and walked around it, looking for something to polish or repair; but apart from a few flies stuck to the front grille and a bit of dust clinging to the paintwork everything was as good as it had been when they left the big house.

He walked to the edge of the track and up onto the verge, leaning on the wooden fence to look out across the fields. Nothing to see but sheep, their lambs alternately skipping and rushing back to their mothers' teats. The house wasn't visible from this part of the estate: only farmland in front of him, the deer park in the distance. Thickets of woodland and the hill with its summerhouse lay behind; and, meandering through Sir Lucien's land, the roughly pitted road, little more than a track. It had been laid for the benefit of horse-drawn carts, but these days was more often travelled by the motor car. The estate cottages were in the grounds behind the house, not on this side. There wouldn't be another soul within a mile.

The sleeve of his coat snagged on a sharp prong of barbed wire, and he unhooked himself, cursing under his breath as it scratched his wrist. He hadn't even realised the wire was there. Funny how things have a way of catching you unawares, he thought, rubbing the trace of blood off the scratch. Nasty stuff, barbed wire: no wonder the animals kept away from it. You wouldn't want to go running into it – it would rip your skin and clothes to shreds.

With nothing to occupy his thoughts it was inevitable that the memories he customarily shut out of his mind would begin crowding in, idleness giving them a chance to sneak beneath his defences. He closed his eyes tightly, but to no avail. He could see Annie's face as clearly as if she was in his arms again.

His heart lurched. The old, familiar pain was there: the raw hole in his chest that made him feel as if his vitals had been ripped out and left to hang on the barbed wire fence for the crows to peck at. He felt a trembling in his knees, warning him they would buckle under the weight of his memories if he didn't either sit down or get moving.

"Where the hell is she?" he muttered, taking out his pocket watch. He wouldn't allow himself to dwell on his griefs, but forced himself to focus on practicalities. Lady Fitznorton had been gone for at least forty-five minutes, and there was still no sign of her. Something must be wrong. He set off in the direction she had taken towards the woods, his legs beginning a swift stride as if of their own volition. There would be solace in activity.

The air in the woods was cool and green, with that characteristic moist, earthy smell of fresh growth. He pressed onwards, wondering if her ladyship had kept to the narrow path or had wandered off somewhere. With no sign of her, he started to fear the worst. She might be hurt; she could have fallen, banged her head or broken her ankle. She could be lying on the ground, her slender, fragile body getting colder and colder. If he didn't find her by nightfall... He shook his head to banish such imaginings. It wasn't as if he should particularly care what happened to her, anyway. Who was she to him? Just his employer's wife. The only reason for concern was the risk of getting into trouble for allowing her to go off on her own and break her neck. But he knew that wasn't really it. There was something about her that drew him in and troubled him in equal measure. The delicacy of her. The way she needed careful handling, like a skittish mare that had been broken in with cruelty and hardly knew how to respond to gentleness. It made him feel protective. If he was completely honest with himself, it attracted him.

He came upon her in a clearing resembling a scene from one of the landscape paintings hanging in the big house. He paused, silent for a moment. Sunbeams slanted between the leaves and lit the bluebells covering the ground in a vivid tapestry of blues, purples and greens. They surrounded her where she sat, head bowed on her drawn-up knees.

She'd taken off her gloves and her hat, revealing surprising glints of russet and chestnut where the sunlight caressed her dark hair, and there was no sign of her coat, so Joe guessed she must be sitting on it. The square neckline of her lacy blouse revealed the creamy nape of her neck, the tender knobbles of her spine below her thick, upswept hair. He so rarely saw her skin, except her face of course, and even that was often blurred by a veil. Seeing her pale neck exposed made her seem more real, somehow – less like a dainty Dresden figurine and more like a woman.

He berated himself. Of course she was a woman. But to him she was a lady, first and foremost, cool as porcelain with that courteous, correct manner; her movements customarily calm and steady, her voice soft. He tried to imagine her shouting or sobbing, and couldn't. Yet there was passion in her, he would swear to that. He had always sensed great depths of feeling beneath her detached exterior.

He was jolted from his reverie by the sudden, awkward realisation that she had lifted her head and was watching him. The bluebells around her stirred and nodded in the faint breeze, beckoning him forward.

She straightened with a sigh.

"Cadwalader. I'm terribly sorry. I've kept you waiting."

"Don't let me disturb you," he found himself saying, taking another step towards her. "I didn't mean to spoil this..." He made an expansive gesture with his arm and saw the way her shoulders slumped, just a little – not enough to relax that determinedly rigid posture, but enough to indicate her relief.

A closer inspection of her face revealed she'd been crying. The thought of it discomfited him, and induced an irrational urge to either get far away from her or gather her into his arms. He opened his mouth to ask if she was alright, but she spoke first.

"It's so beautiful here. So peaceful. I needed to..."

She paused, and he filled in the words for her without thinking.

"You needed to escape."

Her gaze met his for the first time, as if she was surprised he understood. Perhaps he had been impertinent. But she nodded.

"Do you ever feel like running away?" she asked.

He shrugged. "Often. But I couldn't do it. Too many people need me."

She was silent, looking past him towards some distant spot between the tangled trees. Her stillness had him fooled for a moment, before he noticed the tears flooding down her cheeks. She made no attempt to blink or wipe them away, and made no sound, but the despondency in her face was enough to break his heart. His voice caught in his throat. He wanted to kneel beside her and hold her close.

"How fortunate you are. There isn't a living soul in the world who needs me. My parents and brother are dead. Sir Lucien and Charlotte are my only living family, and they don't want me... She has been presented at Court, you know. I received a letter from her this morning. I wasn't invited. Her aunt arranged it all, and by the time I knew, it was a *fait accompli*. I don't know why it should upset me. I wouldn't have been brave enough to go to London, even if they'd wanted me there. But she is my stepdaughter, and she's the only company I ever have here. Now it seems an engagement is likely very soon, so I imagine she'll be married by next year and then I'll have no one. No one but him."

Joe's mouth twisted at the thought of what that would mean for her.

She buried her face in her hands. "I'm so terribly tired of this life. Tired of myself. Of going nowhere and meaning nothing to anyone. I thought that driving on my own, controlling the car, would mean I could go wherever I wanted... I thought it would make me, at last, the mistress of my own fate.

"But I see now that it changes nothing. I'm like a bird that has forgotten how to fly since its wings were clipped. I'll always be trapped in this cage, because I have nowhere else to go, and if I fly he will only find me, and it will be even worse. The only thing that has made life slightly more bearable during these past few months – that's made me loathe myself a little less – is the time I've spent with you. Your patience, your kindness and good humour, your instruction – not since my father died... And now, now that you say I no longer need your help... even that will be lost to me."

Joe swallowed. Even at this low ebb her beauty was so exquisitely delicate. It made him feel like a collector of butterflies, longing to hold her perfection in his hands, to spread it out before him and examine it in all its iridescent colour and detail. Every marking must be noted, every fluttering movement stilled, so his senses could drink her in and be sated on her. His body seemed to groan with the need to make her his, she who could never be his. But he knew it couldn't happen. She wouldn't want it. How could he, a working man, imagine that he could ever join himself to such a perfect creature?

EIGHTEEN
ROSAMUND

Mortified though she was at her own behaviour, Rosamund was powerless to stop the loud gulps of harsh weeping into her hands as if in grief. She tried to swallow the almost animalistic keening sounds, but they came up involuntarily like hiccups, and her feelings of shame only made it harder to stop. Whatever could have possessed her to behave so dreadfully in front of a servant? Even if the servant was Joe Cadwalader, who radiated kindness and had shown her smiles gentler than those of any gentleman she had ever known.

She recoiled in surprise as she felt his hands on hers, pulling them gently away from her face and pressing a soft cotton hand-kerchief into her palm. He was murmuring quiet reassurances, she realised, hushing her as one would a child or an animal in distress. He had come to kneel beside her in the sweet-scented bluebells, and laid a steadying hand on her shoulder, just for a moment, as if he realised at once that he had overstepped the mark. But she had done worse with her outburst. Rigid with the oddest mixture of embarrassment and pleasure at the warmth of his touch, she took deep breaths, unable to look at him for fear of what he must think of her. She couldn't bear it if he dismissed her as a self-centred, self-pitying fool.

"You're lonely," he said. Such simple words, and yet in their simplicity he had managed to sum up everything. She nodded gratefully, fighting back another stream of tears.

"M'lady—" He broke off, and seemed to be searching for words, sitting back on his heels. His eyes met hers, so beautifully intense that she caught her breath. "I understand," he said. "Believe it or not, I've known more than my fair share of loneliness."

She stared at him, uncomprehending. He had a wife, and how many children? She could scarcely remember. Six? Seven, was it? One of his boys even worked with him. How could someone who was always surrounded by people who loved and needed him ever be lonely?

"Please don't feel you have to explain anything to me," she said.

He rubbed a finger along one thick eyebrow, massaging his temple as if deep in thought. "Losing our Annie changed everything..." he began.

Rosamund stilled. She recalled him mentioning a daughter who had died. The pain etched on his face was a mirror of her own: she could hardly order him to stop and take her home now, after her own outpourings had invited such confidences.

"She was such a beautiful child, all soft dark ringlets and dimples, with her older brothers and sisters doting on her. She was only a year old, but she didn't throw tantrums like the others used to when they were little. She didn't need to shout and stamp her feet to get what she wanted – she'd worked out how to get it with charm." A rueful smile softened his lips. "But then we had a bad night with her, crying and fractious with a fever. When I went to work the next morning, my main worry was how I'd get through the day without falling asleep. I never thought..."

Rosamund closed her eyes, sensing what was coming. To look into the face of his anguish seemed too great an intrusion.

"That afternoon, Mary sent Maggie and Dolly, my two eldest girls, to fetch me home. But the foreman wouldn't let me go until I'd finished repairing the lorry we were working on. He said nothing was as urgent as his deliveries, and if I wanted to still have a job in the morning, I'd finish my shift. The way I saw it, I didn't have any choice. I finished the job and went home as soon as I could. By then, Annie was in a bad way. She wasn't crying any more. She was floppy, and her little arms and legs were covered in these great, ugly, purple blotches. Her eyes were open, but I don't think she could see me. Mary had sent the girls to fetch the doctor when they told her I wasn't coming, but by the time he got there it was too late. She died in my arms and my heart felt like it had been ripped from me."

Forgetting her dignity, Rosamund reached out and covered his hand with hers. It felt inadequate; there were no words that could assuage the torment he must have felt. Her own loneliness seemed such a trivial problem by comparison.

"Mary never forgave me. She blamed me for not coming home sooner, for the doctor not getting there, for Annie being ill – everything. I was angry with God; she saved all her anger for me. She said there must be no more babies – she couldn't go through it again, she said. She'd lost two – she couldn't bear to lose any more. As if she had lost them on her own... she forgot that I lost them too. From that day on, she has closed her heart to me. I thought it would pass with time, but it's been more than a year. I took this job to please her, but even so... I live and work surrounded by people – but yes, I get lonely."

He dragged his hands over his face. "When I got into that fight the other week, that's what it was about. Mary had been talking to her sister, Wilf Wilson's wife, saying how we don't – you know – we're not *close* any more, and of course Wilson got to hear about it and thought he'd have a go at winding Stanley up. He said things about you and me – joking, like – how I'd be no threat to you because I was no man, seeing as how I don't even do it with my own wife. I could see Stanley was going to thump him, but I couldn't let Stan get into trouble over me, so I decked the bugger – begging your pardon, m'lady. I remember you looked at me as if I was scum when I told you he deserved it, but believe me, he did. I couldn't let him say that about me, or about you."

"I see." She twisted his wet handkerchief in her lap.

"I'm not in the habit of hitting people as a rule."

"No. I realise that now."

"Although I'd dearly like to hit that husband of yours."

His words were so unexpected, her mouth fell open.

"I've seen bruises on your wrists. And I've seen how nervous you've been around me since that fight. It doesn't take an educated man to work out what goes on." A muscle twitched in his cheek as his face took on a grim expression. The compassion in his eyes was briefly replaced by something hot and fierce.

She was dumbfounded, stunned that he had guessed what her husband was like and that it made him angry.

"He does terrible things..." she whispered. She had never told anyone before. Saying the words out loud was like unravelling a knot that had been twisting up inside her for years. She faltered, her throat seeming to close up to block any further admissions. She couldn't tell anyone about her husband's trips to the most decadent brothels in Paris, or what he made her do when he returned.

In the silence that fell between them, the pure trilling of a blackbird contrasted sharply with the darkness of her memories. Her legs had started to judder, and she realised she had her arms about herself, rocking to and fro like a child in need of comfort. The movement bruised the bluebells, releasing their fragrance, clean like the dappled light that picked out threads of silver and russet in Cadwalader's brown hair.

He had closed his eyes; he must be disgusted by her. She shouldn't have put those thoughts of Sir Lucien into his mind. Cadwalader would think her no better than a whore, if he guessed at the things she'd been made to do. He'd never be able to look at her with respect again. She shuddered, chilled by her thoughts as much as by the coolness of the shady grove, and snatched up her gloves, cheeks flaming from the shame of saying too much. It would be better to go, and say no more.

He caught up her hands before she could put the gloves on, a sad, shy smile making his eyes soften even though his mouth hardly altered. "Do you know, I've never seen your hands before today. You're always outdoors when I see you; always wearing gloves. They are the softest, most delicate, most perfectly lovely hands I've ever seen." He held them carefully in his own, as delicately as if they were made of precious crystal, then pressed a kiss into each palm.

The brush of his warm lips on her cool skin made heat flood through her. She gasped, immobilised as much by the shock of being touched as by his faltering words. Then he said her name, his cheeks flushing as he said it; it sounded extraordinary on his lips, as if she were a real person, a woman, as if her identity had never been swallowed up by her husband's title.

"M'lady... Rosamund. You are exquisite. That vicious old bastard doesn't deserve such a jewel. He should cherish every inch of you. He should put you on a pedestal and worship at your feet. His title and his money might set him apart as a gentleman, but a man like that isn't fit to shine your shoes. The idea of him putting his fat, cruel hands anywhere near you makes me—" He broke off and finished quietly: "You deserve to be adored. If you were mine, I'd treasure you – higher than rubies, more precious than diamonds. Look at you... a pearl beyond price."

Naked admiration lent a kind of rough beauty to his face. His expression, and the closeness of him, the way his eyes had focused on her parted lips, so intent and filled with concentration. It was madness, but she couldn't help herself. She leaned forward, closing the short distance between their bodies, and pressed her lips against his. They were warm, his breath was warm. She'd never before experienced a kiss that was gentle, from soft, generous lips. For a long, golden moment there was a marvellous tenderness that filled her with a kind of molten glow.

But before she knew it, she was caught up in an embrace that made her feel trapped. He had read her kiss as an invitation, and gathered her into his arms. Her heart hammered against her ribs. She hadn't intended this, and the idea that he might use this opportunity to use her body the way her husband did was horrifying. She pressed her palms against his woollen coat and shook her head, arching away from him.

"Don't – please don't!" she managed to gasp out. Her breathing was ragged; her throat felt as if it would close over.

To her surprise, his eyes widened in confusion and he loosed her at once.

"I'm sorry," he said in a voice made gruff by emotion. "I thought—"

Her brain felt overloaded, unable to comprehend how easy it had been to make him stop. She shook her head, unable to meet his gaze for shame, and found herself babbling.

"No, no – please don't apologise. It was my fault entirely. I can't explain my behaviour. I can only ask you to forgive me – and to forget it ever happened. It should never have... It was a moment's folly. Inexcusable."

He was up and walking away, donning his hat and gloves and holding himself ramrod straight. He looked everywhere but at her, and at the sight of his obvious embarrassment, tears pricked her eyes. She had either made him angry or hurt his feelings, and she wasn't sure which was worse. What a fool she was to have tarnished his regard for her with her confessions and that inexplicable urge to experience a still deeper intimacy.

"You don't need to explain yourself to me, m'lady. You were overwrought. We'd better get you back to the house."

Forlornly, feeling as if she had ruined everything, she gathered up her things, dusted the specks of earth off her skirt and coat, and followed.

NINETEEN

ROSAMUND

As much as shame made her try to blot it out, the memory of what had transpired in the woods with Joe Cadwalader kept returning in flashes in Rosamund's mind. It had been so unexpected, like an earthquake that toppled her and made everything seem now as if it had been reshaped. Until it happened, she'd felt as if she was drowning, dragged down by the bitter leaden weight of her marriage like a chain shackled to her ankle. But that was before she'd spoken out to confess the torments and loneliness she suffered. Before she allowed a man who wasn't her husband to touch her. Before she reached up and kissed him.

Joe Cadwalader's lips had tasted so enticing. She knew now what it was to lift her face up from the depths of despair and suck in a breath of clean, fresh air. It had filled her lungs with the scent of possibility, and made her feel energised. And yet it had to have been wrong. She had no right to kiss him, or even to confide in him.

In bed that night, she closed her eyes and revisited the memory, using it to push away any thoughts of the torments she had been subjected to in this room. Those moments of intimacy

with Cadwalader in no way resembled the things Sir Lucien did
to her. On the contrary, the recollection of Cadwalader's kiss
made her body tingle. Although her instinct at the time had
been to tug away in fear, she felt safe to explore the memory of
it now. Her palms traced the path his roughened palms might
have taken if she had let him: over the hollows of her cheeks,
across her throat, cupping the gentle rise of her breasts, all the
while marvelling at the way her nipples peaked in response. She
traversed the flat planes of her stomach, sliding lower. A hot,
tugging urge made her groin turn molten.

With a soft moan she rolled onto her belly. The heels of her
hands pressed against her most private parts and she lay still,
remembering dappled sunlight and adoring whispers, before
starting to move slowly, cupping herself and finding the swollen
nub that ached against her hand. A kind of rhythm built slowly,
until her quickened breathing suddenly came in gasps, and
waves of sensation ploughed over her body from her scalp to her
toes. It was extraordinary, this feeling, this rush of pleasure
almost as fierce as pain. It left her panting in the darkness, tiny
lights exploding behind her eyelids. When it ebbed, she kicked
off the counterpane and sat up, her nightgown clinging with the
perspiration that prickled over her breast; she dragged her
hands across her face, smelling her own sweet, salty scent as she
dashed away the wayward strands of hair veiling her eyes.

Had she always had this power within herself? Was this
something other people knew, this bubbling sense of strength
and joy, the tingling of every pore and hair, the strange,
contented lassitude that made her tip back her head, stretch out
her limbs and fall back onto the bed? She pressed against
herself again and the urge returned, stronger if anything, until
she rolled over and employed this new, secret understanding of
her body to bring it to another peak of pleasure.

Afterwards she tumbled from the bed, drew back the
curtains and crossed the room to stand before her cheval mirror.

On an impulse she shrugged off her nightdress and stared at her pale, slender form, the white linen puddled around her bare feet.

Self-loathing meant that she hardly ever looked at her body. There was something disgusting about it, something that impelled her husband to despicable acts of depravity. Yet tonight she found she could look. Baffling, really, what he saw in it to make him want it so much. Joe the same – he hadn't even seen it, yet she sensed that he had had that same need to plunge himself inside her. Tonight, alone and staring dark-eyed into the mirror, she felt she was seeing the real Rosamund for the first time, silvered where the moonlight touched her. Her collar-bones, ribs and breastbone showed as highlights and shadows. Her breasts were small, the nipples standing erect as cool air touched them.

The round scars of old cigar burns dotting her stomach and haunches were part of her history, but they weren't what she noticed now. What she saw instead was a glowing inten-sity in her eyes, and warmth in her cheeks, and the smooth-ness of her limbs. She lifted her chin and turned this way and that, noticing how the bones and muscles moved in her arms and hips. The dark shadow of hair where she had touched herself seemed now the centre of mysteries. This may be a body that drove men to claim possession, but it was hers, and within it she had something private that they could never take from her.

Men: they were little different from dogs, really; marking the territory they wanted to claim. But tonight, for the first time, the territory seemed wholly hers, not Sir Lucien's, for all he seized control over it whenever he wished.

What would Cadwalader think if he could see her now? Would he still wear that look of stunned awe and admiration she had beheld earlier? Idly she wondered if she resembled Mary, his wife, whom she had wronged by kissing Joe so recklessly. Shame made her drop her gaze; and yet how could she regret her single, fleeting experience of being adored?

Mary and Joseph. Their very names marked them as a holy union. She had sinned against that union, leading Joe into temptation without even realising it until she was so far down the path, she barely knew what she was doing. And if *she* had sinned against Mary, to whom she owed nothing, how much greater was Joe's sin in kissing her back? He was the one tied to his wife by a vow. But if Mary didn't want him, then she must suspect he would eventually find his pleasure elsewhere.

She crossed her arms across her breasts and reminded herself that he, like Sir Lucien, was strong enough to take what he wanted by force. And yet he hadn't used that strength against her. The moment she asked him to stop, he had done so. It occurred to her that Joe might not have responded to his wife's rejection by forcing her to accept his conjugal rights, either. How unlike her own husband he was.

The unfairness of it hit her like a blow – why could she not have been given in marriage to a man like him? Someone who could make her feel like a precious gem. Someone who deferred to her wishes and treated her with gentleness and consideration, even when his passions were aroused? When Joe praised her, it made her feel for the first time since Papa died that she was worthy of someone's esteem.

Tears sprang to her eyes at the thought of being so prized. A longing for love didn't bestow on her any rights to Joe's admiration or praise, to confide the private aspects of her marriage or to press her mouth to his. What kind of woman must she be, to behave like that? Worse, to allow herself to indulge in fantasies afterwards! Tugging her nightgown over her head, she turned away from her reflection in the mirror, disgusted at herself.

Her heart thumped as she clambered back into bed and curled her knees up to her chin, huddling under the bedclothes. Suddenly the desires she had discovered within herself seemed dangerously transgressive, and not something beautiful after all. Fear made her gut twist. No one must ever find out her hidden, lustful nature. If any of her slyly inquisitive staff saw it written in her face, they would tell her husband, and there was no telling what he might do.

One thing she knew for sure: she and Cadwalader would be utterly undone.

TWENTY

ROSAMUND

It was warm in the library with sun slanting through the windows and lighting the corner where Rosamund sat in a wing-backed chair, reading *A Room with a View*. She was entranced by Lucy Honeychurch, inwardly celebrating every time the young heroine spoke out freely, and hating her fiancé Cecil who was so terribly fond of telling her how to think and how to behave. *Don't marry him, don't marry him*, she thought whenever Cecil sneered at someone and expected Lucy to agree. Her heart fluttered at the way Lucy had begun to see the merits of the lower-class George, who seemed open to the goodness in people in a way that reminded her of Cadwalader. He, like George, had shown her that there was a different way for a man to be: a better way, even if he was not well-born or highly educated.

Surely what mattered most was the true nobility that was revealed by behaviour, by gentle words and acts of kindness, and in the balance of passion with restraint? So engrossed was she in willing Lucy on and wishing she, too, was braver in defying the constraints of her class, that she barely noticed Phelps's soft knock at the door.

Reluctantly, she slipped her embroidered bookmark between the pages. "What is it, Phelps?"

"A telephone call, my lady. Sir Lucien wishes to speak to you."

As always, the mention of her husband's name made her heart jump. For a moment she froze; but Phelps was waiting with that look on his face that always made her skin crawl. It was as if he knew exactly what she was thinking, and was laughing at her for it whilst concealing his contempt behind a mask of obsequiousness. He never put a foot wrong, never said anything for which she might reproach him; yet if she truly had the running of the household, she would send him away, glad to see the back of him.

She laid the book down on a side table and steeled herself to walk with every appearance of composure to the hallway where the telephone receiver waited like a harbinger of doom. The sound of her husband's voice made her lean against the wall to steady herself, such was its power to strike terror into her. His words made her feel even worse.

"Tell Dawson to pack your things. You'll remember I told you about Charlotte's intended, Eustace Chadwycke? His parents, Lord and Lady Westhampton, have invited us to dinner on Saturday evening, and your presence is required. I shall expect you to take the morning train to London, and no arguments about it. My sister's chauffeur will meet you at Paddington."

"But – but how can you expect me to attend a grand dinner at such short notice, when you know full well I have nothing suitable to wear, and am not accustomed to society?" Her cheeks felt hot, and a lump rose in her throat. She couldn't help stammering, but dug her nails into her palms so as to deny him the pleasure of making her cry.

"You'll do as you're told. There are seamstresses and clothes shops in London, and my sister will guide you. I can't have you holding things up: too much is at stake. Rumours are circulating about my mysterious, mad wife in the country, and if they reach Westhampton's ears he might forbid the match. I won't have Charlotte's hopes dashed: Eustace's elder brother is a puny sort, so it isn't impossible that my girl could be a viscountess one day if you don't scupper it for her. No, I need you here and I need you to at least appear to be sane. So, for once you'll make the effort to dress up and smile and be pleasant, and behave as a woman in your position should behave. If you let me down, believe me, you will have cause to regret it."

"But you don't understand – Nellie isn't here. I allowed her to visit her mother this week. So I can't possibly come tomorrow—"

He cut her off before she could procrastinate further. "Get her back on the first available train, unless you want to find yourself travelling alone tomorrow morning. There are maids aplenty in London who would be grateful for the chance to take her place. Now, there's an end to it. I trust there will be no further objections."

It wasn't a question, and there was no possibility of refusing his demands when he had so many ways to make her life unbearable. But the idea of travelling to London; of mixing in society with her wardrobe of clothes which were perfect for a simple country life but entirely unsuitable for grander company; and of having to summon poor Nellie back so soon after she had arrived at her mother's sickbed... Her head was already swimming. And there was Phelps, hovering in the background. No doubt he knew all about it already.

"Very well," she managed to croak out before hanging up the receiver, dropping it into its cradle as if it was hot to the touch.

She pictured Charlotte's sneering face and closed her eyes at the prospect of being subjected to the combined forces of her stepdaughter and sister-in-law by day, and her husband's brutality at night. And then – dinner with a viscount and viscountess, and who knew how many other grandees in honour of Charlotte's forthcoming nuptials? A wave of panic threatened to drown her, and she fought to control her breathing.

When she opened her eyes, there was Phelps, hovering in the background in his black and white clothes, like a solitary magpie bringing bad luck.

"I have taken the liberty of ordering a telegram to instruct Miss Dawson to return post-haste, my lady. There is a train this afternoon which should afford her sufficient time to pack this evening."

She nodded dumbly and he bowed and retreated as smoothly as if he were on wheels. She was sorry to call Nellie back so soon, but her pang of guilt was dampened by relief. If she must go to London, and if she must be prepared to spend an evening at the London residence of Lord and Lady Westhampton, Nellie was the closest thing she had to an ally or friend. She needed her, and the sooner she arrived back, the better.

TWENTY-ONE
ROSAMUND

How was it possible for so many people to exist in one place? As if the railway station in Cardiff hadn't been busy enough, Paddington was a hive of bustling activity, with passengers of all classes, ages and even nationalities hurrying in every direction. Rosamund had never been so thankful for Nellie's calm demeanour. She would have been lost under that great glazed roof without her maid at her side to propel her through the throng and out to the sanctuary of one of the Great Western Hotel's many sitting rooms, there to hold a soothing cup of tea in hands that trembled while they awaited the arrival of Blanche Ferrers's chauffeur. Her head thudded and in her half-bewildered state her ears seemed to ring, muffling the sounds around her and lending a sense of unreality to the unfamiliar surroundings. She felt as if she had swum out of her depth and was now sinking, unable to breathe or think clearly, below the surface into murky water.

Nellie marshalled the porter with their luggage and took charge when the car arrived, guiding her into the back. Rosamund went passively, empty as a seashell buffeted by waves on the shore. Given time she felt that she, like the shell, might gradually be ground into nothing more substantial than sand.

On their arrival at Blanche's imposing white stucco-fronted house in Belgravia, Nellie was absorbed into the well-oiled machinery of domestic staff, and Rosamund was left alone in the hallway. It was dazzlingly bright compared with the entrance hall at Plas Norton, with sunlight streaming in through its tall windows and glass cupola to bounce off the gleaming black and white marble floor. Its Georgian proportions were elegant, in sharp contrast to the dark Gothic arches and heavy oak stair of the Fitznorton family seat. Here, the sweeping staircase was of yet more marble, with an ornate balustrade of polished brass that drew her eyes upwards towards a galleried landing. There, gripping the rail with one hand as he descended, was Sir Lucien.

All at once she wanted to shrink and become invisible. But she stood like prey caught in the glare of a predator, pinned by his gaze.

He limped heavily across the polished marble; his gout must be troubling him again. Pain would make him even more ill-tempered than usual. He stood before her, blocking the light, and her heart pounded, partly from his proximity, which always sent it flapping like a wild bird trapped in a cage, and also now at the way he reached out and fingered her lapel. He drew it tight against her neck before dropping it and dusting his fingers off, as if she was unclean.

"Finally you're here. And looking a trifle wan, my dear." He looked her up and down, head to toe and back up again, with a sneer curling his lip under his bristling moustache. "I don't envy my sister the task of making you look presentable. Was this the best travelling ensemble Dawson could find? Time for her to go, I'd say. There are plenty of maids looking for work in London; it shouldn't be difficult to find one who at least understands the rudiments of fashion."

"But you can't—" she began, cutting off sharply at the flash of anger in his eyes. It was never wise to tell him what he couldn't do, and she couldn't afford to antagonise him over this. It was impossible to tell whether he really intended to dismiss Nellie, or if he was merely goading her with the threat of removing her only source of support. "What I mean is – my appearance isn't really Nellie's fault, but mine. I have such silly, simple taste, and I've never needed... Not for the life I lead, in the country. Nellie isn't to blame. She'd dress me better if I only allowed it."

Yellowed teeth bared in the familiar cruel smile that made her own mouth turn dry. "I am not yet persuaded. However..." He leaned in, the smell of cigars and onions fanning her face. "I will allow you to attempt to convince me. Later."

She swallowed a wave of nausea, not daring to contemplate what he might have in mind.

The discreet rattle of china heralded the arrival of the butler with a footman in his wake carrying a large silver tray. Her husband took a step backwards, and she heaved in a deep breath.

"Ah, Garwood," he said, all joviality in front of the staff. "Is it that time already, by Jove? We shall take tea in the drawing room, my dear. Blanche and Charlotte will no doubt join us imminently."

The prospect of facing her sister-in-law and stepdaughter so soon, in addition to her new fears for Nellie and the effect of Sir Lucien's threats on Rosamund's already shredded nerves, was altogether too much. Instead of putting her hand obediently on his arm as he crooked his elbow towards her, she shook her head mulishly and addressed the tall, distinguished-looking man he had called Garwood.

"I'm sorry, but I find myself somewhat fatigued after the long journey. I'd like to rest until dinner, if someone could show me to my room...?"

Irritation flickered across her husband's face, but as she had hoped, he could hardly object to her request in front of the servants.

"Of course, m'lady. Mrs Digby, the housekeeper, will be along in just a moment. I'll arrange for some tea to be sent up."

It was only a small victory, but as Sir Lucien pursed his lips and stumped off to the drawing room alone, it still tasted sweet. Yet, as Mrs Digby swept into the hall and led the way up the wide staircase, Rosamund's limbs felt leaden at the thought of how he might make her pay that night for her lack of elegance, as well as for her disobedience.

TWENTY-TWO

ROSAMUND

Rosamund felt cornered. Blood rushed into her cheeks, not just from self-consciousness at being the focus of everyone's attention, but also from the increasing warmth in Blanche's dressing room. Although it was by no means small, the room was not quite large enough to comfortably accommodate two ladies, their maids, and the tiny French seamstress, Madame Caron, whose accent was so strong Rosamund suspected it might be an affectation. The stifling atmosphere was not helped by the powerful smell of the ladies' eau de cologne, their individual perfumes clashing in the confined space and failing to mask the sour tang of perspiration.

Their task was a challenging one: given the lack of sufficient time to design and make completely new outfits for Rosamund to wear in London, they must identify some suitable gowns from Blanche's wardrobe and adapt them for Rosamund's much slimmer, younger figure. Of primary concern was to create something that would reflect well on the Fitznortons for the forthcoming dinner with Viscount and Viscountess Westhampton. It would need to be elegant, fashionable, and ornate enough to reflect the family's wealth. It must lend her an air of sophistication. In short, it would need to transform her. The more she listened to the comments of Blanche and Madame Caron, the more she had come to feel like a caterpillar who needed to be turned into an artificially gaudy butterfly.

"Not the Poiret," Blanche said, passing a spectacular beaded creation to her maid. Seconds later, she fished another couple of gowns from the rail and the maid found herself laden with yards of silk and velvet. "Keep the Luciles, too. And this one." At last, she stepped back and nodded permission for the seamstress to take a look.

Rosamund was conscious of her cheeks flaming under her sister-in-law's imperious gaze. Although there was no shortage of gowns from which to choose, and presumably Sir Lucien would reimburse his sister for anything the seamstress chose to adapt, it was still unquestionably generous of her to allow Rosamund to take such liberties with her wardrobe. It wasn't a pleasant feeling, knowing she was in Blanche's debt. It gave the other woman even more reason to despise her.

She had already submitted to the Frenchwoman's ministrations with a tape measure, uncomfortably aware of the fresh bruises on the side of her neck and her upper arms from the previous evening when her husband had exacted his price for retaining Nellie's services. The sudden intent look of the seamstress's dark eyes revealed that she had noticed the marks.

"You 'ave a necklace to wear wiz ze finished gown, milady?" the seamstress asked, and Rosamund was quick to nod.

"We brought my mother's diamond and garnet parure."

Nellie nodded confirmation and at the corner of her vision Rosamund noted Blanche's obvious relief that she would not be required to lend out her jewels as well as donating her dresses.

"Zat is good. Very good. You must be careful. Evening gowns reveal the throat, yes? We want nothing but jewels there to catch ze eye." She had lowered her voice for the sake of discretion, but the way she looked at the marks on her neck filled Rosamund with shame. It was bad enough having to suffer her husband's degrading attentions, but knowing that he had left evidence proclaiming them to the world added another level of humiliation.

Having made her final notes, the dressmaker turned to peruse the rail of gowns, her expression animated as she hunted through. After dismissing several items, she held up a pale pink gown with white ruffles cascading down the bodice.

"Zees, now. With your excellent complexion, and with a necklace of garnets, ze *couleur* will be *parfait!*"

She was right about the colour, but to Rosamund's eye the ruffles looked horribly fussy.

"I'm a woman of simple tastes," she said faintly. "I wouldn't feel comfortable wearing anything too... elaborate."

Madame Caron laughed. "'Ave no fear, milady. We do not 'ave time to make anything elaborate!" She tossed the dress onto the chair behind her and continued riffling through the rack of garments.

Suddenly, Nellie spoke up.

"The pink silk is lovely, Madame. But might I suggest – if we snip away these frills from the bodice, making the neckline into a V and taking it a little lower, it will suit m'lady much better. We could add some embroidered or lacy edging if it looks too simple. And what about if we shorten the skirt, like an over-tunic, and add an underskirt in another colour to complement the pink? It would bring it up to date."

Blanche looked doubtful at the prospect of one of her expensive gowns being cut up, but the seamstress seemed excited by the idea, grabbing it again and fiddling with the frills as if imagining the transformation.

"Yes, yes zat could be done. Do we 'ave another gown for ze underskirt?"

"This pale green?" Nellie suggested, pointing to another dress, but the other woman was already reaching out for a mushroom-coloured velvet creation draped in ribbons and lace.

"*Voilà!*" She held up both dresses, the pink on top.

Rosamund had to agree that the colours went well together. She risked a peep at Blanche, whose long face was set as if she would very much like to refuse permission. "Perhaps we can use something else," Rosamund murmured. "Taking two seems a lot to ask."

"No, no. Take both. Madame Caron will transform them, I don't doubt." Blanche gave a frigid smile, little more than a twitch of her facial muscles. "You will have it ready by Saturday evening?"

"*Naturellement*, madame. You 'ave my personal assurance that my girls and I will not rest until it is done. Milady will look… *magnifique*."

At Blanche's nod the maids helped the dressmaker carry the selected gowns away to be packed up and taken away for the alterations to begin.

Blanche closed the door, shutting the two of them in, and Rosamund froze at the look of dislike on her sister-in-law's face.

"You do realise what is at stake, I hope? The only reason I am allowing all this is to help my brother and Charlotte. One can only hope that you will be able to play your part in convincing the Westhamptons that they have not made a mistake in uniting our two families. Are you sure you are up to the challenge?"

Her sick feeling of dread every time dinner with the Westhamptons was mentioned meant that Rosamund was by no means sure, but she wasn't about to make herself look any more contemptible in the other woman's eyes by admitting it. All at once she realised she had had her fill of other people's judgements and assumptions about her, especially those who knew nothing of the difficulties she faced every day. If not for the monster she had been shackled to when she was too young and inexperienced to know what marriage might mean, she could have been an entirely different woman: one who was comfortable in company and at ease in her own skin. She deserved her sister-in-law's support, not her disapprobation.

Taking a deep breath, she managed somehow to keep her voice level.

"Mrs Ferrers, I have faced many challenges since I married your brother. Believe me when I tell you that dinner with a member of the peerage will not be the worst of them."

TWENTY-THREE
NELLIE

It had been an exhausting few days for Nellie, with a whirl of shopping trips into the centre of town, trailing in the wake of the stately and indomitable Mrs Ferrers. All the while she was forced to endure Miss Charlotte Fitznorton's constant sniping criticisms of Lady Fitz's dress sense and figure, and her spoiled bleating about how she had to have the very best for her forthcoming wedding. How her ladyship managed to hold onto her temper was beyond Nellie's comprehension, when Nellie herself would have liked nothing better than to give the nasty little baggage a good sharp slap. Perhaps if she had a job that made her travel hundreds of miles from her sick mother and work twelve hours a day as Nellie did, then she'd have something to whine about.

When they weren't at Selfridge's or Whiteleys ordering lingerie, gloves, shoes, hats and outerwear, Nellie was researching the latest styles in hair and dress. This in addition to her usual tasks of mending, attending to her ladyship, and sewing alterations. Although she felt both physically and mentally worn out, and flopped into bed each night hardly able to spare the energy to wash and clean her teeth, it had been perhaps the most exciting period of her life. The department stores in London were like palaces, with so much to look at, filled with irresistible colours, textures and scents. As much as she loved to see the items on display, she was also fascinated by the other customers, and made careful mental notes of what the most stylish ladies about town were wearing. They sailed through shops with their noses in the air, swathed in gorgeous fabrics and smelling divine. Lady Fitz, on the other hand, seemed to shrink inside her coat. Nellie sensed that sometimes her ladyship was overwhelmed by the experience of London, and struggled to maintain her customary quiet and dignified bearing.

This evening, all their planning and purchasing would achieve its purpose with Sir Lucien, Lady Fitz and Miss Charlotte's visit to the Westhamptons' mansion in Mayfair. Nellie had run through her plans in her mind a hundred times. The dress had arrived and been unpacked, and thankfully it had met with Lady Fitz's approval. Nellie was glad, knowing it would be easier for her ladyship to feel confident in company if she was comfortable in her dress. She had washed Lady Fitz's hair yesterday, knowing it would hold the style she planned more reliably if it wasn't too smooth and clean. The jewels had been retrieved from the safe, cleaned, and placed in the drawer of the dressing table in the room where her ladyship was now resting. Nellie had calculated that she could just about spare half an hour to eat supper with the other servants before she would have to start getting her ready.

Down in the basement, she took her place along with the other ladies' maids at the long table to the left of the butler. From the start of their visit she had decided that Mr Garwood was in every way superior to Mr Phelps. He had intelligent eyes that missed nothing, and a natural air of authority that had the other staff jumping to obey. His voice was deep and low, and he carried himself with an almost regal bearing that seemed fitting, given his absolute rule over most of the servants in this busy household. Compared to him, Mr Phelps was a little man, in a little place, and doing a little job. Puffed up and convinced of his own importance though he was, beside Mr Garwood he would be utterly outclassed.

The staff ate their main course in silence before Nellie and the other ladies' maids trooped out behind Mr Garwood and Mrs Digby to what was informally known as the pugs' parlour for their pudding.

"How is Lady F this evening, Miss Dawson? A bit nervous, I expect. She must know there's been gossip about her, with her being out of the way so much. Bound to make her a bit apprehensive." Miss Sharp, Charlotte Fitznorton's lady's maid, gave an appearance of sympathy, but there was something about her tone that put Nellie on her guard.

"She's resting at the moment, but I'm sure she will be perfectly fine. Thank you for your concern, though, Miss Sharp."

"She's lived so quietly out in the country, though, hasn't she? It must be a bit intimidating for her to dine with a viscount and viscountess when she isn't accustomed to mixing in society."

Nellie set down her spoon and looked her colleague in the eye, determined not to be drawn. She was all too aware of Mrs Digby and Mr Garwood's gaze upon them. "Lady Fitznorton's father was a baron, Miss Sharp. She knows perfectly well how to behave. I very much doubt she will get stuck over which knife and fork to use, or say anything out of turn."

Miss Sharp raised an eyebrow. "I wouldn't be so sure if I were you. Did you know that she asked Miss Charlotte at breakfast yesterday if she was happy about her forthcoming marriage, and told her it wasn't too late to change her mind? It didn't go down well, let me tell you."

Nellie hadn't been aware of this titbit of gossip. She took a sip of coffee to hide her face. It was easy to guess why her lady-ship might have concerns about what marriage might mean for her stepdaughter, given her own experience, but she wasn't about to discuss the Fitznorton marriage in front of strangers.

Miss Sharp took advantage of her silence to press on, still with that pretence of concern which was getting on Nellie's nerves.

"I hope the dress turned out suitable, in the end? There was so little time to create something fitting for the occasion. And Lady F isn't really known for her sense of style, is she? No real spirit in her. No elegance. She's like a brown mouse who'd like to scurry into a hole in the wainscot instead of exerting herself to be charming. It's no wonder Miss Charlotte is so worried that she'll cause some sort of embarrassment."

Nellie had had enough. "Her ladyship is perfectly charm-ing, in my view. She's a woman of dignity and sensibility, and if it's true that she discussed Miss Charlotte's marriage with her, I can only think it must have been motivated by maternal concern for her stepdaughter's future, which is to be expected from a woman with a kind heart. As for her style, her clothes have always been in perfect taste and well suited to her day-to-day lifestyle, even if they are perhaps a little understated for showier London occasions. I assure you she will look very fine this evening. Now, I must go and help her get ready."

Choosing to ignore Miss Sharp's impudent smile, she pushed back her chair and dropped her napkin onto the table.

"One thing before you go, Miss Dawson." Mr Garwood was on his feet, an imposing figure in his immaculate black tailcoat and starched wing collar.

The other servants rose respectfully. His deep voice commanded everyone's attention as much as his physical presence.

"The finest attributes for anyone who wishes to undertake a successful career in service are these: discretion and loyalty.

You would do well to follow Miss Dawson's example, Miss Sharp."

Colour flooded both women's faces, for different reasons. Murmuring her thanks, blushing under Mr Garwood's approving gaze, Nellie nodded and left the room. Unaccustomed as she was to compliments, as she climbed the servants' stairs towards her ladyship's room, it wasn't only the three flights of stairs that made her heart flutter.

TWENTY-FOUR

ROSAMUND

Rosamund was pleasantly surprised at how much she liked her hastily altered evening gown. Madame Caron had been right: the colours complemented her complexion. The updated style highlighted her slender waist and hips whilst the beautifully draped bodice enhanced her bust. Nellie had worked marvels with her hair; her necklace and some judiciously applied powder covered the worst of her bruises; and in her borrowed fur stole, new shoes and long white gloves she felt she had never looked better. Even her husband had nodded when he saw her, and for once remained silent instead of criticising her. Blanche and Charlotte also appeared relieved, as if they had been convinced she would let them down.

In the car, the as-yet unwed Charlotte eyed Rosamund's diamond and garnet tiara with obvious envy.

"Why, look at your tiara, Rosamund. It looks so heavy. When I marry I shall have my mama's tiara, of course, but I shall have it altered and reset in platinum. Yours must be terribly old: no one wears that style these days, and especially not with everything matching. So frightfully *passé*."

Rosamund said nothing. Her tiara and jewellery had

belonged to the mother she had never known, and as such were a precious connection to the blood family who had loved her. She would never dream of having them altered, even if she thought her husband would pay for such an indulgence. More than ever, she wished she had had a child of her own to whom she could pass on the personal items she had inherited from her parents. Her stepdaughter could never understand the true worth of her father's dearest books, with his notes in the margin; or her mother's Bible, with the cover she had embroidered in bright silks. Charlotte would in all probability throw them away upon Rosamund's death, and the few jewels Rosamund possessed would no doubt be broken up or sold. She gazed out of the window on the short journey to the Westhamptons' London residence, painfully aware that she had no legacy to leave the world, and no one who would remember her with fondness. There was a weight of responsibility on her shoulders tonight, and yet her life had never seemed so meaningless and empty.

Stepping down onto the wet London pavement outside their destination, she was forced to pause when Charlotte turned and hissed in her ear: "Don't you dare let me down."

The undisguised malice in the girl's voice made Rosamund's stomach lurch with nausea, but somehow she swallowed it down and followed the others through the imposing entrance of the Westhampton mansion.

She was not so gauche as to complement their hosts on the magnificence of their home. It was indeed very splendid, but having grown up in the sixteenth-century Ambleworth Hall she was not likely to be overawed by beautiful architecture, sumptuous furnishings or *objets d'art*. Slipping her gloved fingers delicately into the crook of Lord Westhampton's proffered arm, she accompanied him to the dining room, where she was seated to his right, as the highest status female guest. Sir Lucien sat at the other end of the table, to the right of Lady Westhampton, and Rosamund was grateful for the distance between them. To her right sat the Westhamptons' younger son, Eustace Chadwycke, with Charlotte on the other side of him to enable the young couple to get to know each other better. It was the first time Rosamund had seen Charlotte's fiancé, and he seemed a likeable enough sort, with a jolly smile and a hearty youthful gusto lending a glow to his cheeks.

Between Charlotte and Lady Westhampton was Mr Rowland Scott, the rangy, blond husband of Maud, the Westhamptons' daughter, who had the misfortune to be seated beside Sir Lucien. At least she had her brother Frederick on her other side. Heir to the viscountcy, Freddie Chadwycke's delicate pallor and slight physique explained Sir Lucien's prediction that he might die before producing an heir, and thus leave Eustace and Charlotte to inherit the title. The final member of their intimate family gathering was Blanche, who presumably shared her brother's hopes, given the way she kept darting speculative glances at the poor young man.

Lord Westhampton was certainly an affable host, and appeared to be enjoying the opportunity to socialise. "How are you enjoying your time in town, Lady Fitznorton? Is it to your liking, or do you much prefer the country? I understand you don't grace London with your presence very often, so we are most appreciative of the honour."

"I've had a most stimulating time in London, but I confess I am more at home in the country, my lord."

"You grew up in Yorkshire, I understand? A particularly fine part of the world, I must say. I've spent many happy hours there, myself. Marvellous shoots on the moors, you know."

Westhampton's enthusiasm was infectious, and Rosamund returned his smile. "The rolling countryside of the Yorkshire Dales must make it the finest place in England, I'm sure. The Welsh countryside where I now live is not dissimilar. Unfortunately, I am less familiar with the moors."

"You must go, one of these days. Do you ride?"

She took a moment to sip her glass of wine. "Sadly, not anymore." She was pleased with herself for not allowing talk of riding to upset her, even though her heart skipped at the memory of her last ride and its aftermath.

"What a shame. My wife loves a good gallop. Nothing quite like the wind in one's face and some vigorous exercise." He gazed along the table towards Lady Westhampton and to Rosamund's surprise a look passed between them: a look of obvious affection, the viscount's eyes crinkling below his bushy brows as he sent his wife what Rosamund could almost have thought was a wink, had it not happened so quickly. Sure enough, the viscountess's lips twitched in a hint of an answering smile.

The sight of this marital harmony gladdened Rosamund's heart, and she beamed at his lordship as they shared tales of their equestrian adventures, surprised at how much she was enjoying herself. The way Lord Westhampton's eyes twinkled appreciatively in her direction lent still more pleasure to the moment.

In a brief lull in their conversation, as they each took sips of wine, Sir Lucien's loud voice rang out at the other end of the table. He seemed to be trying to convince Eustace and Mr Scott that there would be a war on the continent sooner rather than later. The young men seemed more than ready to agree on this point, indeed the topic had been on everyone's lips recently, but Rosamund cringed inside at the way her husband dominated the conversation. Silence spread along the table like ripples on a pond as he boomed his opinions towards his future son-in-law.

"Marriage is like war, and war is like business, my boy: you have to be first. Be in front, not a follower. Sheep follow – I see them all over the hills at Plas Norton. But you don't get anywhere by doing what the other fellow's doing. You have to lead. To strike first. Always be the one who attacks; never defend. Your belief in your natural superiority will give you the fire in your belly that you need to carry you along. I tell you, whether it's business, war or wedlock, a chap must know what he wants, and calculate how best to get it."

Eustace nodded politely, but Sir Lucien hadn't finished.

"When you're done playing soldiers we'll have to see if you have a head for business, young man. And if Charlotte gives you a son, which is more than either of my wives have ever done, then everything that's mine will pass to him in due course. No sense in women trying to succeed in business. It's against their nature; they haven't the stomach for it. I've never involved Charlotte in my businesses, it would be as pointless as trying to teach a hen how to be a fighting cock. So when I'm no longer around it will be up to you to make sure your boy knows what's what. But don't fret, I'll get you trained and ready, once we've dealt with the Germans."

Mr Scott shifted his long, angular body in his seat directly opposite Sir Lucien and spoke up. "I didn't realise you were a military man, Sir Lucien?"

There was an uncomfortable pause, during which Sir Lucien glowered across the table at the subtle challenge to his claim towards expertise.

From her place between the two bristling men, Lady Westhampton made an effort to smooth things over. "I'm sure Eustace is only too glad to be offered advice in advance of his marriage."

"If I was to offer him one piece of advice, it would be this: wives are like horses. The rider must be the one in control, not the animal."

"Even if it requires the whip?" Mr Scott's raised eyebrow emphasised his ironic tone.

Silence fell, before Lady Westhampton poured oil on the troubled waters. "Engagements are such a whirlwind, aren't they? And our two darlings make such a charming couple, don't you think? One can only hope that, if there *is* a war, it will all be over in a jiffy and they will be able to settle into domestic bliss untroubled by the events of the wider world."

With the atmosphere at the other end of the table simmering down, Lord Westhampton smiled towards his wife and raised his glass.

"Amen to that. Ah, how wonderful to be young, with one's whole future ahead. It makes me quite envious, I must say. It seems only a short while ago that we were full of excitement in anticipation of our own wedding. My wife is quite right, we must pray that the impending nuptials come to pass without any tiresome delays."

While he gazed fondly at Eustace and Charlotte, Rosamund felt a lump in her throat. He seemed such a kind, good-humoured man. Her own memories of the time before her wedding were faint, as if she had deliberately smothered them when it dawned on her how awful her marriage was going to be. The girl she had been then was a different person from the woman she was now, already bruised by the loss of her father but utterly naive about the life she was stepping into.

Hopefully it would be different for Charlotte. However difficult it was to like her stepdaughter, she had no wish to see her trapped in a prison of a marriage as she was herself. But with this man to guide him, Eustace might prove to be a gentle husband. If he wasn't... Images of her own wedding night rose before her eyes, as shocking as they had been when the brutal event took place.

At the other end of the table, Lady Westhampton turned the direction of conversation and instead of being the focus of the viscount's kindly gaze, Rosamund found herself the object of Eustace's attention, his blue eyes bright above his ruddy cheeks and lively smile. Fighting off the traumatic memories, she laid her knife and fork down on her plate.

"I hope you will be kind to her," she whispered, feeling her heart might crack in two. "Please, do be kind. Sometimes... some husbands are not... not kind."

Eustace's mouth fell open and he glanced towards his father, as if for guidance. Their mutual discomfort drew attention from others around the table, silence spreading from person to person like a cloud.

At last Eustace cleared his throat. "Lady Fitznorton, are you alright?"

Everything around her seemed unreal. Puzzled, staring faces; her husband's visage turning puce as if he longed to bellow across the table at her. Dimly she heard Eustace's voice repeating her name questioningly: from a distance, as if he was on the other side of a wall, and she was in the dark with only pinpricks of light dancing before her eyes. She mustn't fall into one of her fits of panic. *Not here. Not now.* Closing her eyes, she fought to control her breathing, digging her nails into her palms, hard enough to bring herself back from the brink.

"I'm quite alright, thank you. Just— just..." She faltered and shook her head, unable to explain.

"Jolly good. You looked a trifle green for a moment there. I hope it wasn't the cutlets."

He was trying hard to be jovial. Somehow, she must keep a better rein on her emotions until the evening was over. She took a deep breath and returned his smile.

"Not at all, Mr Chadwycke. I assure you the cutlets were almost as delicious as this Peach Melba."

As soon as the car door had closed behind them for their journey back to Blanche's house, Charlotte began venting her fury.

"What is the matter with you? I have never felt so ashamed. It was quite obvious to everyone that poor Eustace didn't know what to say about your performance. You've been given every advantage, every consideration, and this is how you repay us. If only you had married someone different, Papa. Someone who didn't humiliate us at every turn. Someone who knew how to comport herself in society without looking as if they were about to vomit into their plate. Someone who isn't – well – frankly ridiculous, and embarrassing, and completely and utterly pointless!"

Rosamund endured the tirade, too drained with fatigue to argue. She'd never be able to explain how all the talk of marriage being like a war had made her feel. Her own certainly made her feel she was on the losing side in a war of conquest. One day, for all she knew, it would end in her annihilation.

The enemy glowered at her from his seat opposite, his silence more unnerving than his daughter's venomous outpouring, and she dreaded the night ahead. Up to now, she had managed to avoid the worst excesses of his appetites during her stay in London: he had no taste for her body when she was menstruating. But he might have guessed that that would have finished by now, and decide to visit her room. The thought of it made her rouse herself and speak up.

"You're right, Charlotte. I did my best, but tonight has proved I am of no use to you here. I should return to Plas Norton, where I will no longer be an embarrassment to you. Eustace will understand that my health is too delicate for city life. He will soon forget my moment of weakness when I'm not here."

"You'll go when I say you may, and not before—!"

To her surprise, her husband's eruption of anger was abruptly cut off as Blanche laid a restraining hand upon his arm.

"She's right," Blanche said.

Rosamund had shrunk away into her corner, but now her eyes widened at this unexpected gesture of support from her sister-in-law.

"Let her go, and tonight will soon be forgotten. I observed

her carefully all evening and to my mind she appeared delicate, not insane. You have proven you are no Mr Rochester. Now, people will know that there is no Mad Bertha hidden in the attics at Plas Norton, just a dull, feeble woman who is more likely to bore someone to death than burn their house down. The Westhamptons would not want the scandal of a broken engagement; and besides, from what I have heard, they are too much in need of the Fitznorton fortune to allow your wife's slight peculiarity to stand in the way. Send her back tomorrow, and it will all blow over, mark my words."

The words stung, but not as much as Charlotte's response to them.

"Send her away then, Papa. In fact, I wish you would do us all a good turn and have her shut away for ever, so that we will never have to look at her miserable face again."

TWENTY-FIVE
ROSAMUND

As much as Rosamund regretted causing so much inconvenience to Nellie, who had the unenviable task of packing up all her mistress's new clothes and accessories at a moment's notice, her relief as she boarded the Great Western Railway train was enough to make her giddy. The weight of anxiety that had kept her shoulders rigid with tension throughout their time in London started to lift, leaving her feeling almost free, as if she was shedding a heavy load.

She found herself counting her blessings as she gazed from the carriage window to see rolling countryside again. What a pleasure it was to see the many shades of green, the trees and fields and rivers that gave her a sense of peace she could never feel in the city. And she had, thankfully, managed to avoid her husband's attentions after their return to Blanche's house by scurrying up the stairs and locking herself into her room. When he came and knocked at the door, she huddled under her blankets and covered her ears. He could hardly expose himself to servants' gossip in his sister's house by hammering on her door and bellowing threats, the way he would in his own. At last he had given up, and she had managed to fall asleep, exhausted

and determined to get away as early as she could the next
morning.

By the time the train reached Cardiff, where they were to
catch their connection back towards the west and Plas Norton,
she had made up her mind to allow Nellie to take some more
time off to visit her mother.

"It is no more than you deserve, Nellie, for the help you
have given me; and your last visit home was cut short.
Cadwalader will be waiting to collect me from the station, so he
can speak to the guard and porter about the luggage. Take the
two forty-five train and stay two days – do. I shall manage with
Sarah to help me."

Permitting Nellie to take out sufficient funds for her ticket
back home, plus a little extra for a gift for her mother,
Rosamund had waved Nellie off and settled in her seat, quite
proud of her new-found spirit of independence. Still, now that
the train was moving, it was an odd sensation to be completely
alone in the midst of strangers, with not a soul in the world
paying her any mind. Not that she had many fellow passengers
in her first-class carriage: only an elderly couple wearing shabby
but respectable clothes, who looked as if they had fallen on hard
times; and a well-dressed man whose attention was fixed on his
newspaper.

This unaccustomed feeling of anonymity as the train left
Cardiff behind had her mind whirling with possibilities. There
was no one to stop her alighting at the next station, where she
could buy another ticket. She could go anywhere, without a soul
knowing or caring who she was. To a port, perhaps. If she found
her way to Swansea, she could maybe sail to Ireland. Or she
could travel back the way she had come, into England; not to
London, but to Bristol perhaps, or even Liverpool or Southamp-
ton, and there board a ship that would take her further still.
America? Sir Lucien might never find her there.

These exciting aspirations were soon dulled by the intrusion of reality into her daydreams. Even if she could pull off such a trick, how could she avoid discovery? If she asked a porter to help with her trunks, she'd be noticed. And if she left the trunks on the train and travelled unencumbered by possessions, what would she do for necessities on board the ship, supposing the few coins left in her purse would be sufficient to purchase such a ticket, which seemed unlikely. She had no idea how much the journey might cost. And then, there wouldn't be time to get away before Phelps raised the alarm, as he surely would on hearing that she hadn't arrived on the anticipated train. Before she could even find a ship or a hotel there would be telegrams buzzing along countless wires, instructing policemen to search for her in every railway town in the land.

Even so, when she arrived at her destination, it took every ounce of will to leave her seat and step down onto the platform. Ashamed of the weakness that had allowed the possibility of freedom to pass her by, she halted amidst the bustling passengers who jostled and swarmed about her, each intent on their own purpose. She felt like a husk, empty of all substance and doomed to be blown along by their momentum. But then she glimpsed a familiar pair of green eyes under the black peak of a chauffeur's cap, and it was as much as she could do not to break into a stumbling run and bury her face in his chest. Seeing Joe Cadwalader was the closest she had had to a homecoming since she was a girl.

"Good afternoon," she said, drinking in the sight of him so tall and smart in his uniform and polished leather boots.

His manner was as deferential as it had ever been in public, but she took in the way his face softened as if he was as glad to see her as she was to see him. If he was surprised by Nellie's absence he didn't show it, merely greeting her in the musical Welsh voice she realised she had missed: "Let's get you home, then, m'lady." As if sensing her emotional tumult, he shepherded her out of the station. He handed her into the sanctuary of the car's rear compartment, and his proximity made her heart skip with the sheer delight of being near him.

While he arranged for her luggage to be sent on to the house, she leaned against the back seat, relishing the silence now that the noise of the railway had been shut out. When he slid into the driving seat she closed her eyes, picturing him clearly in her mind: the easy competence of his strong hands at the controls, the thigh muscles shifting under the soft wool of his trousers as he worked the pedals. Her moment of despair earlier was forgotten in the pleasure and relief of being with him again. He drove along the grimy terraced streets of Pontybrenin – so quiet compared to London – until at last they emerged into the relative freshness of the country lanes edged by tall hedgerows.

The idea of returning at once to the house seemed too dismal for words, especially with the sun shining and the emerald fields so beautifully lush out here away from the sprawl of the town. How she longed for some exercise, and to delay the moment when Cadwalader would leave her at the front door to resume his duties in the motor stable. She reached for the speaking tube, watching his head turn towards it as her voice was transmitted to his ear.

"Would you mind taking the southern gate, and stopping at the end of the lane for a while? I'd like to take a walk. After so long in town, I feel starved of clean air."

He drew to a halt as she had requested, in a gateway at the end of the lane where there was room for the car to turn, then handed her down from the car.

"Bring the travelling rug, would you? And your flask," she added on an impulse.

He kept a small flask of rum in the front of the car, and went to fetch it, his expression inscrutable. Tipping her face into the wind, she drank in its clarity and freshness like nectar after the filthy air of the city and the railways.

When they reached a stile, she waited for him to catch up, hampered by her long skirt and petticoats. He held out his hand and gripped hers tightly as she mounted the wooden step. It wobbled, and she almost toppled against him, but he dropped the rug and steadied her with his other hand on her waist, removing it as soon as she was safe. Up on the step she was taller than he, and the distance between their bodies narrower than it had been at any time since their moment in the woods. She was acutely conscious of being away from anyone else's prying eyes: she'd only have to dip her head a little to kiss him. He had caught her gazing at his lips; they parted, and she saw his eyes turn almost black as his pupils dilated.

"Thank you," she breathed, and held tightly to his hand until she was safely on the ground.

His cheeks looked as flushed as hers felt as he dropped the rug into the field on her side and negotiated the stile easily. She was glad of the breeze on her face as she marched ahead of him across the field and towards the wooded hill where the summer-house kept watch over the Plas Norton estate.

It was novel to be leading like this, she who had never led anyone in her life, with a man following blindly and at a loss to know what she was about. The breeze tugged at her hat, and she held onto it with one hand until they entered the more sheltered area among the rhododendrons. His footsteps were steady behind her, gaining on her with his longer stride as she started uphill. By the time they reached the summit his cheeks had a fresh bloom of colour, and she felt light, as if her soul had had an injection of energy.

Above the neighbouring fields a red kite soared, riding the air currents with ease, its forked tail sharp against the stark blue sky. As Rosamund watched, it hovered before tucking in its wings and plunging earthwards, straight and focused as a missile. Knowing what it was like to live vigilantly, always on the edge and half-expecting an attack, she hoped whichever small creature it had spotted had been alert to the potential dangers out in the open.

Buffeted by the wind, the door of the summerhouse swung sharply when she opened it, and she might have been knocked down had it not been for Cadwalader's gloved hand reaching out swiftly to catch it. She smiled her thanks at him and stepped over the threshold while he propped it open with a stone. The windows were cleaner than they had been the last time she ventured up here, and the floor had been swept. The musty smell was gone, replaced by the inviting smell of sun-drenched timber; it was warm inside, sheltered from the wind's chill. She had worked up a glow from the climb, so in a moment of daring she unpinned her hat and unbuttoned her coat, laying both down on the bench in the corner.

Through the window she could see the navy blue of Cadwalader's uniform where he stood surveying the view. He, too, had removed his hat, and the breeze was tousling the curls of his hair. How she had missed looking at him. And not only the sight of him, but the sound of his deep, lilting voice, and the feeling in her breast when she was with him, those moments that made her heart leap like a March hare.

She moved to stand beside him, gazing towards the smoking chimneys of Pontybrenin in the distance and keeping her back to the house, not wanting to look at its forbidding towers before she must.

"If I have a favourite place, this is it," she told him, and was gladdened when he nodded in acknowledgement.

"I can see why. It's quite a view over your domains, m'lady."

"*My* domains?" She frowned at the way he shrugged in response to her question. There was something different about him, as if he was on edge. Less friendly. He hadn't smiled at her yet, she realised; his mouth looked pinched at the corners. "I assure you, my wishes hold no sway here – or anywhere else," she told him.

"Perhaps not with your husband. But I've done your bidding and followed you up here, haven't I? Instead of taking you straight to the house, as I should. And last time we were alone together—" He broke off and she dropped her gaze, unable to deny the truth of what he said. He had obeyed her then, unexpectedly, when she spurned him. Perhaps he was regretting his obedience now. Or, more likely, regretting being alone with her again.

"Last time we were alone, I didn't know what I was thinking." But she wasn't sure if she meant the moment when she kissed him, or the moment when she pulled away. "Come inside, would you? I can't talk to you out here, with the wind in my ears and my hair whipping in my eyes. Spread the rug out on the floor where it's more comfortable."

His reluctance was obvious from the way he hesitated before doing as she asked. The woollen rug took up a good part of the available floor space, and she stooped to smooth it with her hands before settling down on it, pulling her knees to her chest. She patted the patch of tartan beside her, but he let out a harsh breath and scrubbed his hands over his face.

"Look, m'lady – I don't know what your intentions are, but I can't be picked up and discarded again like a toy whenever you decide you're in a playful mood. You made it clear last time that you didn't... that is, you couldn't..." He cursed under his breath, looking as if he would rather be anywhere but alone with her.

She felt suddenly tired. "I know what it is to be another person's plaything, and I assure you, that is not what you are to me. If I have embarrassed you, then I apologise." She made as if to scramble to her feet, but to her surprise he put a hand out to stop her.

"Alright. I'll sit with you." His frown cleared and he sat down cross-legged beside her. "It's not such a bad place to sit, after all, with that view. And at least in here out of the wind I can hear myself think."

It felt as if a barrier between them had been breached. She hugged her knees, resisting the urge to lean her head on his shoulder.

"How'd it go in London, then? Must have been different for you, being in a big city. You got a new hat and coat while you were there, I see."

"We dined with a peer of the realm."

He let out a low whistle. "There's fancy." Was that the faintest glimmer of a smile? His burst of anger seemed to have passed.

"It wasn't nearly as exciting as it might sound. But my time away made me think. I've done a lot of thinking since that afternoon in the woods..." She took a deep breath, then pressed on. "I missed you. Seeing you waiting at the station when I returned, I realised how much."

His face clouded again, and he turned his cap around and around in his hands. "I'm surprised you even gave me a moment's thought. No reason why you should."

A blush flooded her cheeks. "Of course I did. I think of you often – so often. When I am alone. Especially at night. Most of all, I remember how it felt when I kissed you."

He rubbed the back of his neck, shifting uneasily. She wished he would look at her, but he kept his gaze on the cap in his hand, turning and turning it until she wanted to seize it and throw it away, do anything to make something happen between them again. Her breast heaved with the desperate need to feel close to him. But it seemed that if one of them would act, she must be the one. Small wonder that he wouldn't, after she had baulked once.

"If I kissed you again, what would you do?" The words were out before she could stop them.

He fixed his gaze on her, taking the measure of her she supposed, taking his time before answering. "What would you wish me to do, my lady?"

She wasn't sure what disappointed her more: his use of the courtesy, or the way he had sidestepped her question. Blinking away tears, she let out a sigh. He could hardly be blamed for being on his guard with her now. But then, he hadn't said that he would push her away, or that he would go back to the car and report her behaviour to Sir Lucien. And that flicker in his eyes suggested he wasn't as unmoved as he pretended.

"Did you bring your flask? I'd like some rum, if you have some to spare."

He fumbled in his pocket and unscrewed the lid before passing the pewter flask to her. She had removed her gloves and deliberately allowed her fingers to brush against his when she took it. The rum burned her throat going down, and he laughed softly at her grimace.

"Why gulp it so fast if you don't even like it?" His own sip was more restrained. She noticed he didn't bother to wipe the rim first. It seemed an intimate thing, his lips touching the place hers had been only a moment earlier.

Already she could feel a loosening in her shoulders as the rum warmed its way to her stomach. She plucked at the folds of her skirt, sensing that this was a moment of no return. She could risk kissing him again, but she wasn't sure she could bear it if he pushed her away. If he didn't reject her, could she fight her body's instinctive fears and go through with what her heart and loins longed for her to do? If she could, was it worth the possibility of her husband finding out? There was no knowing what kind of punishment he would inflict. But then, what was the point of going on as she was, existing to serve the whims of a wicked man? Surely it was time to live for herself? To follow her own desires.

Her fingers stilled in her lap, and when she looked at Joe she felt she could see his hurts as well as his kindness. He was the only one she could imagine ever wanting; although it wasn't right to ask it of him, there was no one else she could trust to reveal what real intimacy with another person could be like.

"At night, when I think of you, I imagine how it might have been that day if I hadn't been afraid." She laid her hands upon her breasts, the silk of her blouse smooth under her palms. "I imagine your hands on me, your mouth kissing mine. It makes me feel – oh, such a longing. A need that seems to flash through me like nothing else I've ever felt."

In an abrupt movement she rose to her knees, edging so close his breath brushed her face. With her heart racing, she reached to stroke the unruly curls above his ear, allowing her fingertips to linger on the line of his jaw. His breathing was as shallow as hers, his eyes dark like the sweep of his lashes when he gazed down at her mouth.

It wasn't like last time, when he had clasped her in his arms so ardently fear had shot through her like a wound. This time, he barely stirred, except to touch his nose against hers. After a moment, his work-roughened hand cupped her cheek, exquisitely tender, and she tipped forward a fraction to press her lips onto his.

His kiss was hesitant, tasting of the rum they had both drunk. When her mouth opened against his and his tongue slipped inside, its questing was sensuous, not urgent; she felt herself melting against him, reaching around his neck to pull him closer. She pressed herself against his chest, senses sparking at the strength of his arms around her. Heat turned her belly molten as he groaned deep in his throat.

When he lay her down on the rug, he was as careful as if she were made of glass. He was patient, murmuring endearments, hands roving gently over her clothes, pressing those soft kisses onto her face, behind her ears, down her neck, making her fizz like the sparkling wine she had drunk in London. The whole length of his torso pressed against hers, broad and firm in his smart coat with its shiny buttons hard against her breasts.

His hands, hard-skinned yet oh, so gentle, cupped her face like a priest cradling a chalice. There was reverence in his touch, and wonder in his countenance, as if he hardly believed she was real. It came to her in a flash of clarity: to Joe Cadwalader, she was pure. He didn't see the filthy, debased object of contempt her husband's treatment had taught her to see in herself. His touch worshipped her, so light it almost hovered over her, so unlike Sir Lucien's punishing roughness. She felt she was being lifted up, placed on a pedestal to be revered.

He tugged at her skirt and petticoats, pausing between kisses to watch her while his hand explored further, fumbling at her waist, beneath the layers of fabric where the seam was left open. The heat of his hand on her skin was like an electric shock, so startling was it after feeling nothing but linen. And when his fingers stilled on her most secret place, he kissed her again with his eyes never straying from hers, as if keeping vigil for even the slightest flicker of pain. They moved, then paused when she gasped and recoiled from long habit.

Her heart hammered and she lunged past him for the flask, draining it in a few gulps.

"Christ, woman... If you need to be drunk—"

To hush him, she pressed her fingers to his lips and shook her head. She couldn't explain it, the way her body kicked against his touch even though she wanted it. It was as if the scars left by her husband were still controlling her against her will. A spark of anger made her pull him back and crush herself against him to drown out the frightened signals fluttering in her belly. She kissed him until her head swam, the rum making her muscles relax their spasms at last and passion making her forget everything but the need to complete this act.

He can't control me now, she thought in triumph when at last Joe pushed himself into her and paused, trembling. She nodded and curled her limbs around him, pulling him in, filling her view with his broad shoulders above her in his clean white shirt so that her mind emptied of everything but the sensation of him in her. He moved carefully at first, still watching all the while as if terrified of hurting her, until at last his eyes rolled back and he quickened his pace with a low groan that invoked in her a rush of exultation. The muscles of his back shifted under her hands as he plunged into his bliss; she marvelled that her body could induce such rapture on a man's face.

Now her body was hers: she had shared it where she chose, and she was heady with the thrill of claiming it for herself.

Spent, Joe collapsed at her side – even in that, he was different, taking care not to crush her, keeping his arms about her like a shawl. For a while they lay motionless, taking in what they had done; then he pulled down her skirt, adjusted his clothes and reached into his pocket to retrieve a clean, neatly pressed handkerchief.

"Here," he said. "You'd better tidy yourself up before we go back."

She took it and fumbled at the open crotch of her drawers to dry herself. "You can't give this back to your wife now," she said, suddenly awkward. The idea of Mary laundering a handkerchief soiled by adultery was shameful. Nor could she keep it to be sent with her clothes for washing. The Plas Norton laundry maids would recognise that it was not hers, and might guess the purpose for which it had been used.

Colour suffused his face and he stumbled to his feet, stuffing his flask into his pocket and grabbing his cap. "I'll tell her I lost it."

Dusting herself off, she picked up the rug and let him go.

TWENTY-SIX

ROSAMUND

For the past two days Rosamund had missed Nellie even more than she'd expected to. As much as the housemaid Sarah had done her best to please, her touch was timorous, lacking Nellie's confidence. When dressing her hair Sarah dithered and fumbled, dropping the "rats" – the nets of rolled up hair that padded out Rosamund's pompadour style. She chatted constantly, remarking on how little grey she found amongst the chestnut, as if Rosamund was ancient. It made her wonder how much older than her thirty-six years she must look to the young housemaid.

When Sarah wasn't talking about her hair it was her clothes, and how dusky pink became her much better than her usual blue or brown; and how she shouldn't shy away from a little rouge because it was quite acceptable nowadays and would put a little youthful colour in her cheeks. Listening to her prattle and submitting to her clumsy ministrations wore Rosamund out, and Sarah's timid brushing made her want to snatch the brush from her and apply more vigorous strokes with her own hand. But the girl was doing her best, so Rosamund nodded to imply approval and counted the hours until Nellie's train was due to arrive.

She should have sent Sarah with instructions for Phelps, to tell Cadwalader to pick Nellie up from the station. But she couldn't do it. She couldn't wait patiently at home when there was an opportunity to be alone with Joe again. Her heart fluttered at the prospect of sitting beside him in the car.

Usually she dipped her toes cautiously into each day, taking it slowly. There was no point in rushing, only to have those endless hours stretching ahead, stark and empty. But today, the prospect of something to look forward to lent her unaccustomed energy. The thought of those calloused hands so close and his eyes looking at her the way he had looked at her when he made love to her in the summerhouse was enough to make a delicious shiver tingle over her spine.

Besides pleasure, there was another need: it was imperative for her to speak to him alone, to impress upon him to keep what they had done a secret. The journey to the station, without a maid in tow, might be her only opportunity. If there was one thing she regretted about their encounter, beyond the betrayal of Joe's wife, it was the risk of being found out. If he should ever divulge a word of what had happened between them to anyone, it would mean nothing less than her utter ruination, and his dismissal. There would be neither sympathy nor understanding from anyone, least of all from his wife or her husband.

She whiled away the long morning hours in reading and playing the piano, then took a walk through the rose garden before summoning Sarah for one last time to help her change into an outfit more suited to motoring.

"Perhaps just a little rouge," she said, immediately regretting it when Sarah beamed enthusiastically and leapt for the pot. "Actually, perhaps it would be unwise. A dusting of rice powder will suffice." She submitted to Sarah's fussing with the powder puff and waited until she was alone in the bathroom to pinch some colour onto her cheekbones.

"Shall I accompany you, m'lady?" Sarah asked, looking hopeful. No doubt she would enjoy a trip in the motor car. Her shoulders slumped visibly when told that her presence would be unnecessary, and the curtsy she bobbed was sullen as Rosamund swept past her to make her way to the motor stable.

"Good afternoon, Cadwalader. If it isn't too much trouble, I'd like to take the motor out for a drive. Miss Dawson's train is due in at just after four o'clock, so it occurred to me that we might collect her from the station if we set out that way."

He straightened, wiping his hands, and she willed herself not to look at them or to think about how they had felt when he touched her. She noticed the sidelong glance he sent Stanley, who was tinkering with a bicycle at the back of the workshop, and was relieved when he spoke as he would formerly have done.

"Of course, m'lady... but I thought Miss Dawson was due in on the four thirty-five?"

She remained silent, merely raising an eyebrow, and saw understanding dawn in his eyes.

"Well, no matter. I'm sure you have it right. If you'll just give me a moment, m'lady, I'll get ready."

If she stayed inside, she knew she wouldn't be able to stop staring at him, and already her cheeks felt warm, so she nodded and retreated to the yard. Thick, dark clouds were gathering in an overcast sky. No less ominous was the sight of a couple of the stable hands peering at her, ducking out of sight when they saw her looking their way. One of them had a mop of carrot-coloured hair: Wilson, doubtless eager for another opportunity for gossip. *If she did anything to betray herself or Cadwalader...* Perhaps she should bring Sarah, after all.

She lifted her chin, imagining marching over and admonishing Wilson to get on with his work; but she knew she would never have the confidence to do it. She was saved by the rumbling growl of the engine starting up, and stepped aside to allow Cadwalader to draw it to a halt beside her.

His face was reassuringly impassive as he held the door for her and climbed into the passenger seat, giving Wilson's prying eyes no grounds for suspicion as she shoved the motor into gear and chugged out of the yard. Her breath came more easily as they emerged onto the road through the estate, the dust billowing behind shielding them from view.

To her relief, Cadwalader didn't speak; but as she drove on, she knew they couldn't avoid referring to what had happened indefinitely. She risked a glance at him, and caught her breath again at the sight of him watching her. Had he been looking at her like that ever since they left the yard? The steady tawny-and-green gaze subjected her to such an intent examination that her mouth dried up. He maintained his silence, as of course he should until she addressed him first; just went on looking, until the air around them felt hot and stuffy despite the cab's open sides.

Hidden from view on the edge of the woodland about a mile and a half from the house was a gateway, used only when carts were brought to collect logs. She slowed and drew up there, glad to be relieved of the concentration needed for driving. Staring down at her gloved fingers twisting in her lap, she was all too conscious of the gleam in his eyes.

"Cadwalader—"

"I think we've gone past surnames when we're alone, don't you?"

She blanched, rendered mute by the hurt in his voice. She had to put an end to this. "We must be circumspect. And we should discuss... what happened between us."

"I've been reliving it every moment since."

He had picked up her hand and unbuttoned her glove with a flick of his thumb, exposing her wrist. She opened her mouth to speak, but now his thumb was tracing tiny circles over the indigo veins crossing her pale skin, the sudden contact of flesh on flesh making her gasp.

"I've thought of nothing but you for two days and nights. I've gone over and over it. The scent of you, like spring flowers and sunshine. The taste of those soft lips. The feeling of your body underneath mine; of your arms around me; of being deep and hot in you. All morning I've been straining to catch a glimpse of you or hear your footstep. I barely heard a word Stanley said to me."

He pressed a kiss where his thumb had been, then eased the glove down over her palm, following it with his lips. "You've driven me mad, woman. How can I think, when you're this close to me? All I can do is feel. And then... then you call me Cadwalader, as if I was just a servant, a nothing. As if what happened was nothing, when I know that what you want in your heart is the same thing I want."

He took her little finger into his mouth and curled his tongue around it, sliding his lips over its length, making her pulse stumble and flutter. One by one he savoured her fingers as if they were the sweetest delicacy, before nipping gently at the soft pad at the base of her thumb: not like Sir Lucien, not hurting, but making every pore and nerve-ending jangle with life and her belly melt.

"Joseph. Joe..." She found her voice at last, no more than a croak as she uttered his name, broken off as her lips were crushed under his own. His cap had fallen somewhere, and she was dimly conscious of her hatpin dragging at her topknot as her own hat tilted back. His ardour was only slightly dimmed by the awkwardness of their position in the front of the car, wedged against the unyielding wooden steering wheel. Above them came the faint patter of the first drops of rain on the hood.

At length she pulled away. "My hat will get squashed." She needed air, and space to think. He wouldn't press himself onto her like that, confusing her and thrilling all her senses, if they were outside where anyone might pass and see them.

He frowned but fumbled to open the door and stepped back, holding out his hand to help her down. But instead of taking her hand lightly in his, he reached in for her waist and pulled her against him, then pressed her back against the car. His face was only a breath away from hers.

"Someone might see. We must be careful. If my husband should ever find out—"

"Who'll see us?" Laughter and excitement lit his face as if he was a boy going to the fairground, not a grown man risking his livelihood and her reputation.

"Anyone could pass by. You know that."

"It didn't stop you the day before yesterday."

She shook her head. Fat droplets of rain were landing on his shoulders, beading on his woollen coat like diamonds before darkening the navy blue to almost black. Her hat would be ruined if they remained in the open, and Nellie would be sure to notice and question how she had got herself so wet whilst driving to town. He must have realised the same, as he wrenched open the door to the rear compartment and bundled her inside. Her heart leapt in surprise when she realised he had climbed in behind her; her hands fluttered as he dragged her onto his lap.

"What are you doing? You can't be in here with me. If Sir Lucien—"

"Don't say that bastard's name again."

"Joe, *listen* to me! If he finds out, he'll destroy us. You'll lose your job and your home. God knows what he'll do to me. We'll lose everything. Your family will—"

"I need you," he said, as if it was so simple. "I don't know when I'll be alone with you like this again, and I need you in my arms. How can I ever stop needing you, now that I've had you once?"

There was hunger in his eyes, and a desperate need that she had the power to slake. He had told her how Mary's rejection had hurt him. How could she hurt him the same way – Joe, whose hands had been so gentle, almost worshipful in their exquisite tenderness? She inclined her head very slightly, only the merest hint of an invitation but enough for him to reclaim her lips as if they truly belonged to him and they should never be apart. Any reluctance dissolved under the insistent longing in his hands, and she found herself on her back on the seat, with her hat discarded on the floor and her blouse askew. Joe's hands crept under her petticoat where he found the place she touched herself at night when remembering what they had done.

He watched her, his lips parted as he circled his fingers with a boldness that made her tremble.

"I want to taste you," he said, slipping to the floor. Abruptly she sat up and shoved her skirts downwards, trapping him between her knees.

"Don't hurt me. Please..."

It was fear, not desire now, making her heart pound. If he bit and slavered over her the way Sir Lucien did, she knew she couldn't bear it. Astonishingly, once again he heeded her and stopped, pulling up to cradle her face and press kisses onto her eyelids and mouth as if she was everything he wanted.

"I could never hurt you. Let me show you."

It was impossible not to surrender.

There was something different about Lady Fitznorton. Something Nellie couldn't quite put her finger on. An air of something, as if she was living on her nerves the way she did when her husband was at home. She could almost smell it in the atmosphere of the limousine's plush interior when she climbed into the back and took her place on the buttoned seat.

"How is your dear mother now? I hope she is much improved?"

Nellie swallowed hard. "She is quite poorly, m'lady. Her heart isn't strong, so she's mostly confined to bed these days. It's hard being far away at these times... I might need to go to her more often." She kept her gaze lowered, unsure how this news would be received. She could hardly expect Lady Fitz to welcome it, when it would mean Nellie taking more overnight trips home.

"I'm sorry to hear that. Your siblings will be able to take their turn and help, though, I'm sure. You have several, don't you?"

"There are five of us left, m'lady, and of course we all do what we can. But one brother is in Canada now and the other works long days in the mines. I have two sisters, but one is in poor health herself and the other has eight children. It isn't easy."

Her employer's furrowed brow could have been due to either sympathy or impatience. A mixture of the two, perhaps; and no wonder. It seemed young Sarah had allowed standards to slip. The feather on Lady Fitz's hat was broken and sticking out at an odd angle, and her coat looked almost rumpled. Her ladyship was hardly likely to agree to her wish to be away more often if it meant she ended up looking dishevelled.

Nellie licked her lips nervously before repeating her request. "I might have to go home a little more often, m'lady..."

"Of course you must."

The reply was so unexpected, Nellie hardly knew how to respond.

"Thank you, m'lady. I'll help Sarah, train her up properly so you won't..." She paused, choosing her words carefully. She could hardly commiserate with her employer for going out looking shabby. "We can't let standards slip," she said in the end, and Lady Fitz nodded as if satisfied.

"She doesn't have your competence, Nellie. But she's a good girl. She's done her best."

They subsided into silence, and Nellie's thoughts wandered. It wasn't going to be easy, juggling the demands of the two women depending on her. If only her mother lived nearby it would make things easier, but it would hardly be fair to drag her fifty miles away from everyone she knew just to save Nellie from spending all her hard-earned savings on train fares. She had left what coins she could spare with her mother to pay the doctor and to buy medicines. Two days and nights of constant nursing and stair-climbing to tend to her had left Nellie's feet and back aching, but there was little likelihood of any chance to rest, as Lady Fitz would want to change out of her motoring clothes as soon as they got back to Plas Norton.

She'd be lucky even to grab a cup of tea before the next couple of hours were out.

It was puzzling. All the way back here, while the train clattered its way through stinking, soot-blackened towns and past hillsides scarred by workings, she had fretted over her ladyship's potential reaction to her request. She'd wound herself up like a spinning top until she was a ball of nervous energy and her handkerchief a crumpled mess. And yet Lady Fitz, who had been so reluctant to see her go the first time that she'd made her delay by a whole day, hadn't raised an eyebrow. She'd been perfectly equable, even bestowed upon Nellie a faint smile, as if she was happy to grant her time off. This despite Sarah's failings which had made her ladyship so keen to have Nellie back that she had even taken the astonishing step of travelling to the station in person to collect her, instead of sending one of the grooms with the pony and trap.

Nellie was torn. In those long hours at her mother's bedside the knowledge that her employer was so reluctant to let her go had felt like a heavy burden to bear, at a time when she felt weighed down enough. But now she felt strangely disappointed that her request for more time away had been granted so readily. What if her ladyship preferred Sarah, despite her shortcomings?

She'd have to work doubly hard now to make herself indispensable. It was a depressing prospect when all she wanted was to rest. But there it was, and there was no point in choosing a life in service to then complain about hard work. Hard work was all Nellie had ever known from childhood, and she was well aware that her life was not as tough as that of many of the people she had grown up with. She'd spent more years than she cared to recall looking after other people. But who knew if there would be anyone to look after her when she grew old?

TWENTY-EIGHT

ROSAMUND

The crunch of gravel under the tyres roused Rosamund from her reverie. She had forgotten about Nellie, whose shadowy eyes and swollen ankles revealed much about what her time nursing her mother must have been like. Her thoughts had been on Joe, separated from them by the wooden-edged glass partition between the cab and the passenger compartment. She could see only the broad sweep of his shoulders and the back of his head, his cap once again covering the mop of curls that she knew would feel soft under her fingers.

The panel of glass seemed to represent their situation, somehow: once again they had been restored to order, he in his place and she in hers. The moment when he had joined her in the back seat seemed from another lifetime, not a mere hour or two ago. No other human being had been more intimate with her body, apart from Sir Lucien of course.

She closed her eyes, feeling the car slowing down as it pulled up outside the house, knowing that in a moment Joe's hand would reach out to help her out, and then she would have to behave as if he was of no more consequence than the car itself. Against all sense she risked a glance at his face, relieved to see that he, too, wore a mask of cool politeness. For no more than a second she gripped his hand more tightly, then let go and inhaled a deep breath to steady herself before alighting.

The house stood stark against the cloud-laden sky. Phelps was waiting under the portico, his black-coated severity framed by the cold grey stone of the central Gothic arch. As was his custom, the bow with which he greeted her was little more than a nod; a signal, presumably, of the contempt in which she was held. Yet today there was something almost gleeful about his eagerness to bar her way.

"A letter has arrived for you, my lady. From Miss Charlotte, I believe."

It was unusual for Rosamund to receive any letters, let alone one from her stepdaughter, but she recognised the childish handwriting on the envelope even before she picked it up from the salver. Her stomach flipped. What if this was another summons to London? Did Phelps already know what it was about?

Feeling the butler's pale sharp eyes like knives in her back, she went straight into the library and closed the door to blot him out before slitting open the envelope and sliding out the thick sheaf of pages within. It was only teatime, and yet she wished she could justify a glass of brandy.

The letter was written in Charlotte's usual hasty, careless style, with several blots and little attempt at punctuation.

Dear R,

Papa asked me to write on his behalf as he is in such agonies poor darling confined to bed here with another dreadful attack of gout when by rights he should be at home and not grappling with such news as we have had today – that you have been seen making a spectacle of yourself with your utterly ridiculous efforts to drive. Driving is one thing but you may imagine his feelings on hearing that you drove Papa's chauffeur into town with your maid in the back seat acting the lady! – for all the world as if you were the staff and they the gentry! It was so preposterous we didn't give credence to the rumour at first but it has been confirmed and no doubt you are the talk of the town and seen as some kind of radical.

Papa is incensed as you might imagine and just as soon as he is well he will return to Plas Norton but you must make no mistake he will not tolerate any further such displays of lunacy and you are to remain within the bounds of the estate where you will not cause any danger or embarrassment. It is imperative that my Eustace must not have any cause to trouble himself in allying his family to mine so you must think very carefully about what you have done and cease your imprudent not to mention improper behaviour at once before you bring shame and ignominy on us all and we all think you deficient in your wits. Papa is a patient man but even a patient and soft-hearted man has limits and he can only bear so much embarrassment especially after your poor show at dinner with the Westhamptons. He trusts you will show some unaccustomed sense use some rational thought for once and not mistake his will in this matter.

Yours etc
    C.

Rosamund folded the pages up, creasing them sharply with trembling fingers before confining them once more to their envelope. How Charlotte must have enjoyed writing that. She could picture her, the pen in her hand flying across the page, the tip of her tongue poking out between self-righteous lips, scratching her underlinings into the paper with her eyes burning with venom. Rosamund had no doubt that parts of it had been quoted verbatim from one of her husband's tirades.

What had she ever done to earn such contempt from Charlotte, whom she had tried so hard to befriend when she first arrived here? To her, Charlotte had been the only possible light in a world that had plunged into an even more profound darkness than she had known when her father died. But the little girl had been wrapped up in securing her father's attentions, presumably jealous of her new stepmother's intrusion into the family unit, and Rosamund had been too dazed and bewildered to know how to push herself into the child's world.

She tossed the letter down onto the leather surface of the writing desk and crossed to the window, where the view of the gardens might soothe her spirits. But she was too agitated to appreciate it now. Dashing her hands over her face, she sought to regroup as her emotions veered between anger and fear. How dare Charlotte address her so disrespectfully? She hadn't even acknowledged Rosamund's name in her letter, and her scolding tone was so condescending. Who was she to tell a grown woman how to comport herself? And who had started this rumour? Charlotte made it sound as if the whole town were talking about her, but for all she knew it was just one person, two at most. Phelps was the most likely culprit, for he was in his master's pocket and would no doubt be pleased to see her discredited.

If only she hadn't driven beyond the gates of the estate that day. Had she stopped and let Joe drive into Pontybrenin, as she had done today, no one would have thought twice about her travelling to the station. It *wasn't* lunacy for her to drive, not these days when so many ladies were driving – why, Queen Alexandra was said to find motoring agreeable, and some women were even enjoying the freedom of driving all over Britain and the Continent. But if she pushed too hard, her husband could so easily stop her. There would be nothing she could do to prevent him sending Joe away and replacing him with a new chauffeur who would be under strict instructions not to allow her near the motor. Pacing up and down in front of the window, she faced the fear of what might happen then.

She didn't think she could bear it if Joe left. Not now that she was in love with him. She felt she must be: his presence made her heart race, especially when passion lent his amiable features a raw intensity. She had never before made anyone so glad to see her that it lit them from within, and yet that was how Joe looked. He had to hide the spark, of course, keep it dimmed if Nellie was nearby. But those efforts seemed to make it flare all the more strongly in the snatched moments they were alone.

The thought of him made her blush and smile to herself. It was thrilling to have a secret life. Someone whose smile was genuine, not cruel. Someone who wanted to give her pleasure and not pain. Someone who might, perhaps, help her escape...

Of course, the potential for her to escape was the real reason for her husband's disapproval. Sir Lucien wasn't embarrassed by her behaviour. He wasn't worried that she might be involved in an accident, or that she was being unladylike in driving her servants around. What he feared most was what she desired most: that motoring could bring her freedom. And she didn't know what she could do to stop him putting barriers in her way. With her burst of anxious energy depleted, she sank into the chair and buried her face in her hands.

TWENTY-NINE
JOSEPH
JULY 1914

"You need to be careful," Joe said as they rattled along the driveway away from the forbidding grey stone of the house.

"I am being careful. I missed the pothole this time." Her smile was mischievous, lighting up her features.

He looked out of the side of the car, glad of the breeze caressing his cheeks as she drove; the weather was glorious again, making his woollen uniform feel uncomfortably hot and itchy.

"I don't mean your driving. I mean the way you look."

"How do I look?"

It was clear from the playful smile tipping up the corners of her mouth that she knew what he meant. He sighed.

"You're like silver that used to be tarnished and dull, but now has been polished. You shine these days. Only a blind man could fail to notice how you sparkle."

It was true. He had never seen her look so lovely. High spirits suited her. She looked younger. She looked like a girl in love. Her smile grew even wider at his words.

"I can't help it if you make me happy."

His own happiness was tempered by uneasiness. Her face

was like an open door, showing the secrets of her heart too read-ily. She had beamed at Stanley this morning when she arrived for her lesson, and the lad's eyes had nearly popped out of their sockets with surprise. And if Stanley had noticed the difference in her demeanour, others must have too. He had nothing to fear from Stanley, but other people would be different. Other people would speculate.

"Just try to hide it when we're not alone, or people will talk," he said, and softened his words with a gentle smile of his own. Her good mood was infectious: he couldn't bring himself to be cool towards her. He took off his gloves, reached over and rested his right hand on her thigh. His fingers moved stealth-ily between her legs, making the layers of skirt and petticoat rustle. Her eyes met his with a gaze that was as hot as his own.

"We shall have to swap places before we leave the estate," she said, as if he didn't already know. Their fortnightly journeys to collect Miss Dawson from the railway station were their only time alone together.

"Do we have time to stop?" he asked, disappointed by her quick shake of the head. So there would be no furtive visit to the woods or summerhouse today. He knew it couldn't happen every time they went out; indeed, sometimes a kiss was all they had time for. But it didn't mean he couldn't keep her on the boil. He watched her cheeks redden as his fingers began to pleat her skirt and petticoats, bunching them under his palm and drawing her hem up slowly beyond her knee. He sought the skin above her garter and pushed past the hem of her drawers, tracing deli-cate circles on the vellum-smooth flesh of her inner thigh with his thumb. Finally she pushed his hand away with a gasp.

"Joe, you'll make me crash!"

His grin made her laugh. He loved it that he could make her feel so alive – the woman who had once been described to him as an Ice Queen. Leaning back in his seat, he couldn't help feeling smug. He only needed to touch her to make her pant for it: the eagerness of her response to him was like a balm to his male pride after Mary's rejection.

She slowed down to approach a gate, and he hopped out of the car to hold it open while she passed through. She was becoming a skilful driver, he reflected. He hardly ever had to tell her what to do these days. Even when he distracted her, she kept control of the motor.

"Tell me why you married Mary," she said when he resumed his place on the front seat.

The question caught him by surprise.

"Why do you want to talk about her?"

"I want to know everything about you."

"So you can ask me all sorts of personal questions, is it? If I did the same with you, I dare say I'd be overstepping the mark."

The truth was, he hated thinking about Mary when he was with Rosamund. He didn't want to be a married man illicitly fornicating with another man's wife on the rare occasions they could snatch an opportunity to be alone together. He despised the image of himself as an adulterer even more than he now hated his lowly position as Rosamund's servant. He didn't want to be her employee. He wanted to be her husband. Her protector. The head of her household. It wasn't right for a woman to be above her man. And that was how he had come to see himself: as Rosamund's man.

She had lapsed into a silent frown, no doubt taken aback by his harsh words. It was another reminder that he should remember his place. He might consider himself hers, but did she consider herself to be his?

"You go first," he said, to prove a point, even though he would be rubbing salt into his own wound. "Tell me why you married Him." He couldn't bring himself to say the fat old bastard's name. It set his teeth on edge to think of him touching her.

Her frown deepened. "He asked me, and it was likely that

no one else would. My brother had warned me I must marry, as he couldn't support me. He had no choice but to sell our ancestral home. After Charlotte's mother died, Sir Lucien wanted to marry again, and he claimed that before he passed away my father had already suggested a union between our families. The estate was in terrible debt so I had no realistic hope of an alternative. And when he told me about his house in the country and his poor, motherless little girl... it made it seem a less daunting prospect. I believed I could make a life with them. I wanted children of my own."

"But you never had any."

A shake of the head and her downturned mouth told him all he needed to know of her disappointment.

"Now you. Was Mary the first woman you ever... *knew*?"

Her tactful choice of words made him smile wryly.

"No. But the girls I'd been with before weren't the kind I could have taken home to meet my mother. Mary was different. We went to Chapel three times every Sunday – my Mam was a Methodist – and Mary was the preacher's daughter. She was pretty. Quiet; demure. A good girl. The kids in the Sunday School all looked up to her because she was kind to them. When my little sister whispered to me one day that she thought Mary was sweet on me, I started looking at her a bit more. And she did seem to like me – peeping under her lashes, you know the sort of thing. My mother noticed, of course. She told me I could do a lot worse than marry a girl like her. So my fate was sealed."

He laughed, but it was a hollow sound.

They were approaching the gatehouse lodge, and Rosamund slowed the vehicle to a stop.

"Were you happy?" she asked.

"I wasn't unhappy."

"That isn't the same as being happy, Joe."

He considered how best to deflect her questioning. "Marriage to a good, wholesome girl like Mary was never going to be a thrilling experience. For that, I should have defied my mother and stuck with the bad girls."

Her burst of laughter was echoed in his own grin. But his died, frozen into a rictus grimace as they passed two familiar figures walking along the road, coming from the direction of the village with shawls around their shoulders and baskets on their arms.

"What is it?"

She was always perceptive of his moods. He shrugged, but his expression remained grim.

"Those two. My Mary and Dolly. I could be wrong, but I'm pretty sure they saw us laughing."

THIRTY

JOSEPH

Joe wondered all day how much Mary might have seen and what she would make of it. *Just act naturally*, he told himself as he and Stanley stepped across the threshold after work that evening. His youngest daughter, four-year-old Miriam, bounded towards him and he swung her up into a bear hug, planting a kiss on her giggly cheek.

"Did you miss me while you were at work, Dad?" she asked.

"I always miss you when I'm at work, Mim. Did you miss me?"

She nodded solemnly. "Mammy says you're too busy to miss us. She says you don't have time to think about us, you're too busy with Lady Fit-snorting."

"Did she say that? Well, perhaps Mammy doesn't realise what my job is like." His stab of guilt overrode the amusement he might have felt at Miriam's mangling of Rosamund's title. "Have you had your tea?"

Miriam nodded again, her soft ringlets bouncing. "I'm going to feed the chickens," she said importantly.

He set her back down on the ground and followed her into the stiflingly hot room as she scampered off to collect the vegetable peelings from the kitchen. The older children were already seated at the table, waiting for him, while Mary busied herself spooning food onto plates. Their table wasn't large enough for nine people to eat together, so the youngest four children customarily ate first while Joe ate afterwards with the eldest three. Mary would eat later, insisting on serving everyone else first. It was the way her mother had done things, and she stuck rigidly to the same routine.

Joe greeted the children, then washed his hands in the basin in the scullery. Mary was pointedly silent, and he pretended he hadn't seen the uneasy glances passing between his two eldest children, Maggie and Len. Len and Stanley attacked their plates of cheese and potato pie with gusto, ravenous as always after their long shifts at work.

"You and Lady Fitznorton seemed to be getting along very well when I saw you today," Mary remarked at last, when Joe picked up a piece of bread and butter.

"Did we? She's alright, I suppose."

Her dark eyes glittered dangerously.

"You were laughing together about something. It looked like it must have been a good joke. Not quite the way I would expect a lady to behave with one of her servants, though."

She was waiting, arms folded across her apron, for him to respond. He finished chewing his mouthful of pie and then took a sip of tea before answering.

"I only remember laughing after she went over a pothole and it made us both jump. I don't recall any jokes."

He met her gaze levelly, hoping that would be an end to it. It was surprisingly easy to lie when there was so much at stake. When he glanced around the table he saw Maggie's relieved small smile and picked up his fork again.

"She seemed to be in a good mood today, didn't she Dad?" Stanley said through a mouth full of mashed potato. "Very smiley this morning, I thought."

"Don't talk with your mouth full, Stanley," Mary interjected. "But what you said... it's a funny thing, people have been commenting on how much more cheerful she is since she's been having driving lessons. All smiles she is these days, from what I hear."

Joe's lips thinned as he glared back at her.

"If you've got something to say, Mary, then out with it."

She glared back proudly at him.

"It's not for the likes of me to say anything about the likes of her. But other people certainly think she should be more careful of her good name."

"You should be ashamed of yourself, blackening a lady's reputation," he told her shortly. The children were unusually absorbed in studying their plates.

"I'm not the one damaging her reputation. I'd say she's doing a good job of that by herself."

Joe rose to his feet and pointed to the door, furious with her for saying so much in front of their children.

"Out!" he said, and she marched ahead of him to their tiny parlour.

"You should think very carefully about the consequences of spreading gossip," he said, closing the door firmly behind them.

She laughed in his face. "And you, Joe? Are you thinking about the consequences of your actions when you're out all alone with that woman? Poor Sir Lucien – it seems it's true what they say, while the cat's away the mice will play. If it's not true, if there's nothing going on between you and her, then swear it – swear it on the Bible."

She seized her worn copy of the Bible from the arm of the chair and thrust it at him.

A muscle twitched in his cheek and he flexed his fingers, wishing she were a man so he could knock some respect into her.

"I'll swear to nothing. I won't be spoken to like this in my own house."

He snatched the Bible from her hand and tossed it contemptuously back onto the chair, then leaned in until they were nose to nose and growled out his words. "Nellie Dawson is always with us, so what do you think we're going to do – have an orgy on the turnpike? And even if she was climbing onto my cock the second we were out of sight of the house, or I was tumbling her in the woods three times a week, why should you even care? You've made it very clear that you don't want me."

He saw her flinch at his coarse language; her mouth twisted with disgust.

"I have every right to care. I care because I want my children to be able to walk down the street with their heads held high, not having people whispering behind their hands on every corner."

Her eyes filled with tears and she pummelled her fists against his chest. Outraged, he caught her wrists and held them tight while she sobbed.

"I care because I'm afraid of what will happen to us all if Sir Lucien hears the rumours. And I care because there was a time, Joe – may God help me – there was a time when I loved you."

She sagged against him, burying her face against his chest, and wept into his shirt.

In the past, he would have put his arms around her. He would have patted her back and stroked her hair and murmured reassurances. But not now. She had as good as admitted her love for him was dead. He dropped her wrists and turned his back on her, stiff and straight, and gazed out of the window into the darkness of the yard until she left the room.

THIRTY-ONE
ROSAMUND

Rosamund hummed a tune as she descended the stairs, full of happy anticipation for her next outing with Joe in the motor car. She had decided to lend him a book, knowing how much he relied on reading to pass the time when waiting for her to finish her errands. There were a few Sherlock Holmes novels in the library, and she thought perhaps he might enjoy one of those.

Joe filled her waking thoughts as much as he filled her dreams. When she played the piano, she played soaring love songs that filled the music room with passion. When she walked, she pictured him beside her. She talked to him constantly in her mind, telling him her hopes and fears and the minutiae of her daily life, until she hardly knew when they were together what she had actually said and what she had dreamed of saying. She had studied his face so intently that she could visualise every aspect of it: every pore, every little scar, the stubbly patch at the edge of his cheek which he often missed when shaving. Her infatuation was so complete, she could almost hear the rich cadence of his voice and his laugh even when they were apart.

As she neared the foot of the stairs, still deliberating over which novel to slip into her bag, Phelps emerged from a side room and approached her, his soft tread remarkably measured for such a heavy man.

"My lady, I am glad to have caught you before you venture out."

"Good morning, Phelps. I was going to look for a book in the library, and then take it out with me into the gardens. Isn't it a beautiful day?"

He inclined his head, smooth and deferential as always. This morning, though, she thought she detected a faint air of excitement about him.

"Sir Lucien's valet telephoned a short while ago," he said.

She paused, her hand gripping the elaborately carved newel cap at the foot of the stairs so hard her knuckles showed white against the dark oak.

"Oh?"

"He told me to anticipate Sir Lucien's arrival on the two o'clock train tomorrow. Naturally he will expect Cadwalader to collect him from the station. I have taken the liberty of informing Mrs Longford in order that she can make preparations, and I imagine Mrs McKie will want to discuss the menu with you. A celebratory meal as a fitting welcome after so many months away."

He paused, and she blinked rapidly as she realised, belatedly, that he expected her to respond. Somehow, she managed to keep her voice even.

"Thank you, Phelps. That is most helpful. Would you ask Mrs McKie to come and see me this afternoon, after luncheon?"

"Very good, my lady."

He turned and walked away, leaving her frozen into immobility at the foot of the stairs.

She could feel her pulse beating an urgent, alarmed rhythm in her forehead. Her palms grew clammy, her breathing suddenly difficult. There wasn't enough air in the hall: she had to get out. Without stopping to collect a coat or hat, she bolted for the front door and hastened around the edge of the house towards the courtyard and stables. She had to see Joe.

The rising sense of panic made her vision blur and distort. She was panting, struggling to get air into her lungs, her high-necked blouse stifling her like a rope tied tightly about her throat. By the time she reached the motor stable, she could see nothing but bursting pinpricks of light and hear nothing but a roaring, rushing sound that drowned out rational thought.

"He's coming back," she tried to say, though she didn't know if anyone heard. "Oh God, he's coming back."

Joe and Stanley looked up from the task that had engrossed them for the past half hour or more, puzzled by the odd whimpering sound they had caught drifting in through the high doorway. It sounded like an animal in distress. Frowning, Joe laid down his hammer and followed Stanley outside to see what it was.

Never had he beheld such naked terror on a human face. Rosamund was stumbling across the cobbles towards the motor stable from the direction of the house, her eyes huge. Her mouth opened wide as she attempted to gasp out words, but they were incoherent. She lurched, reaching out an arm towards him, seemingly in the grip of some kind of horror or seizure; he knew not what. Something must be terribly wrong.

Stanley turned and looked at Joe, bewildered. Joe didn't hesitate.

"Fetch help, Stan. Go now!"

The lad took off at a run, his boots clattering around the corner towards the rear entrance where the servants came and went. Joe strode the few steps needed to cross the gap between him and the wild-eyed woman who was virtually unrecognisable as the dignified lady of the house. Her legs buckled just before he reached her, and he lunged to catch her before she could hit the ground.

"Joe...?" she gasped out, her breath coming shallow and rapid as if she couldn't get enough air into her lungs. He hushed her quickly, before anyone else could hear her use his Christian name.

"Christ, Rosie – what's happened?"

Her eyes rolled and she slumped, limp and apparently insensible in his arms. The sound of hasty footsteps made him look up with no small measure of relief. Red-faced, Phelps and Mrs Longford came scuttling across the cobbles towards him, like beetles in their black garb.

"Whatever is going on?" Mrs Longford exclaimed, throwing up her hands at the sight of Lady Fitznorton collapsed in Joe's arms.

"I don't know," Joe said quickly. "I think she must be ill – I couldn't tell what she was saying, she was in such a state; the next thing I knew she fell and now she's out cold. We need to get her indoors."

Mrs Longford nodded instant agreement.

"How shall we move her...?" She began, but Joe had already swung Rosamund up and was carrying her towards the servants' entrance before anyone could make any alternative suggestions. His heart pounded with desperate anxiety as her head lolled against his shoulder. Unconscious, she was surprisingly heavy in his arms, but adrenalin gave him strength and the self-possession not to show his frantic thoughts on his face. Concern was proper; fear was not, for a man whose employer's wife had just collapsed in front of him.

"Where shall I take her?" he asked Mrs Longford, who only hesitated a moment.

"Well, I would have said the drawing room – but she's still unconscious. We'll have to call the doctor to her. Mr Phelps, would you please do that now? Mr Cadwalader, do you think you can carry her upstairs?"

His back twinged, making him grimace, but he ignored it and nodded, following the housekeeper across the yard. Rosamund would be better off in the privacy of her own room, rather than in the drawing room with the maids and footman in and out. Perhaps by the time he had carried her there, she might have woken and be able to tell them what was wrong.

Mrs Longford muttered as she led the way through the house. "My, but this is a to-do and no mistake. I don't know what Sir Lucien will say tomorrow when he gets back. Hopefully she'll be better by then. Her nerves were never strong."

His heart slammed: Sir Lucien would be back tomorrow, and there would be no more assignations among the trees or on the back seat of the old man's car. He forced his mind to turn back to the present. Had she heard news of his return? It would explain her panic.

In single file, with Mrs Longford looking back every few steps as if she was afraid he would drop his precious load, they passed the kitchens and along the serving corridor, then through a door into the main hall to the wide flight of stairs. Dust motes floated in the sunbeams slanting through the leaded diamonds in the tall, arched window. Not that they'd be allowed to land: the heavy, carved balustrade was polished to a shine, and the air faintly scented with beeswax and lavender. Mary had trained in a house like this. It explained her obsession with cleanliness, if this was how everything must be made to gleam.

Everything was on a grand scale, oversized even, from the enormous blue and white vase filled with tall flowers on the table in the hall to the height of the family portraits, framed in gold and frowning down at Joe to remind him that he was out of place here. As if he needed such a reminder.

The thick, wide carpet dipped under his boots, like the moss in the woods where he and Rosamund had spent the little time they could snatch away from prying eyes. But he couldn't allow his thoughts to stray in that direction now, for fear they might show on his face under Mrs Longford's perceptive gaze.

As he reached the top of the stairs and paused for breath, Nellie Dawson emerged from behind a door covered in green baize, her mouth forming an O of surprise at the strange sight of him upstairs with their mistress lolling in his arms like a rag doll.

"Would you show Mr Cadwalader to her ladyship's room, please, Miss Dawson?" asked Mrs Longford, in control now that her initial shock had worn off. Joe wished he could feel equally in command of himself.

He followed the two women into the largest bedroom he had ever seen in his life. If he could have measured it, he was sure that he could have fitted all three bedrooms of his own cottage within it, with space to spare. It was a gloomy room, not the frilly, feminine boudoir he had imagined but furnished with a dark carpet, heavy, floor-length velvet curtains that Joe thought must be at least nine feet long, and wallpaper printed with sombre grey-green twining leaves, twisted and tangled with thorns like briars.

Ahead of him stood an enormous four-poster bed hung with richly embroidered silk drapes, topped with a canopy and covered by an opulent damson-coloured counterpane. He crossed to it and laid Rosamund down gently, easing his aching arms from underneath her knees and shoulders. To his great relief, she roused enough to be able to mumble something and look at him in obvious bewilderment.

"It's alright now, m'lady," he said, hoping she would respond in a similarly formal manner. "We've brought you to your room, so you can rest for a bit."

He glanced at Mrs Longford, who was busy at the dressing table, hunting out smelling salts or some such he supposed. Miss Dawson had disappeared into the bathroom.

"What's wrong?" he whispered, hoping Rosamund would be able to read his desperate concern in his face.

Her eyes spilled over with tears, and she silently mouthed the words.

Sir Lucien.

So she had found out he was coming back. His mouth set in a line, but he had no time to respond as the other women approached the bed, Mrs Longford with a small green bottle and Nellie with a glass of water.

Mrs Longford's cheeks lifted as she smiled her relief. "Ah, you're looking a little better already m'lady. You gave us all quite a fright out there in the yard. Mr Cadwalader – thank you for your assistance. We can manage now."

It was his signal to go, and it felt like a physical blow because he didn't know when he might see his Rosamund again.

"I hope you feel better soon, m'lady," he mumbled, touching his forelock, then turned on his heel and left them to fuss over the fragile figure lying weeping on the bed. As he closed the door behind him he struggled to master himself, feeling he had abandoned her but knowing it was the only thing he could do. He had no choice but to leave her on that bed. The bed where her husband had the right to force himself on her night after night if he chose. How much had she suffered in that room already, to make her so terrified of the prospect of his return?

More than anything, Joe wished he could take her away with him. They could steal the car, perhaps; get away to London and sell it, use the money to start a new life where she would be safe. It was worth hundreds of pounds. Joe could get another job as a driver, or even go back to working with horses if it meant they could hide somewhere together.

But he knew it was impossible. He could never pass himself off as her equal, and she couldn't be expected to live as a working man's woman. They wouldn't even get as far as trying to find work, or somewhere to live. Phelps would send a telegram, and the police would be out looking for them before they could even cross into England, never mind get hundreds of miles away to London. He'd be locked up, and his family would never forgive him. He'd never see his children again, and Stanley would be left without a job. The shame of it would destroy Mary, who deserved better from him. No, as much as it killed him to feel so powerless, all he could do was leave Rosamund in that room, in this house with its silent corridors and oppressive air.

* * *

The next afternoon came all too quickly, and Joe waited in the car outside the railway station with shards of dread in the pit of his stomach. His nostrils flared involuntarily when he saw the corpulent, homburg-hatted figure of his employer emerge from the station, closely followed by his valet and a porter pushing a trolley laden with luggage. Clenching his fists, he forced himself to climb out and keep his face neutral.

It had been arranged that the luggage would be taken to Plas Norton separately in the horse-drawn trap while Joe drove the old man in the height of luxury. The motor shone as if its surfaces were made of mirrored glass; the front seats were buffed and slippery with leather tonic. There wasn't a fingerprint or a scratch on the paintwork, not a dead fly on the windshield nor a speck of dirt on the floor. Joe's hat, coat and trousers were pressed and brushed, his face freshly shaved and his long boots pristine as he stood smartly to attention. Everything was perfect. But Sir Lucien didn't wear the expression of a happy man. His jowls wobbled as he huffed towards the car, brows lowered like a bull facing a matador in a ring.

"Cadwalader, look sharp," he snapped in that over-loud voice. "I've been travelling all day, let's get to the house and be done with it. Not the back door, you idiot – I'll ride in the front. Harris can go with the luggage."

Joe hastened to slip into the driving seat and Harris, the valet, closed the front door behind Sir Lucien before stepping back to see them off.

With the old man's bulk filling the space beside him, nervousness made Joe crunch the gears, earning him a sharp rebuke. He put extra care into keeping his movements and his expression as smooth and inoffensive as possible as they proceeded across town towards the Fitznorton estate.

Sir Lucien was silent at first, and Joe stared forward resolutely, painfully conscious of his employer's constant glowering. But after they had travelled a mile or so, Sir Lucien suddenly spoke in that boorish voice that grated on Joe's ears like fingernails on a blackboard.

"I'm surprised my wife didn't come to meet me at the station."

Joe swallowed. "She was unwell yesterday, sir."

"Was she? And yet she has been in positively rude health for the past several months. How very untimely for her to fall ill this week, just when I am coming home."

Joe said nothing.

"Shall I tell you why I decided to curtail my visit to London, Cadwalader?"

"Sir?"

After leaving a long enough silence to prolong his discomfort, Sir Lucien continued, watching him all the while like a predator studying its prey.

"I came home because of the talk that is on everyone's lips these days."

Joe's mouth went dry. He fixed his gaze upon the road and tried to quash his rising sense of alarm. He had a feeling he was being tested. How much gossip had reached his employer's ears? Could Phelps have realised that he and Rosamund were more than just mistress and servant? He doubted it, but it wasn't impossible. Mary had her suspicions, after all.

"What talk is that, sir?" he asked, relieved that his voice sounded much cooler than he felt. Logic told him that if Sir Lucien had any notion of what his chauffeur had done with his wife, he would probably have taken action before now.

"Well, now. What do you imagine everyone is talking about?"

Joe thought quickly. "I can only think it must be war, sir. Everyone seems to agree that it is inevitable."

The old man's harsh grunt could have been an indication of either amusement or contempt. "Of course it is inevitable, you dolt. Give it a week, our army will mobilise. We can't allow the Kaiser to hold the whole of Europe in his fist. He has already declared war against Russia and France, do you really think we can stand back and let him march on Paris or St Petersburg?" His eyes narrowed slyly. "You've got boys, haven't you? Old enough to join up if it comes to a fight?"

"Yes, sir."

"Ha!" His short laugh was a strangely satisfied sound, as if he *wanted* them to face danger. At twenty-one, Len was plenty old enough to join up if the idea of seeing combat struck him as an adventure. Stan was only sixteen, so should be safe. But still. The idea of anyone taking pleasure in the prospect of them facing bullets or bayonets made Joe simmer with suppressed anger, his hands gripping the steering wheel with far more force than necessary. He focused on the road, determined not to reveal his thoughts.

"I hear you've been spending a good deal of time alone with my wife."

The change of subject was abrupt, clearly intended to catch him off his guard. But Joe had his answer ready, having guessed Phelps had probably told him as much. He had already decided to tell the truth, a version of it at least, as far as possible. It left less margin for error and enabled him to remain convincing.

"In a manner of speaking, sir. She asked me to teach her to drive. She wanted to surprise you, she said."

"All the more odd that she didn't drive to the station to meet me today, don't you think?"

"Perhaps she would have done, if she'd been well. I don't know; I'm not privy to her plans, Sir Lucien."

Sir Lucien's voice beside him was little more than a snarl. "You are not privy to her plans, perhaps. But let me tell you, if I find out that you've been privy to anything else of my wife's, you – you and your family – will rue the day you ever set eyes on her."

Joe held back the equally threatening retort that he longed to make. They were travelling along the driveway towards the big house now, its dull grey stone matching the clouds gathering above the four towers that thrust towards the sky. He was relieved when at last he drew the car to a halt, opposite the smug figure of Phelps in the front porch.

Without a word, he inclined his head politely as Phelps stepped down to open the door and Sir Lucien swept past him into the house. He watched them go in, counting in his head until his heart rate slowed back down to its regular rhythm. He got to sixty before he could bring himself to drive to the motor stable.

THIRTY-THREE
NELLIE

As she tidied the muddled array of bottles in Lady Fitz's bathroom back into a neat row, Nellie reflected on how extraordinary it was, the way the gentry invariably forgot that their servants were neither deaf nor blind to their goings-on. The bathroom door was open, and she was able to eavesdrop on Sir Lucien's conversation with the doctor in the adjoining bedroom without the slightest difficulty, as they hadn't troubled to lower their voices.

Given that Lady Fitz had barely stopped weeping for two days after her strange attack of hysterics, Doctor Sheridan had agreed to Sir Lucien's request that she be drugged to sleep, and she now lay curled up in her vast bed while the two old men discussed her condition.

"I have had fears for her state of mind for some time," Sir Lucien said in a sad, confiding tone. "She is quite unstable, you know; prone to these sudden fits of weeping and melancholy. She sometimes stays in her bed for days, refusing to get up or to eat. It isn't normal behaviour, Doctor. Sometimes I even..." He left a theatrical pause, and Nellie heard him sigh. "I even begin to wonder if she is entirely sane."

Nellie stopped, her fingers arrested in mid-air still holding the lid of a jar. She set it down on the basin with exaggerated care so as not to make a sound, and sidled softly towards the door.

She heard the doctor tut sympathetically. "There are options one might consider, should she not recover," he suggested. "It might be kinder, if she simply can't function, to find accommodation somewhere more... well, somewhere more appropriate to her needs."

Nellie went cold as she realised what he meant. Her mouth twisted with the sour taste of disgust. They were discussing the possibility of putting her ladyship into an asylum, as if she was some feeble-minded lunatic – and with Rosamund asleep not six feet away from them. Had they no sense of decency? Had the doctor no qualms of conscience at suggesting such a course of action? Outrage filled her breast, and it took a supreme effort of will not to storm into the room and berate them. She would be more use to Lady Fitz if she kept quiet.

"You know how I shrink from taking such desperate measures," Sir Lucien was saying now in a mournful voice that didn't fool Nellie for a second.

"I understand. But sometimes one must be brave, and take steps that might be distasteful, for the sake of all involved – especially for the patient. Women do have more of a tendency to hysterical behaviour than we men. If Lady Fitznorton's neurasthenia attacks are becoming more frequent, and rest does not effect a cure, it might be necessary to consider a more permanent solution, to avoid further distress and embar-rassment."

"Oh, indeed. As much as it pains me to consider it, one simply can't imagine the consequences if she should display such volatile behaviour in public – at my daughter's wedding, for instance. She has never been comfortable in a social setting, as you know. It became clear on her recent visit to London that she will never master the ability to mix."

Nellie pursed her lips angrily.

"You know I am willing to assist you in any way I can," the doctor said.

Their voices were fading now, and Nellie couldn't catch the rest. She waited a short while, then risked a peep through the bathroom doorway and saw that they had gone.

With a huff, she stomped back into the bedroom, picked up a petticoat that needed re-hemming, and sat down in a chair to sew. From time to time she looked up at Lady Fitznorton, who was sleeping fitfully as if her laudanum-induced dreams were not pleasant ones.

Nellie's thoughts were in turmoil. There wasn't much call for ladies' maids in lunatic asylums. If Sir Lucien succeeded in having his wife sent to an institution, Nellie would lose her position for sure. She couldn't honestly say she loved her job, but she needed it. How many other ladies' maids were allowed time off every couple of weeks to visit family? Nellie's mam needed the money Nellie gave her for medicines and the district nurse's calls as much as she needed the practical support Nellie provided on her regular visits. Besides, Lady Fitz was relatively undemanding. She had been generous in giving Nellie some of her cast-off clothes, and turned a blind eye to Nellie snaffling little things like almost-empty bottles of bath salts for herself. Nellie had never once been slapped, not in ten years. She knew many maids were not nearly so lucky – many employers were far less generous.

Nellie was settled at Plas Norton, too. Although it was out in the country, it was near enough to home to make it easy to visit her mam. She knew the household routine; she had learned to anticipate her ladyship's wants and needs so that little thought was required. Learning the ropes in a new job might be hard. Finding a new job with an employer she didn't dislike too strongly and who would give her the time to go home could be even harder.

As much as Lady Fitznorton's lack of fortitude sometimes irritated her, Nellie couldn't help having some sympathy for the depth of the other woman's unhappiness. If her husband's homecoming was enough to drive her to physical collapse, perhaps Lady Fitz's married life was even worse than Nellie had realised.

When Lady Fitz finally awoke, Nellie was at her most attentive. She brought her a cup of tea, some dainty pieces of toast and marmalade to tempt her appetite, and dabbed some eau de cologne on her temples to freshen her. She hovered while the colour eased back into her ladyship's cheeks and, when she had begun to look a little better, ventured a suggestion.

"Do you feel like sitting up for a while now, m'lady? We could move the chair to the window, and you can look out at the sunshine and the trees. It might help to cheer you up a bit." Anything would make for a more pleasant outlook than staring at the walls in this gloomy chamber.

The other woman looked doubtful, so Nellie continued in that artificially bright tone, the same one she used with her invalid mother and her young nephews.

"How about if I brush your hair? That always soothes you, doesn't it? I'll help you to the chair if you like."

She took silence as acquiescence and dragged the chair across to the window with an encouraging smile.

"There you are now: isn't that lovely? A bit of nice, warm sunshine will do you the power of good. My mother always likes to sit in the window. She's all hemmed in by the other houses, of course, but she's on the hill so she can look across the valley and watch what's going on down below."

Fussing, she gently manoeuvred the frail figure towards the chair, settled her with a soft blanket over her lap and fetched the hairbrush from the dressing table. Deftly, she unwound the braid that trailed down Lady Fitznorton's back as far as her waist, then stroked the brush smoothly through her chestnut brown locks. Worryingly, the bristles rapidly filled with strands of hair, many more than she would usually expect. Nellie glanced across at the pillow: there, too, dark strands seemed a tell-tale sign of extreme stress. She brushed more gently.

Lady Fitznorton remained silent for several minutes, half-closing her eyes at the tugging of the bristles over her scalp. Then, with tears in her eyes, she seized Nellie's hand and clasped it in both of her own.

Nellie almost pulled her hand away from the unexpected contact but stopped herself in time, forcing herself to accept the gesture. She had dressed this woman, seen her dishevelled in bed after nights with her husband; she had sent her menstrual clouts to the laundry, mopped her face when she had been sick, nursed her through several miscarriages. Yet none of those times had ever felt as intimate and personal as holding her hand.

"You've always been good to me, Nellie. Thank you for your kindness."

The words made a lump rise in Nellie's throat; she swallowed hard to squash it and glanced sideways towards the door. She lowered her voice and crouched beside the chair, intent on the other woman's pale, mournful face.

"M'lady, there's something I need to tell you. I overheard things earlier... Things that make me concerned for what might happen to you."

Lady Fitz's eyes widened, prompting Nellie to press on.

"You need to get well, and be seen to get well quickly. You need to get up today if you can, go down to luncheon and even if you don't feel quite yourself just yet, you need to pretend that you're back to normal. I'll help you look pretty, and you can put a good face on it, and make Sir Lucien and the doctor see that you're alright. Believe me, it's important."

"Why are you telling me this?"

She paused, unsure how much to say. She didn't want her ladyship to have one of her fits of hysteria again. But on the other hand, she needed her to understand the importance of convincing Sir Lucien and Doctor Sheridan that she was well enough to remain at home, where Nellie could continue to look after her. Perhaps it was best to be blunt.

"I'm scared of what they'll do if they think you're not in your right mind. Men are cruel creatures, when they're not getting what they want. And the world is on their side, not ours. But I honestly believe that if you're brave, and you can pretend to be stronger than you feel, you could put a stop to their plans, m'lady. I hope you will, for both our sakes."

, They remained still, eyes locked, until finally Lady Fitznorton nodded.

"I understand you, Nellie," she replied in that soft, faint voice of hers. "And I thank you for the warning. Now, you'd better finish my hair and help me dress."

THIRTY-FOUR
ROSAMUND

When Rosamund slipped into the dining room in time for luncheon, she found the expression of surprise on her husband's face highly gratifying. She took her seat at the opposite end of the long table and waited while the footman hastened to lay a place and serve her soup, all the while holding her head high.

Sir Lucien, having seemingly forgotten about his half-eaten mouthful of food in his surprise at her appearance, recommenced chewing and swallowed uncomfortably, dabbing at his grizzled beard with his snowy linen napkin.

"You seem much better, my dear. I must say it is a surprise to see you back on your feet. You were still quite indisposed this morning." The politeness of his words belied the displeasure in his tone.

"I'm much better, thank you." She added a smile for emphasis, enjoying his evident annoyance.

A glance down at her bowl made her stomach twist, rebelling against the prospect of food. Yet she knew she must give the appearance of a good appetite, to maintain a façade of good health in front of not only her husband but also the servants and the doctor, if he should call. She dipped her spoon into her soup and made an effort to initiate what might pass for a normal conversation.

"Did anything interesting happen while I was unwell?"

She sent another cool smile along the table; it froze at his reply.

"Germany invaded Belgium. We declared war. Is that interesting enough for you?"

"Oh, my," she said, setting down her spoon. "So it has happened, as everyone said it would. How terrible, to think of a war so close to home."

"One man's crisis is another man's opportunity, my dear. There'll be fortunes to be made, mark my words. Brass buttons for uniforms; metals for armaments; rations for the troops; coal for the trains and ships; medicines and bandages... The army will need it all, and I intend to supply as much as I can."

She stared at him as he attacked his food with gluttonous vigour. He seemed more troubled by the sauce trickling down his beard than the thought of men killing one another for the sake of territory. He swiped at his chin again with an irritated grimace, then tossed his napkin carelessly onto the snowy tablecloth.

"So, my dear," he went on between mouthfuls. "What are your plans for the rest of the day, now that you're back on your feet?"

"I thought I might take a walk... The fresh air will do me good."

"Hmph. Don't overtire yourself. We don't want to have to trouble Dr Sheridan again, do we?"

She summoned a gracious nod, aware that he would love to do just that. "I'm sure that won't be necessary. I really am so very much better now."

"Then I congratulate you on your truly remarkable recovery. I plan to go into town later. Your friend Cadwalader can take me in the motor. Unless you'd like to drive, of course? Now that you're feeling so much better."

His eyes, small and mean, watched her as she fought to keep her expression neutral. The mention of Joe's name had rocked her, but she didn't dare betray her feelings.

"Cadwalader is not my friend," she said. Saint Peter must have felt equally disloyal when he denied Christ.

"I should think not. And yet, from what I hear, you have squandered a great deal of his valuable time in learning how to drive my motor car. It would be a shame for all those hours spent with your Cadwalader to be wasted, don't you think? So I shall look forward to a demonstration of your new skills tomorrow morning. Shall we say ten o'clock? It will make a change for you to have a passenger of your own rank, instead of ferrying your servants about."

Unable to think of an adequate excuse, she nodded assent, her pulse throbbing in her temples with the conviction that he had some nefarious purpose in mind.

His insistence upon referring to "her Cadwalader" made her nervous, but she couldn't tell whether he knew the truth or was only testing her. Surely it wasn't possible for him to know the true nature of her relationship with Joe – not for sure? She was as certain as she could be that no one had ever seen them in one of their few snatched intimate moments. At least, she prayed no one had.

"I trust Charlotte and Eustace are well?" she asked, more out of duty than interest, and to divert Lucien's thoughts onto safer territory.

"They are. As a Cavalry officer, I imagine he will be off to France in the next couple of weeks. He's very much looking forward to it: like any hot-headed young man, he's eager to get some fresh blood on his sword."

The salacious curl of his lip made the gorge rise in her

throat, but she swallowed it down and started picking at the poached salmon the footman had brought.

"Hopefully it will all be over soon, and he will return in triumph long before the wedding."

"Ha! We'll show the Hun what the British Empire is made of. I have no doubt that our soldiers will be in Berlin by Christmas. Don't you trouble your empty head about it; war is not a matter for women." He sighed and tossed his knife and fork down onto his empty plate. "Now, you must excuse me. I have a lame horse to look at. Damned nuisance if we have to shoot the bally thing, it cost a small fortune."

She flinched, remembering how he had killed her own mare. By the time she had gathered herself again, he had heaved himself up from his chair, resting his hands on the table as he stared along its length towards her.

"There'll be no more trips to Paris until this war is over, and I am needed here to ensure the factory produces whatever is needed for the war effort. So I imagine you and I will be seeing rather more of each other in the coming months than we have done of late. We shall start this evening. I must say, my dear, I'm very much looking forward to some time with you after dinner. Now that you are *so* much better."

THIRTY-FIVE
JOSEPH

At ten minutes to ten the next morning, Joe started the engine of the motor car, listening attentively to its throaty growl. It was running perfectly, he noted with the satisfaction he always gained from a job well done. He loved this car, probably even more than its owner did. He had spent so many hours cosseting it, making small adjustments here and there, polishing it until it shone. He had relished the hours talking and working with his son, seeing him learning all the while; and of course the time with Rosamund, observing her confidence budding and blooming like one of the roses in her garden, falling in love with her gentle spirit as much as her desperate need for love that mirrored his own loneliness.

He thought of her as he manoeuvred the car out of the motor stable and into the sunshine of the yard, and it was as if he had conjured her, because that was the moment she rounded the corner of the house dressed in her familiar duster coat and hat, veiled by a long, filmy scarf.

He left the engine running and hopped out to meet her. His bearing was as correct as ever, but he allowed his face to show his feelings, infusing his gaze with all the passionate ardour that filled his heart. He had been so worried after her collapse. To see her dressed for an outing must mean all was well.

But as she came closer it became obvious that something was badly wrong. The smile he found so delightful was nowhere in sight, not even in answer to his own. Her eyes were puffy, grey-smudged and devoid of vivacity or hope. Her lips were thin, pressed together as if holding her emotions in; and with every stiff step something like a wince flickered across her face. Joe's smile faded and his brows drew together in concern.

"What's happened?" he asked in a low voice as she approached.

She shook her head, a small gesture to discourage further questions, but the pain in her eyes told him what he needed to know. God only knew what she had suffered since her husband's return.

His fingers curled into a fist at the thought of it, impotent fury surging in his breast. But before he could speak again, Sir Lucien marched into view. Joe sucked in his breath. Somehow he mustered a courteous nod for the man who paid his wages, then stepped aside as the fat old brute swept past to greet his wife.

"Good morning, my dear," Sir Lucien said, looming over her. "I expected to see you at breakfast, but you were obviously tired after our late evening. Still, I'm glad to see you're on time for our little jaunt this morning."

He chuckled, tipping up her chin with his hand to force her to meet his gaze. Joe saw her attempt to respond with a brave smile and shoved his hands into his pockets, glancing about the yard to look at anything, anything but that beautiful face so filled with despair.

"Now then, this won't do," Sir Lucien went on in that overly jovial tone that Joe found so loathsome. "You are not dressed for driving, my dear. This tiresome hat, that silly veil."

Joe had been staring at his boots, but his head jerked up at the sound of her whimper. His heart jumped in his chest. Fitznorton was untying Rosamund's gauzy scarf, dealing briskly with the bow under her chin. Once undone, he tossed it down into the dust of the yard before tugging at her hat. She put up both hands to stop him, her eyes filling with tears.

Joe watched helplessly, unable to believe Sir Lucien was undressing his wife in the yard, where anyone might see. Every atom of his body urged him to do something.

"Please stop – you're hurting me!" she was saying, putting up her hands to fend him off.

"Nonsense. Let's have that hat off."

She stifled a cry as he pulled hard and it tugged the bun of hair it was pinned to.

"It's pinned, please don't—"

The old man had taken out the pin, and held it up now before tossing it away onto the cobbles, where it lay in the dust with her veil. Next, he cast her hat aside and crushed it under his heel. Her cheeks had flushed, and locks of chestnut hair were tumbling across her face.

Sir Lucien stood back, as if admiring his handiwork, while she pushed her hair out of her eyes with trembling fingers. Joe had never seen her so dishevelled.

"What you need is a proper driver's hat," Sir Lucien pronounced, turning towards Joe. There was triumph in his eyes – and hatred too, Joe realised. "Cadwalader, give me yours."

Joe couldn't refuse the order. Slowly, deliberately, all the while conscious of a muscle twitching in his cheek, he removed his cap and held it out towards his employer. He knew his face must reflect the murderous anger in his heart, but he couldn't try to disguise it.

Having snatched the hat from Joe's hand, the old man squashed it down onto his wife's head. It looked ridiculous perched atop what remained of her pompadour and topknot.

"That's so much better," he said, his tone spiteful. "Now everyone in Pontybrenin will be able to see what a clever little chauffeuse you are."

Her eyes widened. "I can't—"

"Get into the car," came the cold response.

"You can't mean it—"

"Get into the car."

"But—"

"Do as I say, damn you!" he roared, spittle landing on her face with the force of his words. Joe opened his mouth to speak out, but she had already flinched away and clambered into the driving seat. The old man's cheeks and neck were mottled purple, his gloved fists clenching.

Joe's legs twitched as he saw the desperation in her eyes while she fumbled with the controls. He fought the urge to run over to the car and pull her out, take her to a safe place and hide her from Sir Lucien for ever. But he knew only too well that there was nowhere they could go. She cast a final furtive glance his way as her husband climbed into the seat beside her. Her expression was enough to break his heart.

He remained still while she drove off, watching helplessly while the car vanished around the bend and the sound of the engine ebbed away. Still stunned by what he had just observed, he looked around, trying to reorient himself. Stanley was watching, wide-eyed, from the other side of the yard. He bent to pick up the discarded hat, veil and pin, weighing them in his hands before walking slowly back towards his son.

"What was all that about, Dad? Why did Sir Lucien rip off her hat like that? And why did he make her wear yours?" The boy's face was a picture of confusion.

"I don't think Sir Lucien approves of her ladyship learning to drive," Joe managed to say. "Now, take these to Mrs Longford and Miss Dawson, and make sure you tell them what you saw. Tell them all of it, mind – don't leave anything out – because

God only knows what state Lady Fitznorton will be in by the time she gets back. She'll need them to be ready."

THIRTY-SIX

ROSAMUND

Oddly, now that she was behind the wheel of the car and negotiating it carefully along the driveway, Rosamund felt her fear begin to recede. Her husband couldn't physically force her to drive; and he needed her help now, she reasoned, as he was unable to drive the car himself. Recognising that she now had even a small measure of control over her situation gave her the courage to speak calmly.

"What do you suppose people would say if they saw me like this?"

She lifted Joe's hat from her head and laid it down on the leather seat between them, answering Lucien's tetchy grunt with a reproachful look.

"They'll say you're mad, my dear, to go out looking like that."

She shook her head, and saw that this disconcerted him. "No, they won't."

"Of course they will—" he began, but she cut him off.

"No, they won't. They won't think *I* am mad. They'll think *you* are mad. Who but a lunatic would allow a madwoman to drive him around in a car worth eight-hundred pounds? Who would risk his own safety, not to mention his valuable property, by entrusting these to another person, unless he was either quite convinced of their sanity or was insane himself?"

The disbelief on his face made her laugh aloud with a harsh and bitter sound. It felt good to outwit him and to see defeat in his face.

"Don't worry. I have no intention of shaming you. But I do believe it's time to put a stop to this, now that you've made your point. There's a place further on where I can turn the car around. Neither of us should be subjected to the embarrassment of a visit to town today. Not now."

The car rattled along the track, her confidence growing with every yard in spite of the lingering feelings of distress at the humiliation he had heaped upon her in the yard. She knew what she was doing at the wheel. Thanks to Joe and his patient instruction, she knew she could drive well. It was tremendously satisfying to prove it to the man who had underestimated her more than any other.

"What did you imagine you would achieve by learning to drive?" he asked now. There was spiteful anger aplenty in his voice, but at least he hadn't tried to force her to change her intention to go back.

She was silent for a moment, aware that she couldn't tell him the whole truth: that she had recognised driving as an opportunity to escape from him. Nor could she tell him that Joseph Cadwalader's appreciative soft-lashed hazel eyes, together with the faint aura of sadness that clung to him, had drawn her in and made her long to spend time in his company.

"I was bored," she said at last. "I wanted to do more with my time, to learn something new. And I craved the solitude of being able to go out alone, to walk in the woods further from the house." It was true: she had needed a wider horizon around her, where she was not seen as a failure. Driving had given her that and more.

He snorted dismissively but Rosamund, made reckless by a sudden burst of anger and a desire to prove herself, found she didn't care what he thought. What could his opinion matter to her, when he had made his contempt for her so obvious? She found herself asking the question she had held in her mind for years.

"Why did you marry me, when you dislike me so?"

"I wanted a son. The son you have failed in your duty to provide."

The words hurt her more than the disgust in his tone; she swallowed hard, the taste of injustice sour in her mouth. Four babies she had lost, the first after the fall from her horse, but the other three after he had raped and beaten her. Four times, her hopes dying along with each tiny infant. Four times she had lain in the bed that should have been a sanctuary but was more like an arena for acts of violence, sobbing while she bled out another tiny foetus, the terrible cramps in her womb echoing the agony in her heart. It was as if her own body didn't trust her with motherhood, but let go of her babies, let them fall away before she could even have a chance to hold them in her arms or gaze at their tiny faces, count their fingers and toes. She had been weak then, and despised herself for it. But now she found she was tired of being weak.

"You should have found yourself a widow who had already proved herself fertile, and left me to seek happiness elsewhere," she spat, then stopped, stunned by her own lack of caution. She fixed her concentration on the road, her hands trembling as they gripped the wheel to maintain their course. She had to remind herself to breathe.

"Your father offered you to me. You were a ripe little peach, ready for plucking from the bough. I married you to take possession of you," he growled, leaning so close to her ear she could feel the heat of his breath and the faint spray of spittle as he spoke.

"Never forget that you are mine, body and soul, my little bird. The more you struggle to escape, the smaller and tighter the cage you feel around you will become. I would rather see the life choked out of you than relinquish a single inch of you. Make no mistake: today will be the last time you ever drive a motor car. It will be the last time you see your friend Cadwalader. You've tried to make a mockery of me with your cosy little jaunts, but I'll show you where your true loyalties lie. Where did you go with him, eh? Hmm? Where did he take you? Did you fuck him in my car? Did he take you to the cottage where I've housed him and his brats? Or did you go into the woods? Tell me! Did he lift your skirts and tup you like an animal? Did he tumble you on the ground while you spread your legs like a common whore?"

Without warning he grasped a handful of her hair and pulled it hard, twisting it around his fist while she fought to keep her eyes on the road and steer the car straight. Pain and fear made her shriek.

"Stop!" she screamed, panic filling her as his other hand scrabbled at her breast, squeezing it hard enough to leave bruises. She couldn't focus on the road, had to let go of the wheel to fend him off with both hands. His fierce bulk loomed into her side of the car. "Please, stop!"

She felt his teeth on her ear, champing into the tender flesh, and the agony made her vision explode into white nothingness.

She was only dimly aware of the shock of impact, waking after several moments had passed with the wooden steering wheel wedged painfully against her chest. She touched her ear where it throbbed, and her fingertips came away wet and scarlet. Of course. He had torn out her earring with his teeth, and she had lost control of the car.

Dazed, she turned her head and saw him next to her, his eyes glassy.

"Get help," he rasped, lifting a placatory hand as the sound of his voice made her recoil. He repeated the words, and she saw blood on his forehead. He must have banged his head, she thought, still woozy with shock.

The seat underneath her sloped oddly, and now that she was upright her body began to slide along the smooth leather towards him. She grasped the wheel again and held on tightly, the thought of touching him making her want to retch. Fumbling blindly, she grasped the open side of the car and somehow managed to heave herself upwards and out through the window gap. The effort involved in climbing out left her panting, until at last she tumbled onto the ground and scrambled to her feet, stooping with her hands pressed on her thighs to catch her breath.

No wonder it had been such a struggle to get out of the car. The front wheel on the passenger side was in a ditch, buckled and broken, leaving the driver's wheel poised in mid-air. She heard her husband shout and pummel his fist on the windscreen, and took an instinctive step away.

"Fetch someone, you stupid bitch!"

She had crashed his car. His very expensive car. He was trapped now, but he would be furious later. He would make her suffer, of that she had no doubt. It didn't matter that it wasn't her fault, that he had caused her to crash. Flashes of memory were coming back now, moments of pain and terror.

A thought flew into her head, shocking in its fervency. Why could he not have died in the crash? It would have been a measure of justice for his treatment of her, and his reckless disregard for their safety. Her heart should not hold the capacity for such hatred. It would not, if it hadn't been for him.

She took a step backwards, still transfixed by the sight of the car where it rested at an alarming angle in the ditch. He was hollering again, cursing her and demanding she fetch someone.

She would have to do it.

She took a halting step back along the road, dust rising as she scuffed her shoe in the dirt. They must have travelled at least three miles, she estimated. It would take perhaps an hour or more to bring anyone back here, by the time she walked back and got the servants to fetch a horse and cart. She had no water, and her head ached, her torn earlobe throbbing and her scalp sore where strands of hair had been pulled out. She knew she must look a dreadful sight, with blood darkening the collar of her coat and a bruised lump on her forehead like an egg under her skin.

She would not hurry back. She would take her time, walk slowly and carefully in her heeled shoes so as to avoid any further injury. She was dizzy, still shaking from shock. If she fell, he would have to wait longer for help. So she reasoned to herself as she began her slow, unsteady trek back up the track. She couldn't persuade her feet to move quickly because she knew, hoped even, that if she took long enough, there was a chance he might die waiting.

Rosamund trembled at the sound of hoof beats on the gravel outside, the wheels of a cart creaking behind. Her china cup rattled against its saucer and she set it down abruptly, smoothing the fabric of her skirt with suddenly clammy palms. She was conscious of Phelps's hard gaze, his brow creasing as he seemed to be trying to make sense of her behaviour. He and Mrs Longford had been stunned at the sight of her earlier, dishevelled and worn out by the time she stumbled back to the main door of the house.

She had longed for nothing more than to see Joe, but hadn't dared go to him, and she could hardly compromise herself further by asking for him. Her body ached to know where he was, what he was doing, and whether Sir Lucien would survive his head injury to carry out his threat to ensure that she would never see him again. Going to look for him could only endanger him further, so she waited in the library; waited and listened to the ticking of the clock, jumping every time it chimed the quarter hour, tucking the loose strands of hair behind her ears and occasionally moistening her dry lips with a nervous flick of the tongue.

Nellie had wanted to tidy her up, clean the wound on her ear and restyle her hair; but Rosamund had refused.

"I want to know if Sir Lucien is safe," she said, stubbornly refusing to budge from her chair.

Let them interpret her words as they wished. If they sounded like concern, all the better to maintain the impression of a woman who cared for her husband's safety. No one else needed to know that her words were born of fear and a desperate wish for his demise. If she went to her room to rest, he would come to her, and she would be at his mercy. She must stay in the drawing room until she knew if he was alive. He wouldn't dare shout, hit, kick or bite her with Phelps's disapproving face watching from across the room.

The hoof beats came to a stop, and now came the sound of voices outside: raised and urgent, men's deep voices calling out instructions to one another. Her legs twitched with the urge to rise and run to the window, but she steeled herself to remain seated. By the time the library door opened and Sir Lucien stomped in, her handkerchief had been twisted into a tight knot in her lap. Its lacy edging felt ragged against her fingers.

"It took you long enough to send the men, didn't it?" he snarled by way of greeting on his way to the side table where the brandy was kept. His forehead was grazed, with a bump even bigger than her own, but he appeared otherwise unhurt.

The crushing weight of disappointment settled on her chest like a stone.

Unusually, he didn't pause to allow Phelps to serve him, but poured a generous measure for himself, splashing it over the edge of the glass in his haste. He turned and looked at her, making her avert her gaze towards the grate, even though there was no fire burning in it at this time of year. He must have downed the brandy in a gulp: the sound of glugging suggested he was already pouring another. This time he nursed it in his fleshy palm, swirling it before crossing the room to flop into an armchair.

"Thank goodness you are alright," she said for Phelps's benefit. "I was awfully concerned about you when I went for help."

His glare pierced her, fastening her to the chair like a butterfly pinned to a board. He said nothing, but swirled and swirled the brandy in his hand. It glowed like warm amber in the glass. She picked up her cup of tea again and sipped it nervously even though it was now only tepid.

"They'll have to drag the car out of the ditch," he told Phelps. "Bloody female drivers, they haven't a clue what they're doing. I mean it, Phelps: if Lady Fitznorton so much as mentions going out in the motor again, lock her in her room."

She glanced up in time to see the butler's startled expression before he set his face back into its customary arrangement.

"Wait until Cadwalader has sorted out the motor, then give him and his whelp notice of dismissal. I don't want them to work their notice; I want them gone. I trust you have advertised for a new driver, in accordance with my instructions?"

Phelps nodded. Rosamund realised she was staring at him and made herself look away. Tears stung her eyes; she blinked rapidly, taking a deep breath to steady herself.

"That will be all," Lucien said, sending Phelps scuttling

away. She was alone with him again, and it took every ounce of her courage to speak up for Joe as Phelps left the room.

"Is it really necessary to dismiss them?" she asked. Her voice cracked, soft with fatigue and fear. "None of this is his fault. I asked him to teach me to drive; he acted on my instructions. And you've often said yourself, it isn't easy to find a mechanic of his calibre."

"No one is indispensable, however skilled they may be. But you're quite right that this is your fault. Thanks to you, he will lose his position, and the man's family may starve. How old is he? Forty? Forty-five?"

"I've no idea," she lied, feeling cold sweat trickle between her shoulder blades.

"He won't find anything around here, I'll make sure of it. They'll have to move away, and he's old to be looking for a new post without a character reference. Pity he's too old for the army. I imagine the King's Shilling might be more appealing than unemployment, and with any luck he'd end up shot by the Hun. Still, I expect his boy will join up... Now that Kitchener's Minister for War, he's bound to call for volunteers."

"How long will it take to repair the damage to the car?" She tried to keep the fear out of her voice, needing to know how long she had before Joe would be gone for ever.

"Who knows? A couple of weeks, perhaps. You broke the axle, dented the wing; smashed the headlamp... God knows what else you've done with your careless, stupid attempt at driving. By the time the repairs are completed I intend to have another man in the job. Cadwalader should think himself lucky I haven't dismissed him already."

She remained silent, though she could have sworn she heard her heart break. Her hands twisted her handkerchief over and over, in growing agitation.

"Now that I know you're safe, I think I shall go to my room

and rest. It's been quite a trying morning," she said, rising stiffly from her chair.

"A good idea. I suggest you stay there, take luncheon and dinner in your room," he told her. "I'll come up to attend you later. I can imagine how much you will look forward to that." His rictus smile, cold and wolfish, sent a shard of ice through her belly. Silently she left the room and climbed the stairs, conscious all the while of Phelps's eyes on her back. Her husband's words, couched as a suggestion, were in effect an order. He had made her a prisoner.

THIRTY-SEVEN

JOSEPH

It had been a lousy day, Joe reflected as he swept the floor in the motor stable. It had started badly and so far showed no prospects for improvement. He'd woken that morning in a sweat, the cotton sheets sticking to him like fly paper to a bug. He'd kicked them off to relieve the oppressiveness of the clinging fabric and the dreams that had besieged his sleeping brain.

His waking thoughts were always of her: he only had to close his eyes to picture his Rosie before him. Her smile, lighting up her face until he basked in its glow; her breasts, small and firm under the thin layers of her garments. Her long, slender fingers; the vellum-smooth skin of her white hands and the delicate sweetness of her private parts that enticed him like honey. He only had to inhale to imagine the fragrance of her, and how his own smell changed when he touched her, making his flesh reek of desire. His tongue longed for the taste of her, his ears ached to hear her voice. His eyes sought her even when he knew she couldn't possibly be nearby.

But at night, fears filled him. Last night's dream had been particularly bad. He had imagined her with Sir Lucien, writhing with him in the sumptuous bed Joe had laid her down upon. The scenes in his imaginings were fit to drive him crazy. Sir Lucien, monstrous in the nightmare with hard fists, long claws and sharp teeth, feasting on her flesh like a beast. And in the worst moment, the one that woke him with a start and a cry, he saw her eyes close and her mouth fall open in ecstasy, arching her back the way she had done with Joe in the back seat of the car.

He had risen from his bed, splashed his face and torso with soap and water from the ewer on the washstand to cleanse away the madness, then pulled on his clothes to stagger downstairs and out to the garden. It was early yet, the birds making a cacophony of noise as he stepped outside with his trousers unbuttoned to head to the toilet.

There was something wrong, he realised at once: the coop was suspiciously quiet, with no sign of the hens who customarily scratched in the dirt and greeted him with their soft clucks each morning, expecting food. He went straight to the privy, took a long piss, then swept the cobwebs off the walls, knowing how much Dolly hated the spiders that rebuilt their gossamer homes there each night.

Back out in the daylight, he could see what had happened, and picked up the coal shovel to scoop up what he could of the feathers and flesh the foxes had left. He wasn't quick enough: Jack and Miriam tumbled out of the back door in their nightclothes and rushed over to him, their eager smiles dying on their faces as he tried to conceal the hole in the coop and the ghastly mess on the shovel. He knelt in the dust of the yard and caught them in his arms, his little ones, while they sobbed over the loss of the chickens.

"How could the fox be so cruel?" Miriam cried into his shoulder, clinging so hard he had to strain his muscles to stay upright.

Jack pulled away, rubbing his eyes with his fists, and Joe's heart went out to him as he watched the lad suck in his breath and press his trembling lips together in an effort to stop crying.

"The fox must have been hungry, mustn't he, Dad? Maybe he had babies, so he took our hens to feed them?"

Joe nodded, his chin wet with Miriam's tears. He fished his handkerchief out of his pocket and tenderly wiped her face.

"Do you think they were very scared?" she asked, her eyes filling with tears again, and he hurriedly shook his head.

"I expect it was quick," he told her. "Foxes aren't like cats; they don't toy with the birds they kill. It's like Jack said, the fox was hungry. I expect the chickens didn't even realise what was happening until it was too late."

If only adults were as easily comforted as children, he thought. Jack was looking better already.

"Can we get some more chickens, Dad? Can I help you fix the coop good and strong, so the foxes won't get them?"

"I've got to go to work today, but we'll fix the coop on Saturday," Joe promised. Within a few minutes both children were full of plans to get new chickens, debating what to call them and how they would fox-proof the coop.

Joe trudged off to work with a heavy step, quiet and troubled while Stanley chattered about the motion picture he had seen the night before and the football match he planned to go to on the weekend. Joe's mood hadn't improved all morning and was even worse after witnessing Sir Lucien's behaviour towards Rosamund in the yard. When the grooms had sent for him to accompany them to inspect the motor car in the ditch, telling him that Lady Fitz had crashed and walked back to the house looking like a scarecrow with no hat and her hair a mess, blood all over her blouse and a face as dazed as a knocked-out boxer, his heart had threatened to jump from his chest.

He had endured the other men's jokes about his pupil's poor driving and chuckled along at their comments about Sir Lucien's gout and girth, both of which had apparently hampered his efforts to climb out of the car. Standing silently in the road, Joe assessed the damage to the vehicle he loved before sending to a nearby farm for a Shire horse to drag it from the ditch.

Now, back at Plas Norton, waiting for the Wolseley to arrive back for its repairs, his expression was thunderous and his broad shoulders stiff with tension while he swept. He looked up when a shadow fell across the threshold, darkening the patch of floor he was sweeping, and his eyebrows lifted in surprise when he saw that his unexpected visitor was Nellie Dawson, drab in her dark grey maid's uniform.

"I need to speak to you," she said. He stared at her: she looked edgy, thin-lipped and as tense as he was himself.

"What about?" he asked, so curt as to verge on rudeness. The motor was due back soon; he had too much to do to spend what remained of the afternoon gossiping with one of the maids.

She looked him in the eye and he was reminded of his schooldays, and a teacher who had had the extraordinary ability to control a class of fifty children with her glare, never resorting to the cane as the other teachers did.

"I've heard a rumour," she said.

His nostrils flared impatiently. Which rumour was it this time, he wondered – the one about his impotence or the other one, the more accurate and dangerous one that his wife had heard, about him carrying on an affair with Lady Fitznorton?

"I'm too busy to stand around gossiping about stupid rumours." He turned his back, tossed the broom into a corner and began rearranging the tools on his workbench.

"So am I," she said firmly. "But this one worries me. If it's true, my lady will be distraught. I don't want that, and I don't think you do, either."

There was nothing in her face to indicate disapproval or censure, and something made Joe set down his hammer and stalk out of the motor stable behind her. She led the way to a quiet corner, and he raised an eyebrow at seeing her tug a packet of cigarettes from her pocket. She offered it to him; he shook his head mutely and she took one out, tapping it against the box. He noticed, with a sense of alarm, that her fingers trembled as she held the match to light it, and she drew in a great gulp of smoke with her eyes half-closed. He waited with his hands stuffed into his pockets, resisting the desire to tap his foot impatiently, while she blew out a long grey plume.

"Sir Lucien has told Mr Phelps to give you the sack," she blurted out at last, apparently unable to meet his eyes.

He frowned. While the words came as a shock, they didn't surprise him. He had seen the force of the dislike in Sir Lucien's eyes that morning, and knew he was on borrowed time. He thought of Mary and the children, and rubbed his fingers through his hair. God only knew how they would manage now. There'd be no way for him to find work around here. Fitznorton owned the factories, and there were precious few other families with the money to afford a motor car and chauffeur.

"From what I hear, Phelps has already advertised for someone to replace you," she went on. "As soon as they find someone, you and your lad will be told to go."

His lips tightened with the unfairness of it. It was wrong for Stanley to suffer the consequences of his father's actions. But then, what would Mary say? *The iniquity of the fathers would be visited on their children.* He had been naïve to expect adultery to go unpunished.

"Thank you for the warning," he said. "I'm grateful. But I must admit I'm curious to know why you felt you should tell me?"

She took in another drag on the cigarette.

"She'll never cope if you go," she said, her voice tight. She looked at him now, sideways through the exhalation of smoke. "He's determined to drive her mad, you know. I've heard him plotting against her. He wants to declare her insane, have her put away. If that happens, it won't only be you and your boy out of a job, it'll be me as well. And besides, I wouldn't want to see her go through that. He's already put her through more than a body should have to bear."

His heart was thumping, not only with anxiety for Rosamund's state of mind, but for himself. For all he knew, this was a trap to get him to reveal his feelings.

"I don't see why she'd mind me going—" he began, but she cut him off with an impatient huff.

"Don't waste your breath – I'm on your side here. And I'm not stupid; I've eyes in my head. I saw your face when you carried her up the stairs that day; I've seen the difference you've made in her. She'd started smiling, singing even, for pity's sake."

"Probably only because he was away—"

"Not just because of that. Because of you. Think about it, Mr Cadwalader: you and I are her only allies in this world. If we don't help her, no one will."

He held his breath, knowing her words were true.

"What are you proposing?" he asked at last.

Her words tumbled out in a rush, so low he had to lean closer to hear them.

"We've got to find a way to stop him. He's got her shut up in her room: he'll not let her out for fear of her coming to you. He doesn't know anything for sure, but he has his suspicions. So he'll punish her – you do know that, don't you? He'll beat her and he'll have his way with her, and I'll come along in the mornings and run her a bath to ease the bruises, and I'll get the bedsheets changed, and brush her hair, and she'll try to pretend she's alright. But she won't be, and I really don't think she can take much more of it. If it goes on, she really will go mad. She'll end up as insane as he is."

Joe scuffed the toe of his boot in the dust between the cobblestones, dimly aware that his back teeth were grinding together. He was taut with furious energy, wishing for nothing more than to storm into the house and strangle Sir Lucien with his bare hands. He knew there was no question of doing it: his family would lose everything. No, they'd never live down the shame of it; and at his trial for murder, before they sentenced him to hang, questions would be asked about his motive for hating Sir Lucien so passionately. Rosamund would be destroyed along with him. He needed a more intelligent plan.

He could perhaps tamper with the brakes on the motor car, take Sir Lucien out and deliberately crash at speed. But there was no guarantee that the old man would die; and Joe would likely die himself, leaving his dependants with no one to provide for them. And besides, if they found another chauffeur quickly, he might not even get to take his employer out in the car again.

"You've obviously been thinking about it. Do you have any ideas?" he asked. "If I only had myself to consider... but, you know – too many innocent people could get hurt if I was to..." He couldn't bring himself to say the words aloud.

She shook her head. "I don't know what to do yet. I wanted to talk to you. If we both think, perhaps we can come up with something. Perhaps you could take the motor and use it to get her away, if I can get her out of the house with some of her things?"

"I don't know. It's a distinctive car, the only one like it for miles around. We'd be noticed. One telephone call from Plas Norton and we'd have every policeman in a hundred-mile radius looking out for us. The last thing she would need is to be dragged back here by the police." He didn't add that he would be arrested if Sir Lucien accused him of stealing the car.

She stared at him; an appraising stare that made him feel uncomfortable. "That's true. But we need to come up with something, and quickly. There's the babe in her belly to think of."

Her words hit him between the eyes.

"The... what?"

Her cheeks had turned pink. "Don't say a word to anyone. Not even to her. She hasn't realised yet, but I have. I've not had to send any clouts to the laundry for six weeks. It couldn't be Sir Lucien's, now, could it? He was away until a few days ago, and I'm pretty sure he didn't touch her in London. She's too young for the Change. So there's only one explanation. I can help her hide it for a while, but it won't be long before he either guesses or beats it out of her like he did with the others. You'd better put your thinking cap on, Joe Cadwalader, sharpish. You know where I am when you come up with something."

She flung the butt of her cigarette down to the ground and crushed it under her heel. He remained where he was, reeling, stunned into silence not only by this revelation but by her shocking candour. Without a backward glance Nellie sniffed and marched away, disappearing around the corner of the building while he gaped towards her retreating back.

A baby. He put out a hand to steady himself against the wall, then slid slowly down the rough bricks and crouched on the ground, hugging his knees.

A baby. He said the words inside his head, trying to make himself believe it. He thought of Rosamund, that precious, delicate body carrying his child, and was overwhelmed by a surge of protectiveness. He wanted nothing more than to barge into the house, run to her room and carry her off to a place of safety. He could picture it so clearly in his head: the stunned faces of her servants; Sir Lucien caught by surprise, helpless to prevent him. But how could it ever be?

A baby. If she could get through the next few weeks then perhaps she could pass it off as Sir Lucien's, convince him to take more care with her. The evil old bastard had been with her last night – Joe didn't want to think back to the way she had looked this morning in the aftermath. Perhaps, if it could be kept secret for a few more weeks, she could pretend to have conceived then. The baby would be born a few weeks too soon, but sometimes babies did come early.

He thought about the child. It would never be possible for him to be a father to it. He would never hold it in his arms. He would be lucky even to see it if Sir Lucien had his way and he had to move away to find another job. It was like a knife in his heart to know this child of his must never know the truth of its parentage. If it lived, it must believe Sir Lucien to be its father.

If it turned out to be a girl, it might not have too unhappy a life. Fitznorton indulged his daughter, after all, so he might be kind to this one too. And then – Joe's cheeks drained of colour at the thought – if it was a boy, it would one day inherit all this. Plas Norton, the land and the factories would all be his, the little cuckoo in the nest. Joe gasped out a shaky laugh at the absurdity of the idea that one of his children might grow up to be rich beyond his wildest dreams. He'd be educated at the best schools in the land, grow up like Sir Lucien to be a magistrate or even Lord Lieutenant of the county.

But then he remembered Rosamund's quiet shake of the head when he asked her once if she had ever had children. Nellie's words played through his mind, making his blood run cold.

It won't be long before he either guesses or beats it out of her like he did with the others.

He couldn't allow his child's safety to depend on Sir Lucien's credulity. Rosie needed him to find a way to save her, and their baby too.

THIRTY-EIGHT

LUCIEN

Lucien drank steadily all evening. It aggravated his indigestion and his gout, but at least the brandy gave some comfort as he gazed into its warm amber depths and felt the anger in his brain sharpen into clarity.

He was tetchy, sharp-tongued with Phelps when the fool brushed against his foot where it lay propped on a stool. He shouted at the housemaid when she made a noise drawing the curtains. He grumbled to Doctor Sheridan when he arrived to examine the bump and graze on his head.

"Stupid bitch drove straight into a drainage ditch. It's a wonder I wasn't killed. Thank God it's been a dry summer, so it wasn't full of water. Bally motor's a mess, and I'll have to keep that idiot Cadwalader on a little longer to get it fixed up. I don't know what the hell he was thinking of, teaching her to drive. Jumped-up little turd..."

"It might be wise to make that one your last for this evening." Doctor Sheridan nodded towards the glass of brandy and spoke in that calm, counselling sort of tone that Lucien found so irritating. Who did the man think he was speaking to? What was the world coming to? Full of presumptuous idiots who imagined they knew better than their natural superiors.

"I'll be the one to decide when I've had enough," he snapped back.

"Certainly, Sir Lucien. I'm only – well, concerned. After your head injury. And it isn't good for your gout, I'm afraid..."

"I've got the damned gout anyway, whether I drink or not makes no difference! She's the one you need to be looking at, not me. She's the one mad enough to drive into a ditch."

"Was Lady Fitznorton injured?"

"Banged her head, I think. She was knocked out briefly – I kept telling her to get help but she was insensible..." He narrowed his eyes, choosing his words carefully. "Her ear was hurt, too. Must have caught it against something; she ripped her earring out. God knows how she did it."

He made his voice sound despairing, impatient, and shook his head slightly but the throbbing in his temples made further movement seem unwise. He took another sip of brandy and made what small talk he could muster until the doctor picked up his bag with a sigh to go upstairs to examine Rosamund.

Rosamund: that disloyal, beautiful, cold witch. The thought of her made him sweat with anger and desire. She had never loved him, not even at the start when she had been so fresh and sweet she made him want to devour her, to absorb that fragrant youth into himself, body and soul. She drove him to a wild passion that he couldn't slake even when he forced her to submit to his will.

It was her fault. Her lack of regard for him made him feel unmanned. And now, she had turned those limpid chocolate-brown eyes towards someone else. The thought of her spending time alone with Cadwalader made him sick with fury. When Phelps had let slip that she was learning to drive, a cold hard sliver of steel had stuck in his gullet, as surely and as painfully as if she had stuck a knife between his ribs.

He needed to feel powerful again tonight. He would wait until ten o'clock, but no longer. He would sustain his strength of will until then with more brandy, and picture the act over and over in his mind, imagining every brutal detail to bring himself to a peak of excitement before going upstairs to fulfil his desires.

He would relish punishing her for her lack of wifely devotion. She would feel the full force of his displeasure. He'd make her rue the day she ever looked at Cadwalader and dreamed of driving a car. By the end of the night, she would be in no doubt where her duty lay.

THIRTY-NINE

NELLIE

"You'll have to give her five minutes to dress," Nellie insisted to Doctor Sheridan in her firmest voice. She held tightly to the door, standing in the gap to block his view as he tried to peer around her. She had no intention of allowing him to shoulder her out of the way. If he should examine her ladyship, he might detect her condition, and for this to happen so soon would mean ruin for them both. She remained steadfast, refusing him entry until Lady Fitznorton was ready to be seen.

He huffed and squared his shoulders. "Five minutes, then. I have other patients to visit, you know."

She closed the door in his face and turned towards the woman seated in the chair near the window. Lady Fitz's pallor was worse than usual, giving her face a waxy, greyish tinge. Nellie had cleaned the blood off her ear and neck, undressed her and tucked her into a nightdress and wrap. The blue duster coat that had symbolised freedom to travel beyond the limits of her gilded cage was stained reddish-brown at the shoulder, and had been sent to the laundry, but Nellie guessed the damage was irreparable.

She took her ladyship's hand now; to do so still felt uncomfortably intimate, but it was rewarding to see how Lady Fitz always responded so gratefully to any form of kindness.

"M'lady, Doctor Sheridan is here to examine you."

"Oh?"

Nellie felt the slightest nervous squeeze of her fingers, and moved to ensure she could look directly into the other woman's eyes.

"You need to be careful. Remember what he and Sir Lucien are about. If he thinks that your behaviour or demeanour is... well, if he thinks it odd, if he finds anything to cause suspicion to fall upon you, the consequences for you – and for me – could be very serious."

She could see the confusion in the other woman's dark-lashed brown eyes, and kept her own gaze steady to add impact to her words.

"M'lady, let him look at your head, your ear, even the bruises on your arms if you must... But please, I beg you – don't let him examine you anywhere else."

"Why would he expect to...? And why shouldn't he...?"

Nellie sighed and looked at the scrolling patterns on Lady Fitz's robe. Its softness and delicate prettiness echoed the qualities that made her mistress seem both endearing and exasperating to a woman who saw the world in plain and simple terms, as Nellie did.

"He might want to check that you weren't injured in the accident today. And if he sees the bruises on your body, the ones from last night... He might be inclined to look further. You can't allow him to because—"

"I have no wish to display my shame, Nellie. Do you think I want anyone to know what my husband does to me? Do you think I could bear to see the disgust in Doctor Sheridan's face, any more than I can bear it in yours?" Lady Fitz's voice was suddenly strong, though she kept it low for fear of being overheard.

"It isn't only that. I wasn't going to say anything yet, but... Oh, m'lady..." She lowered her voice to a whisper. "Have you not realised?"

Lady Fitznorton's eyes widened, her hands fluttering to her stomach. Her cheeks flared red; she stammered out a denial, but it was muted almost at once. She cast a sharp, wary look in Nellie's direction, obviously afraid of her disapproval.

"It's alright. I won't say a word to Sir Lucien, or to the doctor. We'll wait a few weeks, and then no one will suspect that it was the result of anything but your husband's happy return from London. Only... you will need to be careful for a while. Try not to let him hurt you, the way he did before."

The terrified tears that sprang into the other woman's eyes at this made Nellie regret her advice.

"What should I do, Nellie? If I pretend to be ill, that won't deter him. If I try to fight him off, it doesn't stop him. If I am compliant, it sometimes makes him worse – it's as if he likes to know he has caused me pain. What can I do...?"

Her agitated words were cut off by a rap at the door.

"Compose yourself now. I'll have to let the doctor in."

Nellie tucked the wrap more closely about her ladyship's slender body before moving to open the door. She stood aside and Doctor Sheridan bustled in, clearly impatient at having been kept waiting.

She watched as he expressed surprise over Lady Fitz's torn ear, held up his finger to check her vision, and examined the bump on her forehead. She saw the patient smilingly deny any further injuries, her hands firmly folded in her lap, and spoke up to confirm her ladyship's story. She gripped her ladyship's hand and looked away, feeling sick as the doctor stitched together the swollen, wounded earlobe.

"She appears somewhat faint," he said when he had finished, as if this was surprising, and ordered Nellie to fetch some smelling salts. Once Lady Fitz had revived, he plied her with questions.

How had the accident happened? How had her ear been hurt? What could she remember of events immediately before she crashed? Had she suffered a fit? Had she fainted? Had she been distressed?

Be careful, Nellie thought, casting a warning glance at her mistress.

"I remember so little about it," Lady Fitz said at last, frowning as if trying to recall the events. "My earring must have caught against Sir Lucien's shoulder when I fell against him. That would explain how my ear was hurt, wouldn't it? As for the accident... I think I was startled by something... Yes, that's right: a rabbit ran across the road, and I swerved to avoid it. So silly of me. What on earth was I thinking? Sir Lucien is probably right, I should give up my foolish idea of learning to drive. It was just a girlish whim. I should never have imagined myself capable of it..."

Her voice trailed away and the doctor sighed, seemingly satisfied.

"You must take more care, Lady Fitznorton. Now, it will be safe to pierce the ear again in a few weeks, but not on the scar that will, I'm afraid, inevitably be left. If you're sure you sustained no other injury, I will take my leave."

Lady Fitz's smile was so beautifully charming and her expressions of gratitude so fulsome as he bowed over her extended hand, his cheeks turned pink above his thick gingery whiskers.

Stupid men, Nellie thought as he left. It was always so easy to fool them.

FORTY
LUCIEN

Lucien's vision swam as the library clock chimed nine and he rose to climb the wide stairway, carrying his glass and the heavy crystal decanter of Cognac that had sustained him through the long afternoon. His ancestors watched from the walls while he lurched upwards, resting against the carved wooden handrail at intervals to steady himself and support his weight. The throbbing in his head and his foot made him faintly nauseous, but he wasn't about to let a bit of pain stop him claiming what was his.

Harris was ready for him, smoothly efficient as ever while Lucien puffed and struggled out of his starched collar and shirt, his stiff joints unwilling to co-operate. He carried on drinking, taking deep draughts of the brandy in between the valet's ministrations, to take the edge off the pain in his foot and the tumult in his mind. At last, he was done – wrapped up in a nightshirt and belted robe, and ready to carry out his plan.

His heavy tread made the floorboards creak as he made his way along the corridor, purposeful if unsteady. When he reached his wife's bedroom door, he paused to lean briefly against the jamb, then used the square corner of the decanter he had carried with him to knock on the polished wood. He didn't trouble himself to wait for an answer, but set down his glass on a convenient side table and twisted the brass doorknob. Damn her: it was locked.

He rattled and knocked again, with his knuckles this time. How dare she lock him out? He'd make her pay for daring to imagine she could deny a man his rights.

"Open this door," he said, conscious that his voice boomed along the corridor despite his attempt to lower it.

He heard her behind the polished wood, whining about being tired or some such excuse. He glanced swiftly up and down the corridor to ensure no one was about.

"If you don't open this door at once I will break it down, strip you naked and whip you for all the house to see."

There was a pause, then the click of the key being turned. He opened the door, caught up his glass again and limped across the threshold.

She was standing perhaps eight feet away, eyes huge with trepidation, holding her silk wrap close over her linen night-gown. Her hair had been braided into its customary night plait, long enough to reach past her shoulder blades.

"Take your hair down; I want to see it loose," he said, placing the decanter and glass on the bedside table. He poured another generous measure of Cognac before settling on the bed, leaning against the feminine stack of lacy pillows to warm his glass in his hand while watching her.

The trembling in her long fingers as she pulled the strands of her plait gave him satisfaction. Her fear pleased him; tonight it was so strong, he fancied he could smell it, sharp like the tang of sweat. He waited until her hair hung loose, swinging its heavy dark curtain across her face as she lowered her chin to avoid looking directly at him. Then he smiled over his glass.

"Get undressed."

"I am really very tired," she pleaded, dread etched in the lines around her mouth. "Doctor Sheridan was quite insistent that I should rest after the shock of the accident and the blow to my head."

He took a sip of Cognac, feeling its fiery fingers curl around his gullet on its way down.

"Do as you're told, or it won't be the only blow to your head today."

She opened her mouth to protest again, but the look on his face silenced her and she slipped the wrap from her shoulders.

"You shouldn't look so sullen about it, my dear. Any normal woman would be glad to please her husband."

She held the wrap in front of her, bunching the fabric in her hands while she hesitated.

"And your nightgown. Take it off. Do it with good grace, or I'll wipe that look off your face with the flat of my hand."

He watched as she fumbled with the buttons at her breast and finally, reluctantly, allowed the pure white garment to drop to the floor. He saw the rise and fall of her ribcage as her breathing quickened, the way she shielded her most private parts from him with her arms, and it amused him.

"Well, my dear. Just look at you." He allowed her to make what she would of his words while he took another sip of brandy, savouring its heat in his mouth. He still loved to look at her, to allow his eyes to trace every inch of her flesh before he took her. But it wouldn't do to let her believe herself to have any kind of hold over him.

"Not the pretty, fresh little thing you once were, are you? Getting a little jaded these days – a trifle frayed around the edges, wouldn't you say? Those sweet little titties have begun to droop, and your skin isn't what it was... You used to be such a ripe, juicy little peach. Now you're becoming shrivelled and dry." He shook his head. "You used to please me so easily; just the sight of you was enough. But now, I fear, with your looks so faded and drab, you will need to put more effort into satisfying me."

The look on her face gave him a savage thrill of pleasure.

"What do you mean?" she asked, as if she had to force the words out from behind her teeth.

He sighed. The cushions were plump and soft against his back, his mood mellowing at the knowledge that he would shortly have her complete submission.

"You must understand, a man has base urges. Up to now, I have spared you – out of respect for your position as my wife, and because I have had my little jaunts to Paris to keep me amused. But Paris seems such a long way away now. With the war, who knows when I will be able to travel back there? The girls... Ah, *les Parisiennes*... They would do anything: whatever I wanted. They are so very obliging. But I dare say you will learn to be equally good. While this damned inconvenient war prevents me from engaging in such delights, at least I can still avail myself of your services."

Her face was surprisingly hard, and her voice sharp. She looked him full in the eye, surprising him.

"What possible degradations could you expect that you have not already inflicted upon me?"

He hardened his own voice in response, allowing the mocking tone to fall away.

"Oh, you would be surprised. Some girls dress up and play the man's part. Others like to be spanked with a paddle. Or flogged. Some allow themselves to be gagged and bound far more tightly than I have ever done to you. Some will submit to various... objects. Some are branded; pierced. Still others will drink a man's piss, smother themselves in his shit."

He wheezed, holding his belly as it heaved up and down with laughter at the revulsion in her eyes. It excited him to imagine himself doing whatever he wanted to that slender body, stamping his authority over it and making her cry out helplessly against him.

"Some will take on two, or even three men at once. Not that I would ever be prepared to share my wife with anyone – but we could have someone watch while we perform. Your Cadwalader, perhaps? Or even Phelps. I dare say they both would find such an experience stimulating."

The way the colour drained from her face, lending it a greenish pallor, was like nourishment to him. But he hadn't had his fill of tormenting her yet, not when she made it so easy. "Well, I shall leave such to your imagination. There's no hurry, after all: we shall have many nights to look forward to." He lifted his glass to take another sip, but the Cognac was gone.

"You make me sick." Her voice came out as a whisper.

"Hmmm. I've been thinking about you all evening, deciding how I shall have you tonight."

He watched her intently as his words sank in. They slurred slightly, but he continued regardless. This was the moment he had anticipated with such relish for hours, and he was determined to wring every ounce of enjoyment from it.

"I've decided to have you three ways tonight," he said, before proceeding to describe his intentions in salaciously graphic detail. He had imagined so vividly how he would heap degradation on her to exact punishment for her wilfulness, and the telling of it excited him.

"You're a monster," she whispered when he had finished. "You're depraved."

He had expected tears, objections and outright refusal; had pictured her struggling, and how sweet it would be to enforce his will. As he'd anticipated, there was a tell-tale sparkle of tears in her eyes as she took in the implications of his words. She'd find the pain and humiliation of what he intended for her hard to bear.

But it wasn't a fearful face looking back at him now. To his surprise she looked furious, watching him with a cold and implacable hatred that made him swell and grow even harder. He touched himself with his free hand, imagining himself forcing her, holding her down while she writhed and struggled. She needed a reminder of who was in control.

"You forget," he said, making his voice cool, like a shiver of silk across the skin, "one word from me and Sheridan will have you put away. If you refuse me, I will still take my pleasure tonight in whatever way I please, and then make the call in the morning. Now, come closer. Be a good girl and pour me another."

He held out his glass and she snatched it from his hand, darting out of reach before moving closer to the bedside table. He sat back, entertained by her reluctance to have him touch her. She could put it off, but he'd do all the touching he wanted when he decided he was ready. He was nearly hard enough now.

She picked up the lead crystal decanter and held it, seemingly weighing it in both hands.

"You don't have a choice," he repeated, smiling. But the blazing directness of her gaze as much as the defiance in her next words left him momentarily disconcerted. His hand on his groin lost its rhythm and he sat up a little straighter.

"You're right," she said. "There is only one choice left to me."

FORTY-ONE
ROSAMUND

Rosamund stood for perhaps a minute, perhaps two, rendered immobile as the sudden vicious rush of adrenalin that had galvanised her into action now dissipated and left her limbs trembling in its wake. The decanter still weighed down her right hand. Slowly, as if in a dream, she lifted it up and bit down on the knuckles of her left hand to stifle the bile that rose at the sight of the blood on its corner.

One crashing blow was all it had taken. Sir Lucien lay unresponsive where he had fallen back on the bed, his jaw hanging loose and a trail of spittle dribbling from the corner of his mouth into his beard. His yellowing eyes stared up sightlessly in shocked and sightless reproach, blood trickling into one of them from the deep wound on his temple. Had she really had the strength to do such damage with one blow?

Her teeth began to chatter, and the jerky tempo of her shaking limbs accelerated until she could no longer stand. She sank onto the edge of the bed, staying out of his reach for fear that he might even now wake to threaten her again. What if she hadn't killed him outright? If he recovered, she would be locked away for ever. But if she had killed him, she was no less lost.

In a daze, she looked over at the cord beside the bed, longing to pull it to ring for Nellie. Nellie could tell her what to do. But she remained where she was, her thoughts racing.

If she confessed what she had done, she would be locked up for the rest of her days. The precious baby she now carried would be born in prison or an asylum, and she would never be allowed to hold it or see it again. Her family name would be tainted by scandal, her reputation ruined. She would be universally reviled. No one would accept that he had driven her to it. There would be no sympathy for her instinctive action, taken to defend herself and her unborn child. Even Nellie would think she had gone too far.

Horrified, her gaze was drawn as if magnetised to the corner of the decanter. A clot of blood was stuck to it, and a couple of strands of white hair. No one could ever argue that smashing a man in the face was the right way to act. But then: what had Joe said to her once about violence? *Some men deserved it.*

If any man did, it was Lucien. If she hadn't stopped him, she could have lost this child, like she lost the others.

Perhaps everything would be alright if she could somehow make it look like an accident... She blinked, touching her fingertip to the blood already beginning to congeal on the corner of the decanter. A sweeping glance around the room gave her the answer. Ignoring her nausea and the shaking in her limbs, she took a deep breath and gathered herself to her feet.

Everyone in the household would have known he was drunk. He had been drinking all evening in the library, before bringing the brandy upstairs. The alcohol, combined with the blow to his head earlier, and his painfully swollen toes, had made him unsteady on his feet. Pressing firmly to ensure she wiped it all off, she slid her trembling fingers over the gobbet of blood and hair on the decanter, then smeared it onto the chamfered corner of the cornice on top of the heavy mahogany tallboy. It was close enough to the bed to make it seem plausible that Sir Lucien could have stumbled and fallen, hitting his head on it.

The rich crimson stain on her fingers made her shudder and retch. She dashed to the bathroom to wash her hands, then remembered the decanter, fetching it to rinse and dry the heavy crystal before setting it down on her bedside table again. Her husband's body still hadn't moved. His mountainous bulk was grotesque where he lay on the bed, his flaccid genitals exposed where his dressing gown had fallen open. She should probably cover him. But then, what had he ever done to deserve to be afforded dignity?

He was already starting to turn pale, and it occurred to her that she should call someone before it became obvious that she had left him dying on her bed without troubling herself to assist him. She felt a strange sense of calm now that she was sure he wasn't going to wake up, but somehow she would have to put on a show of shock. Realising she could hardly call for Nellie in her naked state, she reached for her nightgown and tugged it over her head, feeling like an actress donning a costume. With an increasing sense of unreality, she caught the bell pull in both hands and tugged on it.

She would have to give the performance of her life.

FORTY-TWO
NELLIE

Nellie groaned at the sound of the bell summoning her to her mistress's room. What was the matter, that couldn't wait until morning? It rang again as she swung her legs out of bed, the iron bedstead creaking in complaint, and again as she rose to slip her arms into her dressing gown. Her heart rate quickened. What on earth had happened? It wasn't normal for it to ring more than once.

She knocked on Mrs Longford's door on her way down from the attics to Lady Fitznorton's room.

"Something's wrong," she said. "Her ladyship's bell keeps ringing."

She didn't wait for the housekeeper to follow, but hastened down the back stairs and through the green baize door, along the corridor to where light spilled from Lady Fitz's open doorway. Her ladyship was waiting, jumpy with agitation. There was blood on her nightgown, and her words came out in a stammering rush.

"It's Sir Lucien," she said. "He fell. He had been drinking. He stumbled when he tried to get up for the bathroom and hit his head on the tallboy. I think... Oh, Nellie! I think he must be badly hurt."

Nellie gaped, disbelieving, then stepped into the room. The bed was rumpled, and Sir Lucien lay motionless upon it, gazing up sightlessly towards the pleated canopy with blood congealing around a deep gash in his head. She cast a swift, appraising glance back at Lady Fitznorton just as Mrs Longford entered the room behind them.

"Oh, Mrs Longford!" Lady Fitznorton clutched at her arm. "Sir Lucien has fallen. He hit his head on the corner of the tall-boy, there. And when I tried to get him up, I could see he was bleeding."

She spread her hands and Mrs Longford blanched at the sight of the blood darkening her nightgown. There was more on the tallboy, Nellie saw. She felt her stomach heave and steeled herself to touch the old man. *Strange*: his wrist already felt cool under her fingers as she felt for a pulse.

There wasn't one. She suspected there hadn't been for a little while. Odd that Lady Fitz hadn't called for help sooner, while he was still warm; and that he had fallen backwards onto the bed, not forwards onto the floor when he stumbled. Her mouth twisted at the sight of his exposed genitals, and she cast about for something to cover him, settling on Lady Fitz's wrap.

"You had better sit her ladyship down," she murmured to Mrs Longford, a strange thrill of excitement unfurling in her breast at the realisation that the brute was, indeed, no more. "There's nothing we can do for Sir Lucien now. But Lady Fitznorton must try to remain calm."

Nellie would have to be careful, mustn't let on about the baby just yet. She was acutely aware that this kind of shocking event might be risky to her ladyship's already fragile health. Especially if it hadn't come about in quite the manner her ladyship had described.

Mrs Longford nodded and ushered Lady Fitz to the chair,

her hands flapping. "There, there," she said, as if soothing a child. "You sit there, m'lady. We will send for Mr Phelps; he'll know what to do. Upon my soul, what a day."

Nellie poured a small measure of Cognac from the decanter on the bedside table and crossed the room to press the glass into Lady Fitz's trembling fingers.

"Drink this, m'lady. It will make you feel better."

But the unexpected violence of Lady Fitz's reaction left both Nellie and the housekeeper stunned. She recoiled, batting the glass away and sending it bouncing onto the carpet, the spilled Cognac darkening the front of her nightgown even more. With her mouth covered by her hands, she fled to the bathroom and there threw up over and over, filling the room with the sound of retching and the acid smell of vomit, until there could be nothing left inside her.

The two servants exchanged looks of surprise, eyebrows raised.

"Well," said Mrs Longford, bending to pick up the glass before setting it carefully down next to the decanter. "We had better fetch Mr Phelps and get him to call Doctor Sheridan. Sarah can deal with the carpet in the morning."

Nellie thought quickly. If the doctor came too quickly, might suspicions be aroused? It wouldn't do for anything to go wrong for her ladyship.

"We can't leave him as he is," she urged, before the housekeeper could depart. "He's..." she mouthed the words *not decent*.

The other woman grimaced in distaste.

"Help me with him. We can clean him up, get him laid out nicely on the bed and make sure he's properly covered. We owe it to him to preserve his dignity before anyone else sees him."

Between them, dragging him by the armpits with all their combined strength, they somehow managed to heave him higher up the bed and drop his head onto a pillow. By the time Lady

Fitznorton emerged from the bathroom, pale as a phantom, they had pulled down his nightshirt and rearranged his robe before tucking the eiderdown over him. His folded hands rested on it, waxy against the rich plum silk.

"There," Nellie panted at last, taking a handkerchief from her dressing gown pocket and wiping her brow with it. "If you want to fetch Mr Phelps now, Mrs Longford, I'll get a cloth and wash the blood off Sir Lucien's face. No, no – I insist. I dare say it's the last service I'll ever perform for him."

Mrs Longford nodded, clearly grateful to be spared any further contact with their employer's corpse. She scurried from the room, leaving Nellie facing Lady Fitznorton.

"Oh, Nellie..." her ladyship began, her lower lip trembling. She sank back into the chair as if her legs were about to give out, and buried her face in her hands.

On impulse, Nellie rushed across the room and seized the other woman in a fierce hug that surprised her as much as it seemed to surprise Lady Fitz.

"Hush now, m'lady. There's only one thing that matters now, and that's that you're safe. You're safe at last."

FORTY-THREE

JOSEPH

Mary leaned against the door jamb with her arms folded. "How very convenient for her, to have her husband die all of a sudden, like that. She'll have as much freedom as she wants now to go driving about the countryside, with or without you. If she can keep that great big motor car on the road instead of in the ditch, of course."

Joe picked up a piece of wood to measure it against the chicken coop, stubbornly refusing to look at his wife's bitter face. Deliberately taking his time, he marked a line with the pencil he kept tucked above his ear.

"It's convenient for us too, remember?" he remarked. "There was talk amongst the staff that he was planning to give me and Stanley the push. I heard he got Phelps to put out an advertisement for a new driver, but she's told him to decline any applicants and keep us on. At least our jobs are safe for now, with him out of the way."

Picking up his saw, he rested the length of wood on the garden wall and began to cut, enjoying the rhythmic move-ment of his arm muscles. He had always liked working with his hands, making something that served a useful purpose. If he hadn't found horses so fascinating as a youngster, he might have followed in his father's footsteps and become a carpenter instead of an apprentice coachman. Even now, after all these years and his training as a mechanic, he still found wood-working almost as satisfying as fixing engines.

"Don't you find it funny, though?"

His sour backward glance only silenced her temporarily.

"I mean, in the morning he makes a fool of her, then she crashes his car, and by midnight he's dead on her bed."

Joe threw down his saw and rounded on her in disgust.

"What are you suggesting, Mary? Are you saying she murdered him for pulling her hat off in the yard? You've lost your mind if you think so."

She rested a hand on one hip and tilted her chin, one eyebrow raised as she watched him.

"Stranger things have happened."

"Have you seen her? Did you ever get a look at him? She's as thin as a twig. Her wrists are no thicker than young Dolly's, and I'd be surprised if she weighs much more than her. Sir Lucien would have been more than twice her weight. He used to fill the passenger side of the car; he had to be – what? – six-foot-two and twenty stone, at least. He was a nasty, gouty old man who drank himself into a stupor that day and fell over on his way to take a piss. The only thing I find strange is how he even managed to make it up the stairs to her room."

"You seem to have a very precise idea in your mind of how tiny and delicate she is."

He wiped the sweat off his forehead with his sleeve and turned his attention back to the coop.

"Haven't you got anything else to do?" he asked, weary of her needling. Everything he'd said, and she'd latched onto that.

He popped a couple of nails between his lips and was glad to have a reason to remain silent as he worked, hammering the nails vigorously into the wood one by one. He was conscious of her gloomy presence behind him for several minutes before she finally turned on her heel and stalked back into the house.

His shoulders sagged with relief. Every moment with his wife made him long all the more for Rosamund, who was now, thrillingly, free from the shackles of her marriage. It was all he could do to keep himself from running to her. He knew the way through the big house to her room, and closed his eyes against the mental picture his brain kept conjuring of his feet mounting those wide stairs, his lovely Rosamund falling into his arms at the top with her hair all loose over her shoulders, like one of the actresses swooning onto her beau in the films he and Mary used to watch at the picture house.

How he and Mary had enjoyed those evenings out at the pictures, snuggling together in the plush seats, and then the walk home afterwards when she would tuck herself under his arm as if there was nowhere she'd rather be. His mouth twisted at the memory. There was precious little pleasure to be found in Mary's company these days. It was growing increasingly difficult to remember a time when he had even liked her, let alone felt affection for her. She was shrewish, judgemental and quick to criticise. Even the children were not immune from her peevishness. While Joe understood her unhappiness, it rankled with him when she took it out on the little ones.

The atmosphere at home was thick with their mutual dislike, and he knew by their stony expressions at meals that Len, Stanley and Maggie found it uncomfortable. They were old enough to be aware of it, of course; not children anymore. It seemed no time at all since they were small, yet here they were, young adults and earning a wage. Leonard, the eldest, had talked of getting engaged to Jenny, his sweetheart, and might have a home of his own by next summer if she accepted him. Joe could only hope that his son would make a better job of marriage than he had done.

His thoughts turned to the younger ones. At twelve, Dolly

would soon be leaving school and Teddy wouldn't have many more years of education before he, too, would be making his way in the adult world. Thank goodness for six-year-old Jack and little Miriam: they were still small, fun, and eager to please.

He didn't dare think too much about the two infants he had lost, or the other one, the unborn baby he could never call his own. As far as he knew, it still clung to life. He was sure Nellie Dawson would have told him if it were not so.

He hadn't seen Rosamund since yesterday morning in the yard when she had looked so utterly dejected. He yearned to see her, to touch her and to reassure himself that she was in good health. He knew she would feel no sense of grief at her husband's death, only relief that she need no longer live in fear. It was a relief Joe shared, especially as it absolved him of any responsibility to take action on her behalf. He had racked his brains after his conversation with Nellie, testing out endless scenarios in his mind and rejecting every one as impossible. The unexpected demise of Sir Lucien had let him very neatly off the hook.

He could only hope that other folk would be less cynical than Mary, and would accept the doctor's verdict on the cause of Sir Lucien's sudden accidental death: a fall due to a surfeit of alcohol and an earlier head injury. It wasn't clear from what Joe had heard whispered over lunch in the servants' hall whether the old man had died of a stroke before he fell, or whether his broken skull had killed him. It was immaterial: all that mattered to Joe was that his lovely Rosie was now safe. While it hurt him to know that she must stay out of reach for the time being, it was easier for a man to live with sadness than helplessness. Perhaps one day, when enough time had elapsed for any hint of scandal to die down, they could be together.

The coop was finished by teatime, and after everyone's hunger was satisfied he took the four youngest children with him to the home farm to buy some chickens. It was late in the evening by the time they had walked there and back and settled their squawking acquisitions into the newly reinforced coop.

Miriam insisted on saying an inaugural prayer over it, calling upon God to bless the work of her father's hands. While she prayed in her childish innocence, Joe looked up to the heavens and wondered.

He had lied to Mary. He had wished another man dead, coveted another man's wife. He had committed adultery, not only in his dreams almost every night, but shamelessly, in reality, on several occasions over the course of recent weeks. What right did he have to expect any blessings? Yet he felt no regret. How could he ever be sorry for having known Rosamund's gentle touch, the sweetness of her kisses? He would never forget the sweep of her lashes against her cheek; the softness of her voice when it caught in her throat, snatched into silence by his lovemaking. The memories of her underneath him, gasping his name against his ear, gazing at him with that intently wondering, steady look that told him she had feelings for him almost as deep as his own passion for her.

Miriam finished her prayer and squeezed Joe's callused hand with a smile as pure and fresh as clear spring water.

"We're done, Dada. These chickens will be safe from the fox now, you'll see."

He bent to kiss the top of her head, and was surprised to feel a tear roll down the length of his nose.

May your childish faith be rewarded, he thought as he pressed his lips into her soft, honey-and-brown curls. He had no expectation that his prayer would be answered, any more than God had answered his prayers for Annie or Alfie. It was too late for that kind of hope. Joe's own faith had long since left him.

FORTY-FOUR

ROSAMUND

It was only natural, Rosamund supposed, to dread the prospect of seeing Charlotte. One could hardly murder a man, even in self-defence, and then feel entirely at ease with his daughter.

In the long hours of the night she had been plagued by terrifying dreams. In the first, she was being dragged onto a gallows, a rough rope noose forced over her head to choke the life from her until she woke, gasping and clutching at her throat. In the next, she was hitting her husband with the decanter, smashing a great hole in his skull until splinters of bone and brain spattered her face, whilst still he came at her to force himself upon her. In the last one, he rose from his prone position on the bed to strangle her, taking his revenge for her extemporaneous act of violence.

When she awoke in an unfamiliar bed in the largest guest room, she could still smell the foul scent of cigars and alcohol that had characterised him. She still imagined she could see his blood on her fingers, the blood that she had so deliberately smeared onto the mahogany tallboy to conceal her guilt. There was no question of her ever returning to sleep in the room that had been both her torture chamber and the scene of her crime. She couldn't bear to spend another minute there, or to look upon those furnishings again. Nellie could arrange the transfer of her clothes and trinkets later, when she had finished ordering a suitable wardrobe of mourning garb.

The valet, who had undressed Sir Lucien and helped him into his nightshirt and robe before his final visit to Rosamund's room, had confirmed his employer's state of tottering intoxication, so Doctor Sheridan, arriving near midnight, had been easily taken in by Rosamund's careful recounting of the events leading up to Sir Lucien's 'accident'. One grim glance at the wound and the blood on the tallboy had been enough to convince him.

She could only assume that the stench of stale alcohol from the corpse laid out in her bed, together with the physician's earlier visit to examine their injuries, had lent plausibility to her story. He had shaken his head, as if somehow this kind of thing had been bound to happen, and offered her his condolences, as well as something to help her sleep. Perhaps the laudanum had been the cause of her tempestuous dreams. She would refuse it in future. Better to lie wakeful with her mind racing with terrible memories than to experience those horrors again.

In the morning, her relief at remembering herself free at last was tempered by a crushing sense of guilt, and the fear of anyone guessing the part she had played in Sir Lucien's demise. She had committed the worst possible crime. She, who had always despised violence of any kind, had been transformed into a murderess. However frightened and despairing she had been, she had no right to end a man's life. Not even when that man was a depraved and vicious bully who surely deserved all the punishments hell could devise.

The death of her husband should have enabled her to live without a constant cloud of oppression hanging over her. It would, but the means by which her freedom had come about meant she would have to find a way to live with the weight of her sin – or find a way to atone for it. And somehow, she must find a way to face her stepdaughter, who had been summoned from London and would be arriving tomorrow afternoon.

Charlotte arrived with her aunt Blanche, whose long face grew even more sepulchral at the sight of her brother laid out in a casket on the dining room table. Rosamund had ventured from her new room for the first time, her head still throbbing dully from the accident in the car. Her ear burned yet, a reminder of Sir Lucien's viciousness. She couldn't look at him now, stately in his coffin. They would have neatened up the wound, of course, or brushed his hair over it. Nevertheless, she never wanted to set eyes upon anything connected with his person again.

"You saw it happen?" Blanche demanded in her customarily peremptory tone.

All at once, Rosamund was tired of being spoken to in such a fashion. After everything she had suffered at the hands of the most senior Fitznorton, she was not about to accept humiliation at the hands of her sister-in-law. She turned on her heel and marched to the drawing room, where she took a seat beside the window, folded her hands calmly in her lap, and gazed towards the immaculate lawns outside.

"Answer me!" Blanche had followed, apparently outraged at being ignored. It was more than likely the first snub she had encountered in many a year. "Tell me what happened!"

Rosamund tilted her head, taking her time before responding.

"My husband died. In my room. Half-naked, inebriated and unsteady on his feet, he met with an accident that stoved his head in. Yes, I did see it happen. And yet you ask me to relive that moment?"

Shock registered in her sister-in-law's eyes. Whether this was due to the unexpected details of her brother's passing, or the equally unanticipated challenge in Rosamund's tone, it was impossible to tell.

Charlotte, drifting in her aunt's wake, gasped aloud and pressed a black-edged handkerchief to her mouth. She stumbled towards another chair and sagged into it as if the wind had been knocked from her lungs, then whispered to no one in particular: "I can't believe it. My Papa. How can he be gone?" She rocked as if utterly bewildered, and for the first time in years, Rosamund pitied her.

Rosamund rose wearily, crossed the room and crouched at her stepdaughter's side. "My dear Charlotte, I am so terribly, terribly sorry," she said, breaking off as her throat seemed to close over.

A vision of Sir Lucien's leering face flashed into her mind; she recalled his astonishment as she swung the decanter, her own flaring fury blinding her into madness. She hung her head, unable to say more for fear of betraying herself.

With a shove, Charlotte sent her sprawling onto her back and leapt up to stand over her, clenching her fists and shrieking out wild accusations. Her young face was crimson and contorted with rage.

"You wanted him dead! The whole world knows you hated him. You've been biding your time, wishing he was out of the way so you can live your stupid, mad life without him. For all we know you did it – he always said you were not quite sane. You could have pushed him, or drugged his drink, or goaded him – anything! It should have been you in that coffin, not him!"

Blanche had hold of Charlotte's arm now, almost wrestling her into submission as she remonstrated with her, while Rosamund, hampered by her long skirt, scrambled up from the floor and dusted herself off. Her heart pounded, her mind still stunned by the suddenness of the attack, when Phelps appeared in the doorway, his small porcine eyes round with curiosity.

"Phelps, would you send to the kitchen for some strong, sweet tea? Miss Charlotte is understandably distressed." Rosamund had spoken more sharply than usual, and was gratified to see him scuttle off out of sight. She moved to the French doors, well out of reach of any further blows, and gathered herself.

To her surprise, Blanche had leapt to her defence, her wrinkled cheeks scarlet with embarrassment. "Come to your senses, you foolish girl! You owe your stepmother an apology. To behave so, and in front of the servants!"

"I will overlook your behaviour on this occasion, Charlotte," Rosamund said. "You're overwrought, and little wonder. But I must insist that you withdraw those scurrilous remarks and accusations. Reflect on your words, and I trust that when you are calm, you'll be able to think more rationally."

"You won't get a penny!" Charlotte wailed through impotent tears. She shook off her aunt's restraining hands and pointed in the direction of the door. "Plas Norton is mine now, and for all that Papa tolerated your presence in it, I won't. I'll give you until the day after the funeral to pack your belongings and get out, not a day longer."

"Really, Charlotte!" Blanche sent a half-apologetic, half-embarrassed look Rosamund's way, but it seemed that this time there would be no words offered in Rosamund's defence.

There was nothing left to say. She wouldn't be sorry to see the back of this house. Drained of all her energy, Rosamund paused before the doorway to let Phelps enter with the tea tray.

"You should have given him a boy, if you'd wanted any right to stay," Charlotte said spitefully, over her shoulder.

It was a remark that still had the power to hurt, given the babies Rosamund had lost. But it dawned on Rosamund, standing there alone, with all three pairs of eyes watching her with varying degrees of dislike, that Charlotte had inadvertently given her a way to reclaim her dignity.

"My dear girl," she said, summoning the merest hint of a smile and resting a hand on her belly, "for all any of us knows, I might yet do just that."

Rosamund's life in the Dower House was beginning to settle into a kind of rhythm now that the first month of work was done. Room by room, the decorators were transforming its gloomy walls, removing all evidence of her former mother-in-law's tastes. Even with the windows thrown open, the house stank of paint, turpentine, and new carpets, but at least it was a fresh smell, one that served as a daily reminder of how different her life was now.

Never had she had to make so many decisions. She'd never been allowed to choose her own décor when her husband was alive, but in the past few weeks she and Nellie had scoured catalogues and even ventured by train to the Howells and David Morgan department stores in Cardiff to choose furnishings for her new home. Sometimes she felt almost lightheaded from the whirlwind of change and decision-making, but giddy in a joyful way, far removed from the old sense of panic that had blighted previous years. She had been so accustomed to her clipped wings, the feeling of spreading them to fly was still alien – but they grew stronger day by day as she pushed herself beyond the limits of her previous insular world.

Despite occasional sleepless nights due to vivid dreams, she was enjoying life, and having the freedom to do so felt like a gift. She had avoided any involvement in the arrangements for Sir Lucien's funeral, more than content to leave it to Blanche, and she had surprised herself by coping well with the stream of visitors who had come to pay their respects. The bishop's wife and the Lady Mayoress had even suggested that she might like to join their committees, once her period of mourning was over, and she had found herself smiling and looking forward to the prospect of being useful.

As a new widow, she had been kept busy with correspondence from acquaintances and strangers offering their condolences on the sudden and tragic loss of her husband. Of all the letters she had received, the one spread out on the desk in front of her now was certainly the most surprising. She spread out the thick, embossed creamy white paper and leaned her chin on her hand, taking a moment to appreciate the elegant penmanship before reading it a second time. This time, she would take it slowly and allow the words to sink in. They had taken her back in time to a period of her life that afforded such golden memories, she wanted to linger there.

Dear Madam,

Having read your late husband's obituary In *The Times*, I felt I must write to extend my sympathies to you. I understand only too well the terrible grief of the sudden passing of a spouse. One feels at such a loss; rudderless, even, and most especially when the desire to share a memory or an idea must be left unfulfilled, as the dear one is no longer there to add their own recollections or insights to enrich one's own. Please accept my sincere condolences.

You may be unaware of our connection, since we have not

had an opportunity to meet. In the autumn of 1897 I purchased Ambleworth Hall and its contents from your brother, and I have lived here most contentedly ever since moving from America to take up residence.

Despite the sad nature of the circumstances of tracing you, as a result of your being mentioned in your late husband's obituary, I confess I am glad to have found you. I have been seeking the former Miss Rosamund Pelham for some time, after discovering something of personal significance belonging to her late father amongst his collection of books. Forgive me for not sending it with this letter, but my chief concern is to establish that you are indeed said lady before entrusting anything so precious to the services of the Post Office.

If you are able to reply to this letter confirming your identity as the former Miss Pelham, daughter of the fifth Baron Ambleworth, then I would be delighted to forward it to you.

Your obedient servant,
    Ewart Rutledge III

It was extraordinary. No one had referred to her by her former identity as Miss Pelham in seventeen years, and now this stranger had evoked a vision of her previous happy life with a few words in a letter. Like a spell, his missive had conjured the warm sandstone, the rambling ivy, and fragrant roses of Ambleworth. Her mind revelled in memories of the soft Yorkshire rain and the smell of dust on old books, their foxed pages and tooled leather bindings giving no clue as to the wondrous tales waiting within.

What could she tell this stranger, to convince him to share whatever precious item he had in his possession, this unnamed thing that had been personal to her beloved father and yet hidden away for so long? She cast her mind back to her girlhood. She could describe the Hall's carved panelling, perhaps, or the priest hole; but anyone might be aware of those from reading a tourist's guide. She had to think of something that could only be known by someone who had lived there.

She picked up her fountain pen and refilled it from the silver-topped inkwell on her desk before composing her thoughts and beginning her reply.

Dear Mr Rutledge,

How kind of you to take the time and trouble to contact me. Your condolences are gratefully accepted...

Her eyebrow quirked at the irony, given that the loss of her husband was a cause for celebration rather than mourning. Still, appearances must be maintained, and judging by his letter, his own bereavement was keenly felt after the loss of his wife. She pictured an old man, a trifle eccentric, like her father, and perhaps still dressed in the styles of years past: long, white hair and a Turkish robe and slippers. He would smell of snuff and have fingers stained black with ink.

His words had told her he was kindly, and she imagined he might be a little unworldly, like Papa had been, so absorbed in his research that he paid little attention to his appearance or everyday practicalities like eating at regular mealtimes. Perhaps there would even be a trace of egg yolk on the front of his waist-coat. Smiling at her own absurdity in allowing her mind to indulge in such fantasies, she reapplied herself to her writing.

I confess I am intrigued to know more about the personal item you mention. I have a few of the less valuable books that belonged to Papa, and some photographs, but very little else to connect me to my family. I have considered sending one of those photographs as proof of my identity, but the possibility of its loss in the mail was too great a risk, so I hope you will be convinced by some of my recollections of life at Ambleworth Hall.

Does the portrait of my great-grandfather still hang beside the doorway in the dining room – the one of him as a young boy with a fishing rod, the tail of a perch poking from the top of his wicker creel? The Hall is just visible in the background, but if you look closely you will see that the artist was careless and missed out two of the windows on the south front. The error irritated my father, who was meticulous in his own endeavours, and expected the same attention to detail from others.

What else might I tell you? The third step on the main stairs creaks unless you tread on the far left. The boiler is unreliable and rarely sends any warmth to the bedrooms upstairs, yet the dining room gets stiflingly hot. The windows on the west side of the house have a habit of sticking on wet and windy days, due to the rain blowing against the frames.

My favourite part of Ambleworth was the rose garden, which was planted under the auspices of my mother. It is a source of sorrow to me that I have no memory of her, but I always felt closest to her there, and have inherited her passion for roses. At Ambleworth, the rose beds were underplanted with lavender which was dried and used to fragrance the rooms in the house. Whenever I smell lavender now, I have only to close my eyes to be transported back there.

Does the obelisk still stand at the end of the Camellia Walk? You probably know that the body of my grandfather's horse, Figgis, lies beneath it. Figgis saved Grandpapa's life at the Battle of Balaklava, and came home with him, living for another twenty years. We Pelhams were always fond of our animals. Have you noticed the small brass plaques attached to stones near the Cedars of Lebanon? They mark the resting places of our beloved dogs,

including my spaniel, Remus, and my father's Gordon
setter, Cato.

Please accept my grateful thanks, not only for your kind
good wishes, but for bringing such cherished memories so
freshly and vividly to my mind. My girlhood at Ambleworth
Hall was a golden period in my life, one I remember with the
greatest joy.

Yours very sincerely,
    Rosamund Fitznorton (née Pelham)

Less than a week later, a package arrived bearing a Yorkshire
postmark and the distinctive handwriting of the mysterious Mr
Rutledge. Excitingly, its size suggested he had accepted her
letter as evidence of her identity, and had sent the personal item
to which he had referred in his previous letter. Rosamund cut
the strings with her paper knife, then tore open the brown
paper, eager to see its contents. Inside, a letter lay atop a
battered leather-bound book. Tempted to examine the book
first, her fingertips rested on it for a heartbeat; but she found she
wanted to draw out the moment, so unfolded the letter. She
found herself smiling at the words written in the unusual, bold
hand.

My dear lady,

I hope when you open the contents of this package that you
will forgive any excessive caution on my part in my letter of
last week. What a delight to know that your recollections of
Ambleworth Hall have been a comfort to you in your time of
grief! It is indeed a place that inspires a great sense of peace.
Whenever I must leave it, my mind can never be truly at rest

until I return. Luckily my son already feels as I do, and even at the age of fourteen years he shows a keen interest in his history lessons at school – so I trust the estate will be in safe hands when one day it passes to him.

As an Anglophile and antiquarian since I was old enough to read, I was delighted to have the good fortune not only to move to this corner of Yorkshire from Boston, Massachusetts, but also to take over the responsibility of caring for your late father's collections. Please be assured that I treasure them and have dedicated the past sixteen years to their preservation. I see myself not as their owner, but as their custodian, and have made it my life's work to keep them safe for future generations. The repairs undertaken to the Hall in recent years have been carried out with more concern for its history than for modern fashions. I hope you would approve.

As well as the house and its contents, I consider myself blessed to be able to enjoy the gardens, and my chiefest delight is the rose garden, so it was most gratifying to learn that this was your mother's design and also dear to you. The lavender is still here, and still used for the purpose you described. I am indeed familiar with the plaques you mentioned near the cedars, and have continued the tradition by laying my old Sancho to rest there.

You may already have opened the book enclosed – if we can still call it a book. As it was not a rare volume, for many years I did not trouble to open it, and so the contents remained hidden within its binding until I had an auctioneer visit last summer to value the house and contents for insurance purposes. He was most scrupulous when taking his inventory, and it was he who realised that the book was not what it first appeared, but that the pages were missing and in their place was a package of letters written by your mother to your father, and a copy of your father's Will. No doubt you are already familiar with the latter, as you will have given your permission for Holly Cottage to be sold along with the rest of the estate, but I feel it is only right to send it on to you along with the letters...

Rosamund frowned and read the last line again. What did he mean about Holly Cottage? She remembered it well: not really a cottage, but a modestly sized house with large windows and a sunny aspect. The gamekeeper had lived there in her grandfather's time, but later on her mother used it as a painting studio, and then her father rented it out to a respectable family. Why would she have had to give permission for it to be sold?

She undid the twine that had been bound around the book, and opened it. Sure enough, out fell a bundle of letters, yellowed with age and tied with a blue ribbon; and a separate document, one she had never seen before: Papa's Will. The back of her throat burned with emotion as she laid her fingertips on his spidery signature, then dabbed at her eyes with a handkerchief and blew her nose. So many years since she had seen it. It was easy to picture him writing it at his desk piled high with books and stacks of papers.

Curious, she scanned the contents of the document until she found the first mention of Holly Cottage. The words leapt from the page. *He had left it to her.*

Had she known, in those traumatising early days of her marriage, she could have gone there. Dropping the paper, she slammed her palms onto the surface of the desk, hard enough to make them sting. For all those wretched years, caged within the walls of Plas Norton, enduring abuse and degradation in the belief that she had nowhere else to go, she had owned a house. She scrubbed her face with her hands, her breathing ragged as she held back a tide of frustrated rage.

For a while she allowed herself to picture how different her life might have been if she could have escaped to her own Yorkshire bolthole. She could have lived quietly, in peace and contentment, instead of suffering years of torment. But at last, she shook herself. Like picking at a scab, ruminating on *if only* could do her no good.

Her heart sank as she re-read the last paragraph of the letter. Confusingly, it appeared that the cottage wasn't hers after all. Mr Rutledge said he had bought it. How could it have been sold without her knowledge? The executors of Papa's Will should have ensured that her inheritance passed to her, yet she had not received a penny.

The answer was in front of her. Papa's executors were her brother Tristram and Sir Lucien Fitznorton. Tristram, who had sold the estate to cover their father's debts, must have shared the proceeds from the sale of Holly Cottage – *her cottage* – with her husband, who had controlled every aspect of her life from the beginning of their marriage. For all those years, when she had endured his complaints about the cost of keeping her, adding to her feelings of worthlessness and misery, he had known that he had stolen from her.

He owed her much more than the value of a cottage in Yorkshire. But that would do for a start. Here was proof that she had been robbed, and she would use it to claw back what she could from her husband's estate, not only for her own future security but for the sake of her unborn child.

FORTY-SIX

JOSEPH

Joe stood at the sink and stripped off his shirt, then tugged his undershirt over his head. It was cold in the scullery, the flagstone floor seeming to leech the warmth from his feet, but Maggie had brought a pail of hot water for him to wash with. He needed it: his armpits smelled like cat's piss from his efforts in the garden that afternoon. He had dug over the loamy soil until his back was fit to break in half, his shoulder muscles bulging with the effort. He dug to relieve his frustration, ignoring Mary and the disapproving comments of his neighbours who shared her view that it was wrong to work on the Sabbath.

"If God created these cabbages I'm sowing, I don't suppose He'll mind what day they go in the ground," he had said at last when Mary hissed at him that he should stop; but the pained look in her eyes made him immediately regret his sarcastic tone. She might not like him much, but her fear for his soul was genuine.

Now, he scrubbed the sweat and mud off his torso and arms with a rough cloth, seeing the skin glow pink under the lather from the hard, yellow bar of coal tar soap. He was half sorry to lose the smell of the outdoors. The odour of fresh air and earth invariably conjured memories of stolen hours in the woods with Rosamund earlier in the year.

Much had happened since then, but not between him and her. He never saw her on her own these days. Since the day she was widowed she never took the car out to drive herself. She sat in the back seat, accompanied by Nellie Dawson, swathed in her widow's weeds. It was difficult to read her face behind the dark veil, all the more so because she kept her gaze on the view from the window. She had said nothing to him unless it was to instruct him as to her intended destination, or to acknowledge his greeting with a polite *Good Morning*.

He missed her. He missed her eyes and the softness of her cultured voice and her delicate, clean fragrance, but most of all he missed being wanted. She had desired him for himself, and it was torture to have no way to find out why she had so abruptly cut him off without a word. Being unable to see her or speak to her ate away at him like maggots in putrid flesh. Desperation sucked his thoughts away from the everyday and left him distracted, always on the edge of a fantasy in which they were in each other's arms.

He poured an ewer of water over his head and rubbed the soap over his hair, splashing the floor as the water ran off his elbows. She was free now, he reasoned, with that evil brute of a husband in his grave. She didn't even live in the big house anymore, but had moved out to the Dower House on the edge of the estate nearest Pontybrenin, to allow her stepdaughter to take over her inheritance. If the baby turned out to be a boy, that would set the cat amongst the pigeons and it would be nasty little Miss Charlotte who'd be out on her ear.

He'd heard that a woman from the village went to the Dower House each day to do the cooking and housework, and Nellie Dawson had moved in. But Nellie's mother was sick again, and Joe had learned that Lady Fitznorton graciously permitted her to go and stay with her mother for three nights each week. While running errands in town today, he'd spotted Nellie disappearing into the railway station, which must surely mean she was going for one of her visits home...

If he was right, Rosie would be alone tonight. The idea of it prickled under his skin. His feet twitched with the urge to hurry to the Dower House and demand answers. Most of all, he longed to hold her again.

He rinsed the soap from his hair, shaking like a wet dog before reaching for the towel to rub his hair and chest dry. As he poked the corners of the towel into his ears, a strange sensation on the back of his neck told him someone was behind him. He looked around, the towel still draped around his shoulders.

Mary stood in the doorway, watching him with a steady gaze.

"What are you looking at?" he asked her, wondering uncomfortably how long she had been watching him.

A strange expression washed over her face, so unfamiliar it made him stare. A smile, making a glow illuminate her eyes like the soft warmth of an oil lamp turned down low. It was so subtle, someone less familiar might have missed it.

"I'm looking at you," she replied. "You're still a good-looking man."

"Oh." He turned back to the sink with a frown, feeling uncomfortable. With a tug, he pulled the plug out and watched the scummy water drain away.

"Why shouldn't a woman look at her husband?" she went on. A quick glance in her direction revealed that the smile had grown and was playing about the corners of her mouth. It disconcerted him to see it. How long had it been since she had looked genuinely amused about anything? How long since a smile of hers had been anything but derisive or scornful?

"Well, you don't usually," was all he could think to say in response. He picked up the cloth he had washed with and used it to wipe the soapy grime off the porcelain of the sink. Her intake of breath told him something else was coming, something she had been building up to.

"I haven't bled for six months," she said, taking him by surprise. Her smile was gone, and there was a new intensity in her gaze.

A wave of cold fury sliced through Joe's chest. He crossed the distance between them in a couple of strides, leaned his head forward to narrow the gap between his face and hers, and spat out his response, gripping her upper arm hard enough to leave a bruise as he shook her.

"Whose is it, Mary? Who have you been with, when you won't even touch your own husband?"

The balloon of anger in his breast deflated when she coughed out a startled laugh.

"I'm not having a baby, Joe. I'm getting old."

His eyes widened.

"I wouldn't want to go with another man, in any case," she went on. "There's no one in this world who could hold a candle to you."

It took a few moments for her words to sink in. Abruptly, he dropped his hand from her arm and turned away, back to the sink.

He closed his eyes for a moment, nauseated by his own hypocrisy. He had been infuriated by the thought that she might have been unfaithful, but who was he to criticise her for what he had done himself and would do again, given the chance? He didn't deserve her praise or compliments.

"Speaking of babies," she said, back to her needling again, almost as if she could read his mind. "I heard some gossip at church this morning that's sure to interest you. People are saying that Lady Fitznorton is in the family way. They're saying how strange it is that he managed to put a child in her belly just before he died, when he hadn't managed it for all those years they were married."

Joe's pulse quickened. With a sharp intake of breath he looked up and opened his mouth to defend Rosamund's reputation.

"He did get her pregnant before, plenty of times. Perhaps this one will survive, seeing as the old devil isn't around to beat her these days." A muscle twitched in his cheek.

"Really? I didn't know." Her face fell, as if her dislike of Lady Fitznorton had rushed out of her. "The poor woman!"

He cast her a sidelong glance and was chastened by the horrified sympathy in her eyes.

"How do you know all that?" she asked him.

"You're not the only one who gets to hear gossip."

She was silent for a moment, then nodded. The frown creasing her forehead cleared and she looked up at him, her face empty of any suspicion.

"I'll pray for her. And for her baby – fatherless mite."

The words were simple enough, but he had to look away again so she wouldn't see how they had moved him. He tossed the towel down onto the floor and stooped to mop up the water he had spilled.

"I'll do that," she offered, but he shook his head and carried on with his back turned and his head down. He didn't relax until she sighed and went away a few minutes later. Only then could he allow himself to breathe normally again.

He slipped through the kitchen and upstairs to find clean clothes, and was out of the front door within a couple of minutes, shrugging into his coat and pulling his cap low over his brow.

He was halfway to the Dower House before it dawned on him that Mary had been attempting to give him the glad eye.

It was dusk by the time Joe reached the Dower House. He had walked swiftly and purposefully, his cap low and his chin tipped downwards to discourage any unwanted attention. As far as he could tell, no one had seen him.

He stood outside the gate, pausing with his hand on the cold wrought iron to check that no one was in sight before pushing it open. He felt absurdly nervous, his palms clammy and his mouth dry. His boots seemed to make the gravel path crunch unnaturally loudly as he strode to the front door. Lifting his hand to the brass lion's head knocker, he faltered just for a second before knocking twice.

He had almost lost heart by the time he heard her voice through the thick wooden door.

"Who is it?" she called, sounding as nervous as he felt.

"It's me. Joe... That is, Joe Cadwalader." He cursed inwardly for saying something so stupid. *How many Joes would be coming to her door unannounced?*

There was a pause, long enough to make him begin to doubt his reception.

Tension had made her eyes wide and her lips narrow when at last she opened the door a crack.

"What do you want, Joe? You can't come in."

"Why not? Have you got another man in there?"

"Of course not! I'm alone." She huffed crossly and stepped aside, darting a glance outside to ensure they were unobserved before closing the door behind him.

He stared at her, feeling desire rise in him. Her hair flowed down her back in a long, dark chestnut braid and she was wrapped in a kimono of brightly exotic floral silk. The shadows under her eyes betrayed fatigue, but her skin glowed with health.

"You look well," he said.

Her hands caressed her belly reflexively. Beneath the belted fabric, he could just make out the rounding of her flesh, emphasised by her splayed long, white fingers. He had dreamed of those fingers, their soft warm touch gliding over his skin.

"You shouldn't be here," she said, but there was no heat behind her words.

"I stayed away as long as I could; but I couldn't bear it any longer. I had to see you on our own."

She looked about in agitation, as if undecided what to do, then led the way into the parlour. It was a light, feminine room with flower-sprigged chintz curtains and comfortable chairs upholstered in a fresh shade of green. To his surprise, she didn't sit down, but rested an elbow on the mantel and covered her forehead with her hand. A fire crackled in the grate, sending shadows and flickering orange light to caress the kimono.

"How have you been?" he asked. He had taken off his cap and was wringing it between his hands, her manner making him hesitate to move any closer.

"If you mean the child, everything seems in perfect order."

Her answer puzzled him with its implication that something else might be wrong.

"And you?" he persisted, taking several jerky steps forward until he was so close behind her, he could smell her violet scent and see the wispy tendrils at her nape.

"Joe, don't," was all she said. She lowered her arm and took a step away from him.

It was too much: he seized her by the shoulders and turned her around, forcing her to meet his gaze. He could feel the tension in her muscles, as if she itched to pull away, and frowned in incomprehension.

"I thought things would be different between us, now that you're free...?"

Her breast rose and fell rapidly, and he read despair as well as determination in her fine-lashed eyes.

"What is it? Speak to me, Rosie, for God's sake. Not knowing is killing me, can't you see that?"

He searched her face for any trace of the love that he had once seen there, but there was nothing to see but pain.

"How could you even begin to imagine that you and I could be together? I may be free, but you are not. You've risked my reputation and our child's future inheritance by coming here. What if someone saw you? How long do you think it would be before doubt would be cast over my... Over the origin of my condition? Do you think anyone would continue to believe this baby was my husband's? You'll make me an outcast, Joe. The child, too. I can't believe you want that... Do you?"

His voice came out in a strangled cry: "I thought you loved me. You know I fell in love with you months ago." He hated himself for being so weak, but the pain in his gut was too much, forcing him to blurt out the words.

"Oh, Joe. Nothing good ever came from falling."

He loosened his grip, and she pulled away and sank into an armchair with her head bowed in both hands.

"I can't love you anymore," she said. "You know that, in

your heart of hearts. You should go..." Her tone made it clear that her decision was final.

His sense of abandonment crushed the air from his lungs and blurred his vision. Pinpricks of light floated past him as he stared, disbelieving, at the woman in the chair; a rushing sound filled his ears.

"You can't mean it," he whispered, but without any faith. He waited for his vision to clear, then turned to rub his face, surprised to find his cheeks wet.

"You will always have my gratitude for everything you taught me. But you can't have my love now. You have a wife and children who need you. And soon I will have a child of my own, too. For that, I will be forever grateful. Goodbye, Joe."

With slow steps, she led him back to the door.

"I loved you beyond all reason," he said in one last plea. She only closed her eyes, her face carved in stone.

Stiffly, he straightened his back and fitted his cap to his head. It was pointless to say any more. His arms felt achingly empty as he raised his hand to the latch and opened the door. She should have been in his embrace. She should have thrown her own arms around him when he arrived and led him up the stairs to her bed. They should have been naked together now, luxuriating in the touch of one another's skin against the silky bedspread he could still picture so vividly in his mind.

The evening air had turned cold as he walked blindly down the path and closed the gate behind him with a soft, metallic clunk. He permitted himself one more look at the house, hoping she might be at the window beckoning him back; but the curtains remained firmly closed.

Numb, he set off for home. He was barely conscious of lifting his feet, putting them down again. They were leaden, wanting to disobey him and turn back, run to her so that he could make her change her mind. His brain, shocked though it was, told his limbs it was impossible.

Fifty yards along the road, a man stepped out from behind a tree. He was tall, slim, shrouded in a cap and overcoat that struck Joe as familiar even in his dazed state. He stood in the middle of the road, blocking Joe's path. Looking up, Joe realised with a start that it was his eldest son.

"Len," he said. "What are you doing?"

The lad's eyes blazed with hostility.

"I followed you, Dad. It should be me asking you that question, shouldn't it? What were you doing, visiting her ladyship on a Sunday evening, in your own clothes, not your uniform? You can't say you were planning to drive her somewhere. So what the hell are you up to?"

Joe tried to brush past him, but Len grasped his arm with a hand that shook with a rage Joe could feel even through his coat.

"It's none of your concern," he said, hot and awkward with embarrassment.

"None of my concern? How's that then, Dad? How's that, when my mam's at home wondering where her husband could have gone skulking off to? As if she didn't know. You make me sick."

Seeing the contempt in the face of his son was unbearable. Joe snatched his arm free and lurched away, trying to ignore the booted footsteps that pursued him along the road.

"D'you know what happened today, Dad? Do you? No, of course you don't. You're too wrapped up in that posh floozy of yours to think about what's happening in your own family."

Joe rounded on him. "You! Keep a civil tongue in your head or I'll knock some good manners into you."

"Oh, aye? You reckon you could, old man? I'd like to see you try."

Joe's temper exploded like a burst of light, but he found himself inexplicably on the ground, his jaw stinging and blood in his mouth from biting his tongue. Len stood back, flexing his right hand.

"Don't make me hit you again, Dad. Christ, to think it's come to this." He shook his head as if to clear his thoughts while Joe stumbled to his feet, defeated. They stood apart from one another, each conscious of their own shame, but calmer now.

"Shall I tell you what happened today? A girl came up to me after Chapel." Len's voice choked on the words. "Pretty, she was. She wanted to know why a strapping lad like me hadn't volunteered to fight. Called me a coward for not doing my bit, looked at me as if she despised me. And by the time I could think of anything to say she was walking off with her friends, and even my Jenny couldn't look me in the eye after."

"You should pay no mind to it—"

"But I can't. I can't. So I've made a decision, Dad. Tomorrow morning, first thing, I'm not going to work. I'm going straight to the Recruiting Office instead. I'm signing up for the army. And Stan says he's coming with me."

Panic clutched at Joe's throat.

"Stanley's too young to join up—" he began.

"It doesn't matter. Half of his friends have already joined. If you say you're nineteen, they take your word for it. So there's nothing to stop us going together, in the same battalion."

Len stared at Joe defiantly, daring him to object.

"Your mother will be devastated," he said, hoping this would be sufficient to deter them. There was no point in asking Len to spare his own feelings, not now.

"I reckon she'll be proud. It'll be good for her to have two sons she can respect, seeing as her husband is so despicable."

Joe reached out a hand to stop him, hearing the angry tears in his voice, but Len was already running from him, and Joe had nothing left to give. He felt empty, spent and useless. Despair wrapped itself around him like a sack over his head, smothering him and dulling his senses.

He picked up his cap from where it had fallen to the ground

and pushed it back into shape, scarcely aware of what he was doing. He walked, he knew not where, anywhere but towards home. He couldn't go back, he thought. Not now that Len knew. He couldn't go home and see Mary's face when she learned that her worst suspicions were well founded, only to hear that her two eldest boys were going off to fight in France.

All he could do was keep walking, and hope that somehow the despair and the night would swallow him.

FORTY-EIGHT

JOSEPH

Joe stumbled on until at last he came to the riverbank, where he paused to watch the swirling, stinking waters. Recent rain had augmented the flow; the muddy depths, polluted with God only knew what from the industries upstream, churned with treacherous currents carrying rubbish and broken branches swiftly down towards the distant sea. No one falling in would be able to clamber out, he thought. It would be cold in the water, no doubt shockingly so; but it could bring about a speedy end to his troubles. A couple of steps forward, a few short painful gasps, and then all the pain would be over. It would be so terribly easy to slip into oblivion.

His breathing slowed as he realised he was seriously contemplating the idea of welcoming death. It had taken two of his children; it took his parents long ago. A brother; two sisters in childhood. He could join them all, and be free of grief and rejection. He took in a deep breath, imagining the chilly autumn air transformed into water as he sucked the sweet oxygen into his lungs; then took a step backward. Hesitant at first, but then moving more purposefully, he turned his back on the river and faced life.

He blinked several times as he looked about him in the darkness and adjusted his senses to orient himself. He had been in a daze, but now it was time to shake himself and think. With a toss of the head to sharpen his wits, he began a swift walk in the direction of the big house. He wasn't yet ready to slink home and face Len or Mary.

He knew of a gardener's shed, used for storing tools, which would require little effort to break into. On he went through the wood, avoiding the road and keeping to narrow tracks, thankful for the moonlight despite the eerie shadows it conjured. An owl shrieked once, making him jump and whip around to identify the source of the scream. He heard its wings swoop softly past him and shrugged his shoulders to relieve the tension. His legs were heavy with tiredness, his jaw throbbed, and his back ached with the familiar twinges that told him he needed to stop pushing himself.

When he finally reached the hut a couple of hard blows with a stone were all it took to smash the lock, and he shoved his way inside among the tools and the cobwebs to find some sacks to lie on. Ignoring the rustling and scuttling of the vermin he had disturbed in the corner, he eased himself down, curled up and lay, sleepless and exhausted, in the small and fusty space he had cleared for himself.

His mind raced cruelly, picturing each of his children. How could he face Len again? He had let him down. The shame of knowing his eldest son despised him was like a wound, making Joe pull in his elbows more tightly and huddle against the coarse sacks. In a matter of hours, Len and Stanley would take the King's Shilling and soon they would be learning how to kill other men, for no good reason but that the whole world had spiralled into violence and despair. Stanley was still so young, just a lad. He pictured them as little boys, when they had jousted with sticks, pretending to be knights, and tried to imagine them in soldier's uniforms, carrying real weapons that could maim and kill. Where had the years gone?

Then there was Margaret – his Maggie, so quietly sweet, who had become even more helpful and thoughtful since Annie's death, as if she hoped to make things right. He hadn't really thanked her, he realised now, for being so undemanding and for taking on so many of the small practical tasks with the little ones when he and Mary had been stupefied by grief.

Dolly now, on the cusp of becoming a woman, so different from her elder sister in her mood swings and her emotional outbursts; needing an arm around her shoulders one minute and hating them all the next. He smiled into the darkness at the mental image of her bouncing up to him with her plaits in disarray, full of chatter about her day, what her teacher had said, who had been caught playing truant, and which of her friends had fallen out with whom. She was so lively, so full of energy – like a little lightning bolt.

His thoughts turned to Teddy and Jack, close in age and thick as thieves: two little freckled boys always up to mischief. It wasn't uncommon to find a toad in the bed or beetles under a cup, and hear their giggling scramble to escape his and Mary's dire threats of punishment.

Finally, he thought of Miriam, who shouldn't have been the youngest but had resumed that role in the family after Annie died. So trusting and gentle, affectionate and imaginative. She was the one who needed the comfort of someone else to snuggle up to at night, for fear of monsters in the dark. Little did she know how much she had been a comfort to Joe with her little arms so willing to wind themselves around his neck for a hug when he needed one. He felt abruptly glad that he hadn't made the wrong decision at the river. They all needed him in their way, Miriam most of all.

Almost reluctantly, he remembered how Mary had been that afternoon. Her demeanour had been different from the sour, aggrieved hostility he had become accustomed to since Annie died. He wondered what had changed. Perhaps it was her age, making her moods as changeable as Dolly's. She had hinted as much, making him wonder afterwards if she had been offering an oblique invitation with her comment that she hadn't bled in months. She had excluded him from her bed because of anger and dislike, yes – but also because of fear of pregnancy. Maybe that was lessening. Maybe she had finally decided she wanted a bit of what Rosamund had been getting.

He chided himself for the harshness of his thoughts. He could hardly blame her for feeling upset by the rumours of his affair. The playful smile on her cheeks earlier had reminded him of how she used to be, when the children were small and healthy, and she had worn contentment like a richly embroidered gown.

She was still attractive in her way, when she smiled, at least. If she would only wear something with a bit more colour than dark grey half-mourning. It had been more than a year, after all – eighteen months now, in fact. And if she would just do something more with her hair, and take better care of her hands... He rubbed his palms over his face, suddenly conscious that he was being unfair to her.

It was wrong to compare her to Rosamund, who was probably a decade younger and hadn't experienced even so much as an hour of physical work in her life. Mary's life was a slog of domestic chores, little better than drudgery with their large family, and with scant spare money for luxuries like scent or creams. She deserved better than to be held at fault for her grief, her lack of vanity, and for suffering the inevitable consequences of serving her family's needs.

Gazing at the shaft of moonlight slipping between the timbers at the edge of the doorway, he resolved to treat her better. He must try harder, especially now that he had no one else to want him. He should strive for patience, to afford to his wife the same gentle kindness that he felt for their children. Perhaps then there would be a chance that she would learn to smile more often. Perhaps she might even come to love him again. He tested the thought, remembering times long ago when she would nestle against his chest and kiss his throat just below his ear in a honeyed invitation. His eyes closed, his weary limbs sagged back against the sacking, and he drifted into sleep.

FORTY-NINE

JOSEPH

It was afternoon by the time Joe awoke, stiff and aching and with a bladder fit to burst. His mouth was parched, sour-tasting from sleep, and his head ached. He scrambled up and left the hut to take a piss against a tree, yearning for a drink of water and a chunk of Mary's freshly baked bread to ease the growling of his stomach.

Stretching, he eyed the glowering clouds above the leaves that hung above him, light showing between them as if through the holes of a lacy crocheted blanket. With a yawn and a heavy heart, knowing he had no other realistic option, he turned towards home. A blister stung his toe, as if fiercely indignant at yet more walking, but he pressed on. His dread of Len's contempt and Mary's anger was weaker than the necessity of going back to face them. More than anything, he needed to clean himself up and start trying to make amends.

On approaching his own cottage he spied Miriam hopping on and off the doorstep, humming to herself. Her ringlets bounced with each little jump, framing her small face with its intent expression. She looked up and saw him, and her face cleared.

"Dada! You're back."

He opened the front gate and limped towards her. Her nose wrinkled.

"Pooh, you smell horrid," she said. "You're all dusty and dirty." He ruffled her hair, but his smile soon faded as she continued, "Mam's been in a state all morning. She was talking to Len and Stan, and they made her cry. Then she hurt her hand—"

"Did she? How?" He frowned.

The ringlets swished from side to side as she shook her head and shrugged, still hopping up and down the doorstep.

"Dunno. The kettle or the iron, I think. She had to put her head down on the table for a bit, because she said she came over a bit peculiar, so I went and fetched Mrs Morris from next door. She made her a cup of tea with four sugars – imagine having four, Dad! And before all that Maggie went to work in a huff, and said something about you getting the sack if you didn't turn up soon. Have you got a sack, Dada? I can't see one."

She eyed his empty hands in puzzlement.

"No. I might get it another day; we'll have to see. Mim, I need to go in and see your mother... Give us half an hour, would you?"

She nodded, unconcerned.

"She'll tell you to have a wash," she called after him as he removed his mud-caked boots and stepped into the hallway, his stomach clenching with apprehension as he hung his coat and cap on their hook.

He found Mary in the kitchen, seated at the table with a face as bleak and hopeless as midwinter, her right hand bandaged and cradled in her left. The naked relief in her eyes as Joe pushed the door open made him feel as guilty as a common criminal.

"You came home," she said, and her shoulders slumped. Her face was a mask of pain.

"Yes."

He stood in the doorway for a few moments, debating what to do, then stepped across the threshold and pushed the door quietly closed behind him.

"What happened to you?" he asked, nodding towards her hand.

"I should ask you the same. Look at the state of you."

Her voice was more confused than accusing. He looked down at himself and shuffled his feet, then realised she was looking at the swollen bruise on his face. He touched it with his fingertips, then pulled out a chair and sat down next to her.

"I'm glad you didn't hit him back," she said, and his throat tightened as he realised she must know what had happened between him and Len.

"No. Well... I was the one in the wrong. And besides, these days he's stronger than I am." He made a wry attempt at a smile, trying to shrug off his sense of humiliation. "I spent the night in a shed. I wasn't sure I'd be welcome at home."

"You'll be wanting a cup of tea, then."

He nodded, grateful and ashamed all at once, and she picked up the teapot from the centre of the table, her movements awkward with her left hand.

"Let me," he protested, but she pulled it back fiercely and proceeded to pour him a cup of tea. She added milk from the jug, slopping it over the edge with her clumsy left hand, and pushed the saucer towards him. Stewed and dark though it was, it felt warm and tasted like nectar on his parched tongue.

"She turned you down, I take it?"

He looked up from the cup and placed it carefully back on the saucer. She was avoiding his gaze, pulling at a loose strand of yarn on the gaudy knitted tea cosy.

"Yes, she did." He couldn't quite keep the bitterness from his voice. She was watching him now, her eyes still filled with hurt.

"How did you know?" he asked.

"Len said you were only in her house for five minutes, ten at the most. You couldn't have done much with her in that amount of time. So I guessed you must have gone there to try your luck, and that she sent you off with your tail between your legs. I suppose I should be grateful that she, at least, has some morals. What were you thinking of, Joe, trying to seduce a pregnant woman, one who's recently widowed?"

He stared. Clearly, she didn't know the full extent of his wrongdoing, hadn't realised the seduction had happened ages ago. His eyelashes swept down to disguise his thoughts. Should he admit the truth, or let her think the fault was all his? He settled for a half-truth.

"I had feelings for her. I thought she had feelings for me. Turns out I was wrong."

"You fool."

He was silent for a while.

"You'll be lucky if she lets you keep your job after this."

"I don't want it anyway. Look, Mary – I've been thinking. I was thinking all night. We should move somewhere else, have a fresh start. I'll look for another job, one that gets us away from Plas Norton, away from... from her. I'll try harder, be a better husband to you. I'll do whatever you want. But let's move away."

Her eyes were reproachful, her lips thin and twisted by inner hurt.

"We came here to get away after Annie died. Running away doesn't help, Joe. It didn't make any difference then, did it? If anything, we've ended up in a worse state than we were before, with all this. And I'll miss Peggy if we move again. Besides, Len and Maggie are settled – or Len was, before he took it into his head to see if the army will take him."

"I know. I'm sorry. But it's the only solution that makes sense." Desperation made him manipulative. If he appealed to her beliefs, made her fear for his soul, he'd have a chance of winning. "Please... Deliver me from temptation, Mary."

He saw her swift intake of breath, her eyelids fluttering as she took in his words. At last she nodded unhappily.

"Thank you," he breathed, reaching out for her hand. She flinched away, holding her bandaged fingers against her chest; but he took hold of her wrist, oh so gently, and pulled it towards him. He nursed her hand in his as if it was a wounded sparrow.

"What happened?"

"I burned it taking bread out of the oven. I wasn't thinking, I was in a state after talking to Len, and I tried to pick it up without a cloth. You're not the only one who's a fool." Her voice trembled, catching on a wobbly breath like a sob.

Carefully he unwound the bandage. He could feel the tension in the slight jerk of her arm that told him she wanted to tug it away, but he carried on until he had exposed the burn. He winced when he saw it, his heart flooding with sympathy. She had been through so much inner pain in the past eighteen months, and now the angry blister on her palm and fingers must have caused her physical agony too. Avoiding the burn, he kissed her fingertips with exquisite tenderness and wound the bandage softly around her hand again. Tears had welled in her eyes, he saw.

"That burn must have really hurt," he said, feeling useless to express his feelings. She took her hand back and put it in her lap.

"Not as much as my heart hurt when I thought you weren't coming home. Even Leonard and Stanley going off to enlist this morning didn't feel as bad as that."

He frowned. "I'm surprised you minded. Don't you think you'd be better off without me? It's only my wages that you'd miss, after all."

"Is that really what you think? After twenty-three years of marriage, you think all I need you for is money?"

"Well, that and jobs around the garden and the house, I suppose..."

She cut him off, eyes blazing. "Then you're a bigger fool than I took you for. I love you, Joseph Cadwalader. Whatever you might think, I've loved you since I was a girl. I've fought it, God knows I have. I've tried every way I know not to want you since we lost Annie. I've tried to hate you, to keep my thoughts from fixing on you, to keep from dreaming of you, to keep myself from flinging myself into your arms and never letting you go. I've fought to find the strength not to look at you because it so nearly kills me to see you within reach and not touch you. But you couldn't see it. All you could see was her. Oh, don't get me wrong – I don't blame you. She's beautiful, I could see that when I saw the two of you laughing together in the car. God forgive me but I hated you both that day, because I couldn't bear to see you enjoying her company when you dislike mine so much. We haven't so much as smiled at each other in nearly two years, and you looked so happy in that moment. Why would you want me when you thought there was a chance you could have her? She's got everything, after all, and I'm just stuck – a bitter, horrible old woman stuck in a cage of my own making, trapped by the pain of losing Alfie and Annie, and too frightened to let myself love my own husband even when Lord knows I should."

Joe rose to his feet to catch at her arm as she tried to rush past him.

"But you made me think... You told me to leave you alone. You pushed me away for months; you wouldn't so much as let me touch you. You said – Christ, Mary, you said you *used* to love me. What was I supposed to think? How was I to know?"

She shook her head, blinded by tears as she leaned against his arm.

Joe felt as if his head would explode. How could he have got it so wrong?

"You know why," she whispered. "I didn't want another baby; to go through it all again. And I knew that if I let you near me, I couldn't stop myself, so I pushed you away."

"You did a good job of it," he gasped out on an incredulous half-laugh. Slowly, he eased his arm around her shoulders. They heaved as her long-repressed tears burst forth; he held her and let her cry, pressing soft kisses onto the top of her head where the dark hair of her bun was threaded with white.

The door flung open, banging against his shoulder. Keeping Mary close within his arms, he turned his head to see who had come in.

"Oh!" Miriam said when she saw Mam and Dad hugging. It had been ages since she'd seen them snuggling like that, with him leaning his cheek against her hair and her with her cheek pressed against his dusty coat. She hesitated, then ran to be swept up and held tightly between them.

"Has it been half an hour yet, Dad? I'm hungry."

She let Mam hug her and didn't fuss when Dad ruffled her curls, even though she always got annoyed when he messed up her hair. She couldn't understand how Mam could bear putting her nose so close to his smelly, unwashed clothes; but she did understand that something had changed. She didn't know what it was but, squashed between her parents as they whispered above her head, she knew that it was good.

FIFTY

ROSAMUND

Rosamund remained motionless in her chair for what seemed like an age, still reeling from the shock of Joe's visit. Seeing him again had reawakened feelings she thought she had buried weeks ago. She kept her feet firmly on the carpet, pressing against its softness under her slippers, to stop herself running to the door after him.

Continuing their affair was impossible; she recognised this, even if he didn't. Of course, he wasn't fully aware of the circumstances that made it so. She couldn't risk being with him, talking to him, for fear of telling him her secret. He couldn't know what she had done. He might not despise her as an adulteress, but if he realised she was a murderess it would be another matter. It would be so terribly easy, wrapped safely within the circle of those strong arms, to confess everything. And if he then felt compelled to tell the authorities, she would lose everything: her good name, her freedom, her child, perhaps even her life. For the selfish chance of brief happiness by continuing their secret affair, it wasn't worth the risk of the truth coming out.

The baby had changed everything. Its existence made her want to live. For the first time since Papa died, she had someone who needed her. The baby would have no knowledge of her past. Together, they could start afresh. They would love one another, and their love would be pure and unselfish, untainted by class or sex or history. She had denied it a father by rejecting Joe, but she could be father and mother to it, of that she was sure.

Had she ever really loved Joe, she wondered now, or had it been what he represented that fascinated her? She had been drawn to his looks, that shared sense of grief, his obvious love for his family; and she had been enchanted by the awe and desire in his eyes when he looked at her. He was a handsome man, physically commanding in his smart uniform and so unlike Sir Lucien in that she had never once felt threatened by him – not even tonight, when he had seized her arms so firmly, or when she had seen him in the fight with Wilson. While he was of a lower class, his sensitivity and standards of behaviour were superior to her husband's in so many respects. The love he had given her had been a gift, as much as the driving instruction: both had helped her see herself differently. The past self who had believed she was broken, a victim of a curse that kept her in a prison of a marriage, was gone. At last, she could see that she had strength. She was capable of defending herself and her child. She had proved that she would do so to the death, if she had to.

Tomorrow, she would attend an appointment with Sir Lucien's lawyer to pursue her rights as a widow, and the rights of a child born posthumously. Having been kept in the dark as to her financial situation throughout her married life, she would find out whether she should have inherited anything from Tristram when he died, as her continuing correspondence with Ewart Rutledge had proved that Sir Lucien would have kept any such bequest from her. Given everything that had been stolen from her over the years, she meant to reclaim whatever she could.

She looked up at the mantelpiece, where Ewart Rutledge's most recent letter was tucked behind the clock. She would reply to it in the morning and accept his invitation to Ambleworth Hall. Why not? With no one to answer to, she could go where she pleased. The thought brought a bubble of soft laughter to her throat.

Spreading her palms over her belly, she pictured herself in a few months' time, holding her baby in her arms. A rush of protective love washed over her, overwhelming in its intensity. Her child was everything now: a second chance to live. A chance to get things right.

She hadn't needed a handsome prince to ride up and rescue her, or a fairy godmother to save her from the curse that had been laid upon her. She had slain the dragon herself. And while she may never be completely free from the grip of memory, or from the pangs of conscience, from now on she would be the driver of her own destiny.

The future lay before her like a gift.

EPILOGUE

NELLIE

Dear Mam,

I hope Polly is taking care of you, and making your tea good and strong, the way you like it. Make sure she doses you up with your tonic regularly, and keep nice and warm. Provided her Ladyship keeps to her original travel arrangements, I should be back in Wales by the middle of next week, and I'm hoping I'll be allowed a few days to visit you as soon as we return.

Our train journey up north was just as long and tiring as you'd expect, especially for Lady Fitz in her condition. We had to make three changes, and the last train was a proper bone-shaker on a little country branch line up to the local halt. By the time we got here we were both worn out, and as grubby as railwaymen from the engine smuts. Luckily, our rooms at the Pelham Arms are very comfy, and the food is hearty. Although we are so much further north, the weather is still quite mild for late October, so we are not getting cold and wet at every turn as I'd feared.

I wish you could see how different Lady Fitz is up here in

Yorkshire. On our journey, she chatted away nineteen to the dozen about her childhood and what she thought Mr Rutledge would be like. You'll remember I told you about him: the aged American who bought her father's house and collections of old books and curiosities.

The morning after we arrived, he sent a carriage to take us from the inn to Ambleworth Hall, and I watched her get more and more excited as we came closer to her old home. It's a fair bit bigger than Plas Norton, and a lot prettier – built of light brown stone, same as the other buildings around here. Very quaint, and hundreds of years old – much older than Plas Norton – and probably very draughty to live in I should think. It wouldn't suit you, with your arthritis!

Mr Rutledge came out to greet us, and you should have seen them both. I watched their blushes go racing up from their collars to their hair when he took her hand and kissed it to welcome her. She'd been expecting an old man, scruffy and short-sighted and round-shouldered from all his time poring over books, almost a fossil himself – but I suspect he's not yet fifty, and he's a bit of a looker I can tell you. Neat and tidy, a paragon of health and vitality with a full head of fair hair and all his own teeth as far as I could make out. His accent is different from anything I've heard before, being an American, but his voice is perfectly pleasant to listen to. Lady Fitz certainly seemed to hang on his every word.

From the way he stared at her when we arrived, I reckon he was just as surprised as she was. I swear he could hardly believe she was real. Perhaps he'd been expecting her to be a dumpy, middle-aged matron, all gloomy and depressed in her widow's weeds; not a lovely looking woman still in her prime with bloom in her cheeks. She's still wearing black, of course, but by adding those creamy lace collars I told you about, the effect isn't too harsh, and especially with the glow she has about her from being back in her old home. On our first visit she wasn't too worried about how she looked, but you should have heard her on the second day, after she'd met him. It was: *Do you think a little bit of powder and rouge would suit me, Nellie?* and *Could you do something prettier with my hair today, Nellie?* I'm not puffing myself up when I say I made her look a picture. And with the girlish blushes Mr Rutledge caused, the rouge wasn't needed.

We've been up here for three days now, visiting the hall each day, and on all those visits they've hardly stopped talking. If they haven't got their heads together over some old story book, they're walking in the grounds and pointing things out to each other. He listens carefully to everything she says, and is always asking about her memories and her opinions.

Watching her reminds me of doing an embroidery, the way it grows richer and more complete with every hour that passes and bits of colour are added here and there. That's what she's like. Even his dog has taken to her – it's a wolfhound, such a massive hairy beast it makes my palms sweat I can tell you, but she seems to love it. From the look on his face when she pats and fusses it, I reckon he wishes he was the dog.

Even her condition doesn't seem to have put him off, judging by the way he keeps talking about how it's an idyllic place to bring up children, and how empty the house seems with his son away at school. I've a feeling she might be getting an offer before too long, and although I never thought I'd see her want to get married again, if anyone could change her mind about that it would be the handsome Mr Rutledge.

You mustn't worry, though. As much as it's very pleasant here, Yorkshire wouldn't suit me as much as it obviously suits Lady Fitz. With that in mind, I've written back to Mr Garwood in London. Do you remember me telling you about Mrs Ferrers' butler, who was kind enough to write to me? He says he hopes we'll be able to renew our acquaintance next time Lady Fitz visits Mrs Ferrers and Miss Charlotte. With everything that's gone on, I can't imagine her ever doing that – but it was good of him to offer to put in a good word for me, if I ever need him to. The way things are going up here, there couldn't be any harm in me having some contacts in London. I could get back to visit you a lot easier from there than I could from Yorkshire, that's for sure.

I heard a couple of bits of gossip before we came up here, and I know how you love to hear all about everyone at Plas Norton, so I expect this will be of interest. When Mr Cadwalader arrived at the Dower House to take us to the station, he stopped for a cup of tea and told me and Ethel that his eldest son will be off to start his military training soon. They had been thinking of moving on, but his wife won't hear of it now, as she says their son needs a familiar hearth to come home to when his soldiering days are done.

The other bit of news is that Mrs Longford the house-keeper had a letter from Mr Phelps. Apparently he's now helping his sister run a seaside hotel in Tenby. All I can say to that is, I hope his sister keeps her wine cellar safely locked.

I must finish here Mam, as Mr Rutledge has invited Lady Fitz back to the hall for dinner this evening, and she wants to look her best. I'll see you next week, all going well. Give my regards to Polly.

Your loving daughter,

Nellie

A LETTER FROM THE AUTHOR

Dear reader,

Huge thanks for reading *The Gilded Cage*. I hope you were hooked on Rosamund's journey. If you want to join other readers in hearing all about my new releases and bonus content, you can sign up for my newsletter.

www.stormpublishing.co/luisa-a-jones

If you enjoyed this book and could spare a few moments to leave a review that would be hugely appreciated. Even a short review can make all the difference in encouraging a reader to discover my books for the first time. Thank you so much!

I've always loved history, and have read historical fiction since I was a child, so it has been a real treat to go back in time to write this story about an unhappy woman whose life changes in unexpected ways when she learns to drive.

My writing explores the dynamics within relationships and the pressures that mental health issues can exert on the strongest of people. The character of Rosamund was inspired by the testimony of people I love and admire who have survived abuse and PTSD. Even though Rosamund has been made to see herself as cursed and broken, she possesses powerful inner resources, and is much stronger than she or anyone around her realises. It was a joy to have her overcome her cruel circumstances to achieve the happy ending she deserves.

Thanks again for being part of this amazing journey with me and I hope you'll stay in touch – I have so many more stories and ideas to entertain you with!

Luisa

www.luisaajones.com

HISTORICAL NOTE

It was fascinating to research life in Britain in 1914, an era caught between Victorian mores and the modern age. It's difficult not to see parallels with our own time in some respects, as it was a time of rapid social and technological change, with huge disparities between the lives of the rich and the poor, and a growing threat of conflict between powerful nations out to expand their interests.

By 1914, motoring had become a popular pastime in Britain for those wealthy enough to afford a motor car. There were several British manufacturers: the most famous of them, Rolls Royce, is of course still in existence, although now owned by the German firm BMW. When researching this book I decided to celebrate one of the less well-known marques, and settled on a Wolseley 24/30bhp limousine-landaulette as a suitably luxurious and powerful model to be owned by a wealthy industrialist in 1914. These veteran cars are rare today, with only twelve of them known to the Wolseley Register, dispersed around the world. Slightly earlier but very similar models from 1909 and 1912 are held in the Shuttleworth Collection in Bedfordshire, and at Holkham Hall in Norfolk.

According to the 1913 Wolseley catalogue these models cost £800, but optional extras such as a spare wheel, silk blinds, leather upholstery and a number plate would have increased the cost. (For comparison, a lady's maid at that time might have expected to earn around £32 per year.) The interior details I've used in the book are based on photographs found online relating to both the 24/30 and the slightly less powerful version, the 16/20bhp model.

There were electric lights in the passenger compartment and a speaking tube to facilitate communication with the chauffeur, who sat in considerably less comfort than his passengers, as the front of the car was open to the elements at the sides. I have referred to the speaking tube and also to the glass sliding screen between the chauffeur and rear compartment, which had a brass communication flap on one of the models I looked at. The conversation in chapter three, in which Rosamund is embarrassed by Sir Lucien's tactlessness, couldn't have been overheard if Charlotte hadn't insisted on Joe dropping the glass window down behind his seat.

In the book I describe using the hand crank as the method of starting the car, which was not yet completely outdated by 1914, but I feel obliged to point out here that by 1913, with engines becoming more powerful and more owners wanting to drive their own cars, Wolseley had developed a "patent compressed air self-starter".

From the earliest days of motoring, there were female drivers who were just as excited as men by the speed and independence afforded by motor cars. The Ladies' Automobile Club was founded as far back as 1903. Around half of its founding members were titled ladies, and their first outdoor event was observed from the balcony of Buckingham Palace by no less than King Edward VII and Queen Alexandra. The club's annual subscription fee of two guineas provided these ladies with technical advice and information, driving instruction for ladies and their servants, organised motoring tours, competitions, garaging to rent, and a social space to meet at the luxurious Claridge's hotel in Mayfair. Lectures were held on topics such as "Hints on Motor-Car Driving" and "Motors and Morals". As time went by, the club expanded into charitable work, providing funds for a hospital bed for those injured in road traffic accidents, and setting up a motorised field kitchen during the First World War.

Some famous women drivers of the day include Dorothy Levitt, whose book *The Woman and the Car: A Chatty Little Handbook for Women Who Want to Motor* provided me with much inspiration (and a fair bit of incidental detail) for Rosamund's experience of driving. As Levitt says, "Motoring is a pastime for women: young, middle-aged, and – if there are any – old. There may be pleasure in being whirled around the country by your friends and relatives, or in a car driven by your chauffeur; but the real, the intense pleasure, the actual realisation of the pastime comes only when you drive your own car [...] It will fascinate any woman who tries it."

Levitt was a Jewish Londoner whose talent for motoring and boating led her to set land and water speed records for women and made her a well-known celebrity. She took part in (and often won) many speed trials, and loved to drive with her Pomeranian dog, Dodo, on her lap. It was Dorothy Levitt whose suggestion of carrying a hand mirror when driving to see the road behind led to the development of the rear-view mirror.

Other notable female motorists included Aileen Preston, who had a motoring school in London and called herself "the first woman to take up motoring as a career"; and Muriel Thompson, a talented racing driver who won the first Ladies' race at Brooklands in 1908 and went on to become a volunteer ambulance driver in the First World War, winning the Military Medal and the Croix de Guerre for her brave service. Vera "Jack" Holme was noted as Britain's first female chauffeur in 1911: a committed suffragette, she was Mrs Pankhurst's chauffeuse-cum-getaway driver. It struck me that such role models would be an inspiration to Rosamund. For so many of us, whether male or female, the skill of driving opens up a world of independence that can be truly life changing.

ACKNOWLEDGMENTS

As always, I would like to thank my family for their unwavering support and belief in me. My husband Martin, in particular, for encouraging me to write when my motivation and confidence falter, and for bringing those vitally important cups of tea to sustain me during my hours at my laptop. I'm so grateful to him, and to my children and my parents, for letting me know they are proud of me.

My superb editor, Kathryn Taussig, deserves a special mention. Her astute, insightful comments have never failed to inspire me. She's also kind and good-humoured. Together with the brilliantly sharp-eyed Natasha Hodgson, I couldn't have asked for better support in polishing *The Gilded Cage* ready for publication. Sarah Whittaker has produced a stunningly beautiful cover that has surpassed my best hopes. I can't thank the team at Storm Publishing enough for the wonderful job they've done in turning Rosamund's story into a book.

Thank you to Ciara, Chloe, David, Linda, Meryl, Natalie, Pauline and Siobhan, who kindly gave their time and energies to read and reflect on a previous draft of *The Gilded Cage*. I couldn't have got this far without their constructive feedback.

A word of thanks is due to Andy, and to Mike from the Wolseley Register for putting me in touch with him. Andy was hugely generous in supplying information about Wolseley veteran cars. He sent me videos, articles and photographs as well as taking the time to answer my questions about such topics as the top speed of a Wolseley 24/30 Limousine-Landaulette, and whether the driver's side front door actually opened – it doesn't, which led to quite a few edits!

Thank you to Angharad, owner of the gorgeous Rooftop Atelier sewing school in Barry, for help with research into the mysterious world of ladies' undergarments in 1914.

The incredibly talented authors of the Cariad chapter of the Romantic Novelists' Association deserve a special mention for their kindness and helpful advice. I am grateful for their collective wisdom and the warm welcome they extended to me during the Covid-19 lockdown.

Finally, I would like to thank you for reading this book. Writing Rosamund's story has been an emotional journey, and I do hope you enjoyed it. If so, I'd be thrilled if you could take a moment to leave a review or rating on Amazon or Goodreads. It can make all the difference in encouraging other readers to try books by authors who are new to them.

Printed in Great Britain
by Amazon